Shadow of the Castle

Matthew Macleod

ISBN: 978-1-365-54148-3

PublishNation
www.publishnation.co.uk

For Alana

*Alpha reader, Beta reader, non-editor and
long-suffering partner*

Same team

Chapter 1

The rain beat a tattoo on the window pane of the flat, echoing through the dark. Outside on Victoria Street, the water was gathering in the gutters and sweeping down the pavements towards the Grassmarket, the rubbish of the day being carried along in its wake. The luminous face of the bedside clock indicated it was 03:58 and from the look of the downpour outside, Luke Calvin reckoned even the most reluctant drunk would have found his way home by now.

A solitary taxi cut through the gloom with its headlights, searching the sodden street for a fare. It bumped slowly up the cobbled street before rumbling on past leaving only the constant rainfall to fill the silence. Edinburgh in the night-time. Despite the fact that most people thought a major city never slept, Luke had always felt like it was at least dozing between four and five. If he looked up through the haze and water he could see the castle looming ominously over the Old Town. A stoic watcher. Throughout the day it seemed a landmark and a point of focus; a destination for the throngs of excited, yammering peoples from here, there and everywhere to gather. To point and to take photos. Once dusk fell though, the impression shifted. Once the tourists had taken shelter from the dark and the wet, the castle looked down on the people and saw everything that was being done in secret.

From the window ledge where he sat, Luke saw all this. His bed felt far from inviting and his bedroom was probably just as chilled as the rest of the flat by now. That was the issue with these old flats: the high vaulted ceilings and listed facades looked glorious by day but there was just no way to keep the heat in them by night. The thermostat clicked back on for the hundredth time that night. Across the wooden floorboards came the creaks and moans of contraction or expansion, whichever one was happening. He could never remember. The living room where he sat was sparsely decorated; a simple table and chair by the old fireplace, no longer usable but retained for 'aesthetic purposes' by the owner. A three-piece sofa with one seat clearly used more than the rest. The TV flickering on its unit, spilling an ambient glow onto the rug under the coffee table. All were ignored in favour of his favourite perch: - the deep window sill. Wide enough for him to lean with his back against the side of the glass, the way it protruded from the room on both sides meant you could see up and down the whole street. When the night fell and the darkness closed in, when the light retreated and the roar of traffic and people died down, when the rest of the world was dreaming and resting, he often sat here. Watching the castle watching them. The most peaceful he could be.

There had been many nights like this. An attempt to sleep while staring at the ceiling through the dark. A cigarette. Watching the wisps of smoke meander endlessly up into the black through the orange glow. The long slow look to the alarm clock. The mental calculation of how much sleep he would get if he fell asleep right this instant. A sigh. An acceptance. Clicking on the lamp. Padding to the kitchen. Putting on the coffee. His mind worked better when everyone was asleep anyway so he'd pour his coffee into his mug, take his cigarettes and sit in the window and watch.

This flat was his home. Ever since he got out of the service, he'd been put up here. Never had a bill to pay or a mortgage to worry about, just cover his overheads, sparse as they were. The day he was handed the keys, there was also a mobile phone. Even now it sat in its charging cradle, constantly scanning, waiting for the signal to smash the silence with its obnoxious ring. The phone was never to be switched off and never had been. The phone was never to be out of his immediate vicinity and never had been. That phone was his job, his co-workers and his 9 to 5. Sitting, scanning, waiting; it was his very own custom fitted golden handcuffs. It would be silent for days - silent for weeks even sometimes - but whenever it eventually did ring it would be answered before the third chime. There was a niggling anxiety that was brewing inside him about his phone. A subtle pressure; building, growing, constantly expanding. It had been a fortnight since it had gone off last and his subconscious had been waiting for the next ring. For 2 weeks he had waited. For 14 days he had gone about his business, feeling the phantom vibration in his pocket with ever increasing frequency. For 336 hours (well 342 technically, but who was counting), he had waited and watched and slept less and smoked more. With every single one of these 20,000 odd minutes (20,508 technically) his unrest and unease had grown. Snowballing inside him. The fear of the unknown sat heavy on his chest and made it harder to relax. It lay beside him in bed and stole away the covers and his peacefulness. It lurked in every cup of coffee, sharpening the knives that needled his brain. It was the slow transformation in the condemned man from anxiety about the impending doom, to acceptance and finally impatience to have the sentence carried out. The sweet release of all the worry.

Still the rain fell and the floorboards creaked and the television spilled light onto the table. The phone sat in its cradle, waiting for the signal. Luke sat in his window, watching the phone. Watching the street outside. Watching his coffee grow cold and his cigarette smoke pooling lazily against the topmost lintel of the frame. And the castle loomed above it all, seeing what was being done in the dark.

Up on Arthur's Seat, you could almost make out the outline of where the castle was although the constant downpour had reduced visibility to practically zero. A car was waiting in the gloom on the slopes of Edinburgh's iconic hill, with the engine cut and lights off. The man in the driver's seat kept his hands on the wheel and wished he could turn the engine over, just to get some heat through this icebox that the car was steadily becoming. He could see nothing out the windscreen: the massive droplets smashed into it from all angles, creating a cacophony of noise that was infuriating and setting him on edge. The knuckles on the wheel whitened as he gripped harder and muttered under his breath, 'Hurry up, hurry up, hurry up.', fogging up the inside of the windows.

The passenger window suddenly darkened for a moment and the click of the door handle startled him. His companion lowered himself into the seat with an audible squelch and tossed something into the back seat before slamming the door shut again. Dripping water on the floor and mud all over the upholstery, the passenger huffed and puffed, blowing hard into his hands. The mud was caked all over his legs and most of his arms. Even the cap under his hoody was speckled and ruined. The driver shot a disapproving look at the mess and the carelessly tossed shovel that had turned the back seat into a Jackson Pollock. He turned the key and once the engine had taken its time and decided to turn over, blasted the heat on. The wipers opened up his vision and settled into the rhythm of the fastest setting. It was almost enough to make the driving conditions safe. The passenger had his hands stretched towards the hot air and was starting to breathe a little better, taking a proper lungful every time. The car pulled away from the roadside and started its journey off the hill, back towards town. They would dump it in the agreed place. They would change into clean, dry clothes. They would torch the car with everything in it and then that would be that. The rain kept on and the wipers were catching briefly on the upswing, echoing his thoughts from earlier, louder and more intense.

'Hurry up, hurry up, hurry up, hurry up......'

When the phone finally rang that morning, it filled the room, jolting Luke from his uneasy sleep on the couch. Sitting upright, his hand fumbled for the receiver and picked it up just before the second ring. The familiar pressure in his chest was no longer there, replaced for the moment with too much smoke and not enough sleep.

'Luke speaking.'

The sun had begun to shine through the windows. People had begun to wake and go about their day on the streets outside in drips and drabs: human traffic flowing down the pavement just like the overnight rain that had disappeared without a trace.

'You have a job.'

The voice on the other end of the phone was high and girlish. Laura, his usual point of contact in the "office". She was always business down that line but still sounded as though she was stifling a constant giggle and struggling to do so. Luke had yet to see her in person in the two years they had been conversing but had built up an image in his mind, adding and correcting details here and there, yet the main themes remained. He had decided that she was blonde: hair shoulder length and straight. Relatively young: no older than 30. Her accent was pretty much absent leading him to believe she was an Edinburgh girl or had lived here a good few years. All of this remained to be confirmed but he maintained the utmost faith in his baseless deductive reasoning. She broke into his thoughts with more information.

4

'The client will be visiting in person at 1000 hours at your address. I have passed him all your details but he was very insistent that he would only discuss the nature of his visit with you himself.'

She was wearing bangles of some description - He could hear the faintest jangle as she moved the phone on her end. That was a new thought, he'd never thought of her as a bangle sort of girl. He tried discreetly to clear his throat before replying.

'Laura, this isn't the normal procedure, usually...' he broke off to cough and instantly felt better for it. 'Excuse me. Usually...'

This time it was she who cut in abruptly, her voice rising slightly, her bangles (or could they be bracelets.... he hadn't considered that option) jingling down the line.

'I am fully aware of what the procedure usually is and I appreciate this is a deviation from the norm but I spoke with the Major who vouched for his credentials absolutely and insisted I did as he asked.'

She had said all of this so quickly that Luke believed her. Up until now she had done everything by the book and she was not the sort of girl to break fundamental procedure without express command to do so. In truth she seemed more upset than he was with the alteration of normal routine. He imagined that she always waited for the green man before crossing. Never put her feet up on the seats of the bus. Had never littered in her life. Her desk was probably meticulously organised and she remembered to put the bins out the night before. She probably wore cardigans all year round.

'I was just checking Laura. Please don't think I was accusing you. As if I could do such a thing.'

His attempt at being coy felt flat and forced. It was too early for their usual one sided banter but she probably blushed anyway.

'No offence taken. Mr. Calvin. Your client will be arriving at 1000 hours. Will there be anything else?'

He was sat in his boxers, the bright day dawning, the old town full of promises and possibilities. Last night's stress was gone. It had evaporated along with the rain, been soaked up in the sun and absorbed by the unknown client. He imagined she was sitting at her desk with a pencil skirt on and matching glasses. She'd probably have a salad for lunch. She probably drank Latte Machiattos.

'Not unless you're going to let me take you out for that drink like I've been asking for two years...'

She probably didn't wear lipstick. He doubted she was out of tights even in the hottest summer. It was probably just his improved mood but he was feeling much better and he was sure she was smiling down the phone.

'Goodbye Mr. Calvin.'

She probably went crimson right down to her sensible shoes.

Chapter 2

When the flat buzzer rang out it was exactly 10 a.m. Luke had just finished his breakfast of bacon and eggs and was enjoying a second cup of coffee when it broke the silence. Now dressed in dark jeans and a plain grey t-shirt, he crossed to his door. The buzzer was a standard front door entry system with a button for each of the 6 flats below and his larger flat on the 3rd floor. There was no difference on the street level but while most flats simply had a receiver to lift and a button to press if they wished to allow access, he had an advantage they did not. Secreted in the woodwork of the common entry door frame was a minute camera which fed directly to a display just by his front door 3 floors above.

On this display he could see a man in a suit and hat crouched over, studying the names on the other buzzers, obviously unsure if he had pressed the right one. As he straightened up and pressed the buzzer again, Luke made some initial guesses as to his proportions: - probably 6' 4" or thereabouts, a comfortable 18 stone. It was always difficult to gauge things too accurately from the screen since the angle had the habit of skewing proportions like a fun house mirror. The buzzer was being held longer the second time. Luke sipped his coffee and kept his eyes on the impatient giant. His guest was looking around, clearly becoming increasingly exasperated. Pressing the button one final time, he fumbled in his pocket for his phone and raised it towards his ear. Only then did Luke pick up the door handset at his end. He opted for feigned ignorance.

'Hello! Hello. Hello?'

The visitor lowered the phone slowly and turned to face the speaker. It disappeared into the pocket of his suit jacket as he stooped down slightly to be closer to the speaker.

'Yes. Hello. I am here to see a Mr. Calvin. I have an appointment for ten.'

The voice was cool and confident. Educated perhaps; definitely English. (The two were pretty hard to distinguish sometimes in his experience.) It carried authority and weight. Luke didn't like it. This time he adopted for a polite and gracious tone.

'Ah, yes. Please come in. I am on the 3rd floor. Right the way up the staircase to the very top and the red door.'

He saw the man lean down again to express thanks or understanding but Luke pushed the door open button and held it down. His guest waited a second for the buzz to stop before realising it wasn't likely to and decided to push the door and enter the building while the offer still existed.

Luke reckoned about 90 seconds would see his visitor comfortably to his threshold, so he took the opportunity to refill the coffee maker. A fresh pot always seemed to set thing off on an even keel. The kitchen was arranged neatly; he wasn't one for hosting or cooking too often. The 4 mugs on the stand were usually 3 too many and the cupboards were all but empty. The American style fridge/freezer only really served to emphasise how little food he required and if it weren't for the takeaway containers the bin wouldn't need emptied for weeks. Out of the few appliances, the coffee maker saw the most action by a long chalk. He emptied the grounds out of the filter into the bin and replaced the filter paper. The cupboard directly above housed a myriad of different brands and strengths, purporting to be from many exotic locations. Reaching for a new pack that promised a relative strength of 4 (out of 7 for some unfathomable reason) he was stopped momentarily when the doorbell rang. Not seeing the point in leaving the job half done, he grabbed the packet and was dumping a few heaped spoonfulls into the filter paper when the doorbell rang out again, shrill and persistent. The avalanche of grounds grew steadier and larger and once the doorbell had silenced once more as he added an additional spoon for good measure. It was obvious already this was going to be an ordeal.

With the water gurgling and dripping through into the pot he walked slowly across the cold kitchen tiles and along the floorboards of the corridor to the door. The peep hole offered another distorted image, a fish eye lens this time, making the face on the other side appear grotesquely misshapen. There was only one way to get a proper impression of his guest. He yanked the door open and the man on the stoop started for a moment before regaining his composure and introducing himself.

'Ah, Mr Calvin I assume? Geoffrey. Geoffrey Reid. So good to meet you. I've heard a lot about you and all of it good I might add which is unusual within these sort of circles.'

All of this tumbled out in one long tirade and as he spoke he swept off his hat and let himself into the flat. Luke's hand was grasped, pumped and discarded as Geoffrey strode through to the living room, his voice quieting by a measure, reducing now to the sound of an idling jet engine rather than a roaring one as he reached the threshold of the front room. Luke reckoned his estimation had been out. Mr Reid was probably a good 5 inches over the six-foot mark, with at least a 3-inch advantage over himself. His initial estimation of 18 stone may have been on the conservative side and he thought he would make mention of this if his "guest" kept up his bullish behaviour.

Luke followed him through to the living room where Geoffrey was now poised awkwardly, halfway in a sitting position on the seldom used end of the couch. He gestured with one hand directly behind his ample backside and Luke nodded. He sighed as he sat, clearly having reached the sort of mass and girth that required noise to conduct any sort of sudden strenuous activity. His greying hair was damp with sweat that ran freely down his face. Clean shaven and pitted with acne scars, it was the only part of him that didn't scream authority and the voice that boomed out from it was a deliberate attempt to offset this notion. The expansive jacket was hastily unbuttoned in the middle with sausage fingers and the collar loosened so that his neck was not being dug into quite as badly. The tie was silk and fastened in a knot that Luke doubted he could tie if he were given years to practice yet that too was yanked loose and Geoffrey Reid seemed to slightly deflate inside his tweed suit, relaxing into the sofa. Luke wasn't overly concerned: he could always throw that seat cushion away.

'Sorry for being so rude, I simply had to have a seat as soon as humanly possible.'

There was a wheeze to his voice and the red rising in his face and neck made Luke fully believe that he would indeed have had some sort of dramatic cardiac episode had he not sat down then and there. The breaths came deeper and slower and a handkerchief the size of a small African country had materialised in his paw as he mopped the perspiration from himself.

'Not a problem Sir.', said Luke, 'Make yourself at home. Would you like some water? The coffee won't be long if you'd prefer to wait for that?'

This time the manners were not quite as false. Hideous images had flooded his mind of the behemoth expiring right there and then on the sofa. It wasn't that he had suddenly become enamoured with his guest but merely the thought of the poor paramedics who would have to carry him out. Back problems like that never really go away. They linger in the background just enough to give you an uncomfortable reminder of that time you struggled down three flights with a well-dressed walrus on your gurney. Luke was a man of the people. He would not want to force that on any fictional working man.

'Coffee my good man. Coffee please. Lots of cream. Lots of sugar.'

There was a healthier sound to him now. His breathing had slowed considerably and the grim reaper had undoubtedly slunk away, almost as disappointed as the last time a flight of stairs had assaulted his portly pal. Now he was even making references. Maybe they'd get on OK after all. Luke took a moment to place it.

'Pulp Fiction? Winston Wolf, played by Harvey Keitel. Excellent film.'

The handkerchief stopped wiping and a look of confusion flashed on Geoffrey's face. Oh well, never mind. Must just be how he actually liked his coffee. Pouring a healthy mugful, he dumped in two big spoons of sugar and opened the fridge. There was no cream. In fact, the carton of milk looked as though it had seen better days. He took a sniff and grimaced before pouring it in anyway. Needs must. He brought the mug back through with his own black coffee in a black mug. Nondescript. Boring. Safe. There was nothing in his guest's manner any longer to suggest he had just crept back from the brink of oblivion. As he took the mug in his ample hand he took a large gulp and nodded approvingly.

'Excellent. Excellent.' he coughed, 'Quite excellent'.

The mug went down on the table right beside the coaster. Luke smirked. He doubted it would be picked up again. Settling carefully in the seat opposite with his mug cradled close, he eyed Geoffrey Reid through the haze of the steam. His suit was enormous and probably cost an enormous amount of money. Perfectly tailored; doubtless real tweed. Double breasted jacket and waistcoat. Timepiece? Check: - Inside pocket with chain to waistcoat. Handkerchief? Check: - Refolded in the breast pocket. Either embroidered or monogrammed. Cufflinks? Check: - They sparkled like diamonds because they probably were. His shoes were wing-tip patent leather; so shiny he probably saw himself reflected whenever he was able to see past his stomach. The whole ensemble screamed money. Not new money but wealth. It spoke of power and authority and it was once again definitely all intentional. Luke addressed him from over his mug.

'Why don't you tell me about yourself? You seem to know about me and you have me at a disadvantage there.'

Geoffrey's eyes brightened. This was obviously a subject close to his heart and Luke got the impression he was about to be buried under an avalanche of irrelevant information. He gulped down another mouthful of scalding coffee and braced himself.

'Well, where to start? As you know, my name is Geoffrey Reid. You may have heard of my work as a magistrate?'

The blank look he received did nothing to quench his enthusiasm. Seated more comfortably now, he appeared to expand even more, as if swollen by his own bluster and self-congratulation. The tone of voice implied that it was Luke that was in the wrong for having made the mistake of not knowing who he was and most certainly not the other way around. The next ten minutes were a highlight reel of a privileged life well lived. Born in England, studied at Fettes College in Edinburgh before moving on to the University. First class honours and distinctions, top of the class. The room was his echo chamber. The compliments he lavished on himself vibrated the windows and filled up the space all the way to the ceiling. A man about town. A cornerstone of society. Respected. Loved. Listened to.

The more he boasted the more animated he became. A grand sweeping gesture in the vague direction the court accompanied a particularly detailed story of his wise judgement. A conspiratorial

11

lean, hands braced on his thighs, eyes wide with delight; this was when he received a personal letter of congratulation from an unspecified important figure for his ongoing efforts within the judicial system. A firm slap of the knees preceded the recovery to the couch back. Mercifully, he was done. Luke took another long swallow of coffee and let the silence settle between them. It was always good to know your man but there had been no indication of why he was here or what service he expected from him. What could a man of this purported position and status need him to do that his many connections within the police and justice system could not? It was usually a woman. He eyed the hat perched on the arm rest which probably cost more than most people's first car. It might be several women.

'Well.' Luke stood with his mug and went to the kitchen for a refill. He shouted over his shoulder. 'That is all very impressive but it doesn't tell me why you're here.' He returned and retook his seat, this time folding one leg underneath him. 'Or indeed why the Major allowed you to see me without giving me the details on you or on what you wanted.'

The very suggestion that there had been anything different or untoward in the manner of their meeting was dismissed with a wave of the hand and a vague reference to how he and the Major knew each other from before. Privately or professionally was not specified. The implication seemed to be both.

'A favour. Let's just call it that.' he concluded. 'A special exception for a friend.'

This was not a sufficient explanation to Luke. He made a mental note to call the Major as soon as his settee had been relieved of its burden. All he really wanted out of Geoffrey was the reason he required his services and nothing more or less than that. Slowly, Luke was growing tired of playing the part of the audience in this dramatic monologue. His private analysis of the interaction so far was less than favourable. (1 and a ½ stars – Although interesting in sections the extent of self-indulgence and the suspension of disbelief required to fully become engrossed in this so called epic tale becomes ever more difficult as the bulky lead drags you through a quagmire of bloated and overreaching dialogue towards a tired and entirely predictable outcome. One to avoid.)

Geoffrey Reid grasped his chin gently between his thumb and forefinger and turned slightly to look out the window. He couldn't see the castle from where he sat.

'It's about my son.'

The tone had shifted. There was almost a hint of pain at the edges of this statement. The eyes returned from the window and rested firmly on Luke. This was not a man who was used to needing anything from anyone. His nature was resisting the horrible notion that there was something in his life over which he did not have complete and utter control and his blue grey eyes told of desperation.

Luke reached from his chair for the pad and paper on the table. His empty mug sat opposite his guest's full one. He placed his bare feet on the floor across from Geoffrey's £1000 shoes. He might have 3 inches, 5 stone and a disgusting amount of money more than Luke Calvin, but at this particular moment, he was not in the driver's seat and he knew it.

'Tell me all about it boss. We'll sort something out.'

Chapter 3

The pad was filled with notes, the sofa was empty and the flat was warming up from the sun streaming in the window. You couldn't trust the weather in Edinburgh: it had a nasty habit of changing on you without any warning. Luke sat and reread the lines he had taken down. The details were deliberately sparse but the overall message was clear. Geoffrey Reid had a son who was more the thorn in his flesh than the apple of his eye: a disappointment and an embarrassment. It was plain to see that his father thought him a failure, which was the ultimate insult to a man of success. He leeched off his father's reputation and money not realising that wealth might trickle down but respect did not. That notwithstanding, the errant son had been "off the grid" for two days now and there was no sign of him anywhere. The impression Luke had gotten was that this was not entirely unusual for him.

One thing was certain. Luke had not been his first option. Neither was he the last resort. He was a grey area in-between the law and order of the police force and the dark interactions of the serious criminal underworld. Geoffrey's nature and vocation forced him to begin his tentative enquires in the correct manner and through the proper channels, regardless of how little faith he might have had in their likely success. The Magistrate had not appeared to be a patient man and his efforts to involve the police force had been just as turbulent as Luke expected, if not more so.

When he had arrived at the police headquarters on Fettes Avenue, Geoffrey had exploded at whichever Sergeant had been in the Chief Superintendent's bad books enough to be placed in the firing line first by having to inform Magistrate Reid, straight to his face, that there was nothing further they could do. Once he had stormed into a higher officer's office the process had been repeated. His jowly face had been glistening with the sweat of fury and the doors rattled in their frames as he made his way up the ranks and through the corridors. Each subordinate was left quivering with relief when he stormed out and each superior dreading the human tsunami stalking from room to room, until he finally landed in front of the main man himself. The Chief Superintendent was a man of about 60; tall, slender and extremely serious. Even the Magistrate would normally respect him enough to make an appointment but he had gotten himself too worked up. There were no brakes on this runaway train, just as the Superintendent had anticipated. As soon as his secretary's polite protestations had been buried under a furious verbal barrage and the door nearly ripped from its hinges the Superintendent raised one hand and the big man silenced. In his other hand, he offered a scrap of paper with a handwritten phone number.

'Phone this Geoffrey. Speak to the Major. Off the record.'

The voice was a soothing balm: a yacht cutting gracefully through the bow wave of a tramp steamer. The older man raised himself to a standing position and looked down at the Magistrate from across his desk, seeing his eyes dart from the Superintendent to the paper and back again, radiating anger. The Chief had been renowned as a brutal man in his days on the beat but he was older now. He knew the merit of avoiding a head on collision and had learnt the benefits of deflection and distraction. Through years of experience, he had gradually realised that earning respect was easier without being loud, brash and burning your bridges everywhere you went. This was a lesson his intruder had staunchly refused to take. He placed a strong hand on Geoffrey's heaving shoulders and made the decision for him by clamping his bony fingers and turning the whole man towards the door and escorting him to it. Geoffrey Reid was as compliant and docile as a child now. He was calming down by degrees and felt his ire being replaced with rising shame at his behaviour. He looked one final time at the paper and spluttered slightly trying to convey an apology or thanks. The Superintendent didn't even bother to find out which.

'Anything for a friend. Now Geoffrey, I have other matters to attend to.'

There was no arguing with the polite request and he allowed himself to be escorted across the threshold. The secretary stood up with a start but the Superintendent shook his head to indicate no action was required. The Magistrate began the long walk back down the corridors to the exit and the Superintendent closed his door. Reseating himself, he could see Fettes College to the left and Broughton High School directly in front. There was only a road separating them geographically but they were streets apart in every other sense. How funny it seemed that he had gone to the High School with the rough and the ready while the Magistrate had gone with the privileged and rich. Education was clearly not the making of the man. Calm had descended over his station again and he felt at ease. He pressed the intercom and spoke.

'Karen? Take an early lunch. I'm very sorry about all that. I don't expect you back any time before 3pm OK? I'm big enough and ugly enough to field my own calls.'

Having had a reply in the affirmative he locked his hands together behind his head and leaned back in his chair. There was no way of knowing how this would play out yet – only time would tell.

Having finished reading and rereading the notes he had made, Luke decided to call the Major. There was something entirely different about every aspect of this scenario and the Major was not a man who tolerated deviations from the norm; far less approved them personally. Throughout his sparse interactions with his most senior employer, it had been kept deliberately unclear whether he actually held that rank or not. Luke doubted it: - he was probably much higher than that. Still, just another voice on the phone and another blank canvas onto which he could project his mental impressions. It was a generally harmless pastime of his but one that he enjoyed immensely.

The mobile handset had two numbers pre-programmed into it, one for the 'office' (which was just Laura's number) and one for the main man himself. As he pressed it and the number was dialled quicker than any human hand could manage, he had the sudden realisation that this was the first time he had actually called him rather than the other way. As it rang, he hoped he had startled him. As it rang a second time, he hoped that he was in the middle of something important. Just as it started to ring a third time it was picked up. "Three rings Major? Oh dear oh dear oh dear...." ran through his head but did not slip out of his mouth.

16

'Good morning Mr. Calvin. What can I do for you?'

Polite and trite. Every syllable was even and measured; his manner unruffled and crisp. The voice belonged to a man of precision and 'correctness'. Being an ex-military man himself, Luke knew how difficult it was for many to drop the manner once they were back in civilian life although the impression he got was that the Major had been born with perfect elocution and had spoken his first words with authority. Or maybe was reading too far into it.

'Sorry to bother you Major. I've just had a friend of yours visit with my assignment.'

'Ah. The Magistrate.'

Luke wondered why all these people referred to by their titles? Had they transcended the doubtlessly common practice of having names? How did they refer to him? Dogsbody? Cannonfodder? The mind boggled. Inwardly he bristled, but ever the true professional, he refused to allow even the slightest hint of this to enter his voice.

'Yes. The Magistrate.'

The ball had been deftly chipped back into the oppositions side of the court. It hung in the air alongside the silence. The Major was probably sat in full parade regalia. The number of medals on his chest lessened or increased depending on how charitable Luke was feeling that day. Some days, when congratulations were in order, he was a sweet old man in a suit just doing a job. Others, when there were questions or misgivings about a job, his chest was emblazoned. When he was being as evasive and difficult as he seemed today, he didn't even polish them himself. He had a polish-boy. Probably treated him terribly: short smoke breaks and a 45-minute lunch. The monster.

'He is a man I know from before, Luke. In a difficult position which required sensitive handling.' The Major positioned himself to smash the return down the line for the win; "I knew that a man of your calibre would understand that exceptions have to be made for exceptional circumstances.'

Luke weighed the words. He was going to do the job and he was going to do the job well, as he had before and as he would in the future. However difficult the Major was being, there was nothing to be gained from either pointing it out or acting on it. Today, the Major had a waxed moustache. He wore aviator goggles on top of his flying squadron cap. His scarf streamed out behind the chair, cartoonishly suspended on the horizontal.

'Very well sir. I will keep you informed on any and all developments.'

The Major was prepared to respond but Luke had already realised that the conversation was pointless and was going to be from the start. He decided to level a parting jibe that could be interpreted as innocent; no point blatantly sticking the knife in for a reaction. The man was, after all, his employer and significantly his superior.

'Yes Sir. I will keep you informed. Through the *usual* and *correct* channels of course. Goodbye Major.'

He hung up and the line went dead. In his mind, the ball smashed into net and the Major's monocle popped out in horror and disbelief. Point; Calvin. The crowd that existed nowhere except for in his own mind went wild.

It was high time to leave the flat. The best way to start always seemed to be by making an exit as if he had a purpose and the purpose would soon present itself. The Yale lock clicked softly into the latch as the door closed and he drew across the deadbolts with two separate keys. The latch style locks on the main door and his own weren't worth the cheap metal they were made from. Even a relatively tame kick would admit entrance to a burglar or more commonly, a drunk without keys. The issue wasn't necessarily the lock but that the frame that would splinter and allow the latch to jump free. The fact that his own door and frame were both reinforced with steel was not known to any of the other tenement occupants or to anyone with a mind to rob that might happen to make the grave error of attempting to enter his flat. After all, he had always reasoned that a padlock was only a deterrent to an honest man.

Victoria Street was busy with tourists. Making his way through the throng, he registered the many faces from the many places all clamouring around, alternately in a massive hurry then stopping to attempt to make sense of a map the size of a tablecloth. Heading downhill, he made the Grassmarket and paused at the corner. To his left, there was the road under George IV bridge: he could nip into the Three Sisters or Bannerman's for a quick half and make his way towards Waverley Station or North Bridge? If he jinked left, then right immediately right he would have to walk back uphill past Greyfriars Bobby and end up on George IV Bridge itself but that was likely to be even busier with tourists than here. Grassmarket it was then. He could cut up King's Stables and onto Lothian Road. That would be the West End of Princes Street and the best options for busses to wherever he needed to be. It seemed to be the most sensible option available. Besides, there were a myriad of decent boozers on the way, should the sudden exertion leave him a little bit dry.

He strode to his right through the pedestrianised area, over the cobbles and through the masses, internally revisiting the sparse facts he had. The son - Robert Reid. When jokingly questioned about whether he was called 'Rab' the client had become irate and dismissed the question as irrelevant. This tendered two pieces of information: 1) He was in all likelihood called 'Rab' by at least some people and 2) Daddy did not approve of nicknames. (Luke had made a mental note to refer to the Magistrate as 'Geoff' or 'G-Dog' or 'Jam Master G' if he was given even half an opportunity.) They were of similar ages, he and Rab. Both in their mid 30's. Highly unlikely they went to the same school but they were doubtless educated around the same time in the same city. At least they had that in common once he found him. They could even bond over how little they enjoyed the scorn of his father? The possibilities were endless.

In lieu of a physical description, the Magistrate had produced a photograph from his inside pocket: obviously printed for the purpose of giving to him. It was pristine and glossy, a head shot from a graduation. The man in it was smiling broadly with a large meaty arm draped over his shoulders. Luke had winced at the thought of a congratulatory hug from the Magistrate - his rib cage would need to be rebuilt from scratch. He bore only a passing resemblance to his father – the face was more angular with pronounced cheekbones and a narrower jaw. Possibly just because he was yet to put on the weight the Magistrate had presumably piled on during his late 30's. There was a diamond studded earring in the left ear and the only concrete resemblance between father and son were the blue grey eyes. The face was framed by blonde hair, oiled or gelled for the occasion. As he ran a hand through his own dark untidy curls, Luke knew that this picture was not a true reflection how Rab would look in everyday life.

Having reached a convenient pub and despite the fact that it was only halfway to the bus, he decided to nip in for a quick pint. As he swapped the glaring sun for the gloom inside he wondered about the man in the picture. How much of his success in education had been financially supplied by his father? Was he even bothered about the degree? As he paid for the pint, sipped a little to make it easier to carry and took it over to an empty table by the window, he wondered what it was like having a father who would choose to use that sort of a picture to aid in the search for his son. How would it feel to know that your own father chose to preserve the facade of your successful life, even if it potentially damaged the chances of finding you? Luke took a long swallow of lager and watched the people passing by the window. He very much doubted it felt good, but he wanted to hear it from the man himself. Still, the afternoon had barely begun. There was money in his pocket, a picture in his wallet of a strange man and a glass beading in front of him. It was good to be back at work.

Chapter 4

The number 37 bus ran all the way from Penicuik through the town and out to Silverknowes. The route went through deprived areas and rich areas alike, coasting over the Bridges and along Princes Street to the West End, down across the Dean Bridge and up to Crewe Toll roundabout. Beyond that, it ran through Pilton and Muirhouse before terminating in Silverknowes. Luke jumped on along Queensferry Road and settled himself in a seat on the lower level. The destination for him was a pub in Pilton called 'The Archer'. There had never been any serious trouble for him in these areas but he understood the apprehension that people tended to feel going there. The stories they'd heard and the reputations that had been built surrounding these areas were really a throwback to the 80's at best: when the skag had really taken hold and thrived. When Muirhouse was the heroin capital of Europe and the problems that came with that made it a tough place to live and an easy place to die. No matter the changes that are made, a bad reputation was hard to shift. And to a certain type of person, a tough reputation was hard to build and the benefits of willingly shirking it were almost entirely outweighed by the respect that seemed to come from living in these areas.

Depending on who you asked, these streets had either been some of the most dangerous in Edinburgh at one point or still were today. The only people who ever professed to think any different lived there. They would talk about the great sense of community. They would refer to any trouble as just being the 'young ones' running wild. Or even just dismiss it entirely as boys being boys. The best place to go for information in a time like this was the sort of establishment he was headed to now. You could trust the people to be honest without the grandstanding or pretension you tended to get in the more reputable places.

The Archer was the sort of boozer that people were warned about before they visited the city. Even if they had no intention of visiting the area, they would doubtless hear stories. It became less clear with each retelling how much of it was bluster and legend but Luke Calvin had been brought up in the area and he knew the script. People would say it didn't even have a ladies' toilet; apparently the most damning indictment of an establishment that polite society could place on a location. The implication was fairly straightforward – No ladies' toilet: No women. A watering hole so rough and ready that it wouldn't be graced by anyone of the fairer sex. This was untrue.

The second most prevalent story was that it had no windows. Not a single source of natural light, the drinking and fighting all taking place outside of the gaze of even the sun itself. That it was a low brutish building made of brick teeming with low, brutish men with fists of stone and hair trigger tempers. This was partially true. There were indeed no windows in the pub and it did look as though it was built to survive nuclear war. In fact, he genuinely believed that should he find himself alive in the post-apocalyptic wasteland, all he would have for company would be the cockroaches and a few guys taking liberties with the unmanned taps in The Archer. In terms of the clientele, the rumours were closer to the truth. He supposed that if you were used to sipping Mimosas in a bar on George Street with a seemingly random word as a name, an inexplicable door policy and happily paying £12 a pop for the privilege you could possibly become unstuck as soon as you walked in the door. These opinions were held by men who had watched too many Westerns. They would push the door open and every head would turn. The jukebox box would skip and fall silent. All the chatter would stop. Then someone would wrap a pool cue round their head and that would be the end of that.

Anyone who had ever been there knew this to be nonsense of course. It was true that there was a higher proportion of 'amateur' pugilists than you would usually have but no one ever went out for a quiet pint looking for trouble. One of his favourite characters was a man who insisted he was 70 but was probably a fair bit older by the name of 'Tam'. He hadn't volunteered a second name when they first met and Luke saw no benefit in asking over the intervening years. He was his first port of call if he needed information; all the man appeared to do was sit in the local pubs and drink. He knew everyone and everything and unusually for these areas, he was well liked by everyone. Slightly hunched and occasionally making use of a tripod style walker, he had a scruffy white beard down to his chest. The hair on his head was equally strikingly coloured and hung past his ears. Aside from these two things, he was always impeccably dressed – blazer as a minimum, usually a waistcoat underneath and a great overcoat all year round. Tam had once volunteered to Luke the exact explanation for a so called 'rough pub' that he said fit the bill for any establishment of that reputation…

'You see son, the problem with somewhere like this is that people decide this is a rough boozer.'

He swept his hand behind him, gesturing across the stained pool table. His half pint and nip sat in front of him and Luke was in the middle of attempting to salvage some pride after losing two frames badly. For a man that struggled to walk when it was cold, he could certainly still work the cue.

'Someone decides that this is rough. Then he tells someone. And they tell someone.'

His hand was listing off these connections one by one. Counting up on mangled fingers. 'And maybe someone kens someone who kens someone who once got a hiding in here off someone and that's it. It becomes fact.'

Underneath his right eye was a long hook shaped scar, looping up through his broken nose and into the centre of his forehead. The bright blue eye was framed on the top by another scar which was conveniently covered almost entirely by his bushy eyebrows but Luke had been forced to feel it during a particularly dramatic retelling of the origin story. Both eyes were fixed on him now and a smile beamed broadly through the fuzz.

'All hearsay mind. But now. Now.' He wagged his finger and took a sip of whiskey.

'Now someone who reckons he's a hard case gets telt. And he reckons he'll decide. So in he nashes. Chest out and the boys behind him. Causes bother and gets the script read to him. And that's the cycle started.'

Luke rapped a red towards the top left hand corner and it thumped deep into the pocket and dropped. Chalking the cue with the remnants of a cube, he glanced back at Tam who was now staring reflectively at nothing in particular somewhere in the nicotine stained ceiling.

'Aye son. That's it then. Folk will come in looking for trouble and they'll find it. No because it's here waiting, but because they're bringing it in with them. The boys aren't bad boys. Nah, they're jist normal gadges wanting a quiet bevvy and a bit of crack.'

The next red rattled in the jaws of the centre pocket but rebounded luckily and dropped opposite. Luke raised his hand to apologise for the luck but Tam was still educating him and hadn't even noticed. Only one more ball to go now and the black was sitting nicely in the centre. As he chalked up, the older man looked back at him again and pointed a finger.

'You played it right son. You played it right. You walks in that door there, didnae give anyone any lip. Nae dodgy looks. Just ordered a pint and drank it. Just another gadge in for a drink. I ken't as soon as I seen you that you'd be nae bother to anyone.'

Tam took another swallow from his half pint and chased it with another nip. Luke cracked the final red straight into the top corner and landed the cue ball directly behind the black in the centre of the table. Although he was pleased he'd behaved correctly the first time he'd come in, his pride was hurt somewhat by the suggestion that he'd come across as a wet blanket or a pushover. As he settled down to line up the black he glanced at the old man who was looking at him, beaming. He drew back the cue as Tam concluded.

'A knew you could handle yerself son. I can always tell a scrapper when I see one. Dinnae be getting yir pampers in a twist just yet eh?'

The black ran slowly into the top right pocket as Luke straightened up and smiled back at Tam. The old man raised the last of his whiskey to his mouth and winked.

'Mind the in-off there son.'

The white was trickling straight for the top left pocket. It teetered on the lip for a moment before dropping in to the sound of Luke's groan and the rest of the pub laughing.

Hopping off the bus at Pilton Bank, Luke raised his hand behind him and murmured the customary 'thanks driver' to the heavily tattooed gent behind the wheel. It felt a bit like asking a taxi driver if he'd

24

been busy or what time he was on 'til – somehow these statements were hard-wired into everyone regardless of age, class or status. Striding off down past the old arcade, he headed for The Archer. There was the usual array of bookies and chippies down here but the old arcade had at one time housed a reasonable number of decent shops of all varieties. When they closed it had hurt the community and apart from the endless cycle of big brand supermarkets buying out the large shell at the top of the road and closing down due to harassment and shoplifting, not many had ventured in and remained for any length of time.

All the establishments around here had the same steel shutters that rolled down every night and rolled up every morning. Like a housing association of vandalism and terror, any newer place that went without had their windows panned within a week and the steel erected within two. When the shops were shut, the signs above read as normal – the big chain bookmakers, the post office, the family owned take away place – but the shutters proclaimed a different tale once they were down. Disco Dave had been here "2k13" and by his own assertion and lacking any other proof, Luke was forced to believe that he must indeed be "on top non stop". It made no difference that the local shop had been "Established 1972" because the real scoop was that the readers mum had apparently been established in 1972 by "YMR – Kick to kill. Kill for fun." Night would fall and the shutters would hide the contents of each shop and replace it with their own particular brand of petty rivalry. Tags scrawled over mentions scrawled over nonsense. The many layers of shifting alliances and dominant gangs.

Luke raised the cigarette packet to his mouth and extracted one with his lips. Replacing the packet, he grabbed the lighter and flicked it deftly at the end until it was sufficiently glowing. The number of smokers in these allegedly impoverished areas never seemed to decrease, regardless of how often or how much the price was increased each budget. Money wasn't as much of a concern for him as it seemed to be for most people, but every time he saw the pitiful amount of change he got out of his ten spot for 20 cigarettes, he made a mental note to quit. It was a mantra he repeated several times a day; every one that he didn't really want or need was accompanied by the thought, no matter how fleeting, that this could be the last.

Reaching the door of The Archer, he leant against the brick to finish smoking before he entered. The smoking ban had been an unmitigated fiasco when it was first introduced but he could not deny the merit in it now. Gone were the days where you'd sit inside, the air thick with smoke, and just crush one after the other. He'd easily gone through forty of an evening if the booze was taking control enough. The absence of the large glass ashtrays was also a boon: one less weapon in a pub was never a bad thing.

For the first couple of weeks and onwards, people had moaned non-stop about having to get up, leave your pint and stand in the cold and wind to smoke. It was an inconvenience. It was an interruption to half a century of tradition for some of the older boys who would light up inside out of habit and be escorted out on their wobbly legs as quickly as the barmaid could manage. Luke took a long drag and exhaled through his nose as he took the final pull. Crushing it out in the metal tray that looked like a letterbox, he thought that the inconvenience was worth it. It probably helped people cut down. And the camaraderie that existed between smokers now was stronger due to their being shunned together. Huddled outside, away from the warmth and the others, they became closer and stronger. It was not entirely unlike Pilton itself, he thought as he pushed open the door and walked into the dull roar of The Archer.

Chapter 5

Geoffrey Reid was sitting in his office on The Mound, not quite 100 yards from the High Court. His wing-tip shoes rested on a desk that wouldn't have looked out of place in a banquet hall – rich mahogany, polished to a high shine and with countless drawers and compartments. It was a legitimate Victorian writers desk complete with ink well and the remnants of blotted and dripped stains all left for the sake of authenticity. He had paid £5000 for this desk – a fact that he was more than happy to disclose that to anyone who asked and indeed a few who didn't.

When it came to the law, there was always the assumption that justice was blind. Not in the sense that most people would jokingly take it, but in the sense that it treated every person and every circumstance on its own merits. Not on any pre-existing status, colour, creed or religious persuasion. This was the law executed as it should be; based purely on the facts. Anyone with half a brain cell rolling around in their head knew this to be false. Even with the best of intentions, a man is prone to prejudice. A suit and some nice shoes will get a lot more respect and better treatment in the exact same circumstance as a man who is dressed shabbily. A good education and a reputable occupation can buy you more leeway than the most watertight alibi in the world.

This was a point that the Magistrate felt very strongly on, but not in the way that one would expect. He believed that justice should not be blind: That a man of good standing was allowed some form of elasticity in terms of all things legal and especially when it came to sentencing. People of a certain calibre didn't deserve to be cooped up with reprobates and criminals like rats. This was his opinion and this was how he ran his courtroom. Never to any extent that would lead to any sort of professional repercussions but enough to satiate the innate need in himself to cement his ongoing belief that he was – in fact – better than the rest of them.

Stretching backwards, he clasped his enormous hands behind his head and leant back in the chair further. This suit was different from the one he had worn in Luke's flat but no less extravagant. The silk shirt strained slightly in opposition to his reclining but the blazer was tailored so well that it barely rode up: no pull at the armpits and no tightening at the waist. A more subdued dark navy was the choice for this afternoon, with a grey waistcoat and matching trousers. There was not a single component of this outfit or any of the rest that he kept at his home or indeed in his office that had cost less than the top prices and as he leant his head back to fix his eyes on a point somewhere among the cornices on the ceiling, he knew he would not have it any other way.

His son was the prime example of the exception that proved this rule of his. Robert had been given every opportunity. Raised in privilege under his own roof and treated to the best food and entertainment that money could buy or the man himself could offer. An enviable academic career which was thankfully no true representation of his seemingly endless capacity for stupidity and disinterest. All of this he had provided because he was his son and for better or worse, he was a representation of himself. Ungrateful. That's what he was. Unable to see beyond his useless lowlife friends and the fun they had together (which seemed to him to consist of nothing more than sitting in the darkened games room playing on the consoles and smoking endless "cigarettes"). His constant source of shame. The spoiled fruit of his loins. Heaving a deep sigh, he levered his massive frame forward and sat upright, pressing the intercom button briefly. It was answered immediately by a curt voice.

'Yes Sir.'

His secretary, Claire, had been with him for almost a year now: a true testament to her staying power and thick skin. Geoffrey Reid prided himself on being a firm man and this notion of "firm but fair" was for the birds.

'Would you come through here please Claire?'

The lack of response was in the affirmative and the Magistrate leaned back once more in his seat, listening to the muffled traffic roar outside on the street. The soft 'tip tap' of high heeled shoes pacing towards his office down the long corridor became louder and louder until they paused right outside the heavy door. There was a

28

tentative tap that resonated through the wood and he allowed himself a brief pause before speaking.

'Enter.'

One word. One syllable. Through many years of practice, he had got it down to a fine art - the duality of command and politeness. The undeniable instruction which was seemingly an invitation all at once. As the door opened soundlessly, his head turned, still rested on his arms to watch Claire walking in. It was a treat that never got old.

The timid knock had belied the creature that was now closing the door firmly and walking towards the desk. Tall and slender, she had dark hair down to her shoulders tied back in a severe looking ponytail. She carried herself entirely erect, soft shoulders deliberately squared and the heart shaped face atop her neck held upright. Through the square rimmed spectacles, her eyes were a burning brown. The overall look of a stern librarian made most men come over all a quiver or at the very least tone back whatever lewd and boorish behaviour they had been undertaking or even planning. Geoffrey Reid bore her gaze lazily.

'Yes. How can I help you?'

Even the voice was severe. He truly understood why the timbre and cadence of this imposing woman's speech when coupled with her appearance and manner had reduced many of his powerful and occasionally hostile guests almost schoolboy like obedience. His head turned back to the window as a raven landed on the sill. Even as he watched it looking through the pane, head cocked in confusion as if wondering what to make of the supine giant whose head was also rolled to the side, he could feel the irritation begin to emanate from Claire. The fire in her eyes had taken hold now and they were attempting to sear a hole in the back of the Magistrate's greying head to get his attention. She made an indistinct noise of annoyance. On the granite window ledge, the raven had concluded its leeward inspection and now had its head pointed to the other side. Its beady eyes surveyed the room briefly; the impatient secretary, the Victorian furniture, the tapestry and diplomas on the wall. They ran across the fireplace, for display purposed only now, and the ornaments that sat heavy and imposing on the mantelpiece, but they returned to the Magistrate. Claire coughed and Geoffrey's head whipped back round.

'Oh yes. Sorry Claire.'

The warmth of his tone was not entirely false. He took a great amount of pleasure in attempting to rile Claire. The smile that split his great face like a razor, flashing his unnaturally white teeth and the kindness that appeared in his eyes did little to quench the furnace building inside his secretary. She crossed her arms across her chest and looked at him pointedly, breaking the heavy silence with a single tap of her shoe. With her head lolling slightly to one side, she put him in mind of the raven on the window. Only the raven was less likely to try and peck his eyes out at the moment.

'I was getting rather hungry. Would you do me a favour and order me something in?'

Under the bridge of the black glasses frame, her small nose twitched. This was the tell that Geoffrey had noticed: - the one chink in her armour. It was the reason he did not fear her like most did and he often thought how funny it was that this was all it took. She had spent years being cold and distant. She had remained professional and stern and endured a lifetime of building a wall to keep these so called men of power where they should be – on the outside. But Geoffrey saw her nose twitch when she was close to losing her temper and he knew it was all an act. The anger that she was showing, however, was not. She liked order and routine and here he was dragging her out of it to order him a sandwich. It was just because he could and they both knew it. She informed him that she would and turned to leave. The Magistrate looked to the window but all he could see was the traffic whizzing up and down the mound. As the click clack of Claire's shoes echoed through the halls, he raised his eyes to the ceiling once more.

After lunch, he supposed he'd check in on this Luke Calvin character that was supposedly going to find his son. All the recommendation in the world couldn't give him faith in a man he had only just met and he would not accept anything less than quick and decisive success. Once Claire had cooled off to a medium boil he'd ask her to bring the files she had found on his detective, through the correct channels and the very shady ones alike. It was difficult to get references for this sort of work. There wasn't usually a manager to call and check if they'd had a good attitude or shown up drunk all the time. He reached for the telephone and dialled the Major's direct line knowing full well that he wasn't meant to have it. He knew the Major would be polite but unimpressed. He knew that checking up on a job he'd issued 3 hours earlier would probably look unprofessional and pushy. But this was just how Geoffrey Reid was wired and he would apologise to no man for it. As the final number was punched into the phone, he glanced outside once more, hoping to glimpse his bird. Two carnivores, eye to eye. He had sensibly remained gone.

'She'd have scared me off too buddy.' he murmured as the line began to dial.

Leaving The Archer, it was close to 2 o clock. An unnatural warmth was flowing through Luke's body and it wasn't entirely down to the sun that seemed to hang overhead. Tam had been in at the bar and had furnished him with what sparse information he could. Information, facts and possibilities were what he required to make headway but they usually came at a cost. Luckily for him, the old man had never upped his prices – giving out the goods both large and small for nothing more than a few rounds of drinks and a bit of company in the meantime.

Tam had known of him and promised to ask around, graciously accepting the smaller copy of the headshot that the Magistrate had provided. Luke paused outside the high rise flats to light up again. As the smoke hit his lungs, he held it briefly before exhaling. The taste of whiskey subsided temporarily and he made a mental note never to quit. There was something about the way it hit the spot when you had a drink in you that made it all worthwhile. Walking down past the playgrounds in-between the flats, he took the small black notebook out of the back pocket of his jeans and opened it to where he had begun writing inside the pub. The hand with the cigarette reached upwards to sweep back the hair that was threatening to curl down over his eye and obscure his vision and he began to read.

The first thing he had written was always the same; "Stop writing in notebooks". Aside from the date and location, this was the main pointer in the numerous notebooks that lay in his flat that it was Tam who was helping him out. He always insisted on making him write it down at the top of the page; a bizarre habit that had started the very first time they had become acquainted. It was one of Tam's favourite stories to tell…

It had started when the older man had eyed him warily as he took the pen and paper out to write during their first chat, a good few years ago. Tam had jabbed his whiskey in an accusatory manner towards Luke's hands.

'That's not normal son.'

Luke viewed him with confusion. 'How?'

Tam's head shook sadly in response to the question. It was a gesture of disappointment. His mouth was puckered upwards and the wise old eyes avoided Luke's. The whiskey took a neutral position in-between them around shoulder height.

'There's only three types of people who use notebooks.'

As the whisky made its shaky way towards Tam's mouth, Luke waited for the rest. A sip later and the glass returned to the table but nothing more was forthcoming. His face was placid as if trying to recall a memory just outside his grasp. Luke raised his glass almost to his lips but then paused and pressed the issue.

'Well. Who uses notebooks then?' he asked, trying to keep the irritation from his voice.

A great amount of air emanated out from the bushy white beard. The head began to shake again and the whiskey glass rose.

'Imagine not knowing that.' Luke took a sip instead of taking the bait. 'Imagine.'

Tam swirled the dregs of the amber liquid round the glass slowly and drained it. Turning on his stool with one mangled hand on the arm of his walker for support he faced his younger companion. The hand not being utilised for support was raised in front of Luke's face with the index finger extended upwards.

'Reporters. Nosy bastard reporters. Always asking questions. Asking who and whit and how come. And it makes nae odds whit you say, they'll be scribbling away in that notebook and ye ken that they'll be twisting it to suit them.'

There had been only two other men in the pub at this point, besides Brenda the barmaid. Both were known to Luke by sight but not by name. Stalking each other around the pool table, they were smashing every shot. He had clocked them on the way in and between the ink on the hands and the 'whit you lookin at' glances that he had gotten, he didn't reckon they were there to make friends with him. Tam had been sitting at the bar right by the pool table, to decrease his journey time should he want to play. Both of the players' heads whipped round on the announcement of Tam's next point. Luke fancied it was more out of habit than anything else.

'Cops.' A second gnarled finger made its way up to join its companion. 'No matter whit you're up tae or whit ye say it aw goes intae that wee book. They write and they nod but they watch ye and ye can tell they think they're better than you.'

Luke could feel the pool players' eyes on him. Being pegged as a reporter or a cop could literally be a death sentence in this place. Brenda had sidled up to the end of the bar and taken the empty glasses from in front of him. She clocked the intensity of the glares and the growing tension between the men on the stools so made an effort to kept her voice as breezy and light as possible.

'Same again boys?'

The white hair and beard rose and fell slowly to indicate "yes" but the eyes never left the man sitting opposite. Brenda began whistling to fill the silence as she started the drinks and made a note to get the jukebox on as soon as was possible. Luke remained calm. The iciness of the old man's eyes cancelled out the heat he could feel building behind him. He realised it had been a long time since he'd last heard a shot being taken.

'If you're no a cop.' One finger curled painfully back down to the fist. 'And yer no a reporter'. The second joined it and the fist clenched tight. 'Then you must be the third kind of person.'

Scar tissue ran thick and deep across his broken knuckles and Luke eyed him warily. The two men were now very interested in what the older man was saying and he could almost feel their breath on the nape of his neck. Brenda was in the middle of pouring the second pint, far too far down the bar to intervene. It felt like there was something coming and Luke gripped his empty whiskey glass tight in his right hand, ready to spin and smash it on whatever part of either pool player he could reach before the cues came down. Tam leered through narrowed eyes and reached the fist forward until it was just touching Luke's chin. His voice when it came was coarse and breathy.

'Yer a traffic warden.'

The two pool players behind him laughed so hard and so close that Luke nearly glassed them anyway as a reflex. He let out a long breath that he hadn't even realised he'd been holding and looked up the bar to Brenda who was pretending not have heard yet seemed to be finding the pint she had just poured somehow hilarious. Tam had both hands braced on his thighs and was rocking back and forward, eyes glistening with both tears and mirth. He reached out and clubbed Luke's shoulder playfully, nearly sending him flying.

'Ah, I cannae put the shiteners on you son. But I'll keep trying.'

Chapter 6

Robert Reid never went anywhere without Grant. Grant Ferguson could rarely go anywhere without Rab. They had started the same day at Fettes College, sat next to each other in registration and never really properly separated. Starting into the "big school" at the age of 12 is a harrowing experience for anyone and just because someone comes from a well off family, it doesn't mean they are above the usual childish bullying that you expect in a "normal" school. A "free" school was the derisory description of choice among the self-proclaimed elite who had nothing to earn the money that sent them there but felt they deserved the respect regardless.

Grant was big for his age; strong and broad; whereas Rab was and always remained rather slight. Short, slender and quiet, he struggled to raise his head from his shoes when spoken to and was even less inclined to do so when the interaction consisted primarily of name calling and cuffs around the ear. The Ferguson's were a local family who had made their fortune in the fitness industry. Their house had improved but they stayed in the same place they always had and they made the best effort to keep their only child in the precarious balance between enjoying the avenues opened by their wealth and keeping him grounded and grateful. They both agreed that the merit of a private education was well worth the investment in their son but Mrs Ferguson feared daily. The first day that they had deposited him in front of the main building and waved him off, she had spoken to her husband about her worry:

'We've stuck him in there with all these snobs. God knows what they'll do to him or how they'll change him.'

Mr. Ferguson had put an arm across his wife's shoulders as they looked together at the grand school building looming over them. He shared her fears but one of them had to keep the sensible head on or Grant would be withdrawn and placed in a normal school before the day was out.

'He'll be fine. This is the best opportunity we can give him.' The confidence in his voice surprised him. He pulled her head sideways onto his shoulder and smoothed her hair as gently as a man with hands the size of ping pong bats can. 'Who knows, maybe he'll change them?'

The very first lunchtime, Grant and Rab took a walk down to Stockbridge for some food reasoning that they had sat together so now they might as well eat together. Young Master Ferguson wasn't yet entirely sure what to make of his diminutive companion – with his blonde hair cut short and the eyes that tracked the toe of each foot as it shuffled along the pavement seeming watery to the point of tears at all times. When he did speak, he mumbled indistinctly, although Grant was sure he had almost looked at him when replying most recently. It was a minor improvement, but an improvement none the less. None of this behaviour made sense to a boy who was bigger than his classmates. Who bore any name calling with the indifference of a man who knows it won't escalate beyond that. On they went. Rab shuffling and mumbling. Grant striding easily, head up, eyes forward. They came upon a group of their classmates standing around eating who noticed their approach and fanned out to block the way. Grant paused two feet in front of them and held his left arm out across Rab's body to stop him since he wouldn't have noticed otherwise. Rab glanced upwards briefly and seeing the boys in the path, thrust his head back down towards his shoes, furiously avoiding eye contact.

This was the main group that had been riding him all morning. With their matching haircuts and expensive shoes, they looked like copies had been made of one original toff and the details changed ever so slightly with each iteration: a transmogrification by Chinese whispers. Even though Rab had the same style as them; the pricey satchel, the £100-pound haircut, the shoes and even the affluent upbringing; they had had all been to school together from the start and knew that he didn't belong. Grant knew he didn't belong either but no one had chosen to mention that: in fact, the guys had treated him well and even now they greeted him warmly.

The question was asked about why he chose to associate with the Reid boy. A sly dig about his father's reputation for backhanders and biased judgement was made. Grant stood impassive as they all drew closer, beaming smiles at him that excluded the scrawny blonde who had begun to sniff audibly. He was cordially invited to reconsider his choice of friends. He scanned the faces of each of the boys in front of him as the subtle implication came that Grant would be more than welcome to carry on and go eat but they needed to speak to his friend about something. Rab's shoulders had begun to tremble slightly and his nose dripped clean onto his patent leather shoes. As his despair and shame built, he knew that Grant would walk on and leave him and he felt he almost deserved it. With the ever increasing heave of Rab's shoulders, Grant's eyes went once more from the face of one boy to the next. Each of them had the pride and unwashed arrogance of a boy who had never been given the kicking he had deserved.

His mind had been made up from the start but just as a hand stretched to grasp Rab's shoulder, Grant planted his legs and drove up with his fist, twisting from the waist to get his whole weight behind it. The hand crunched into a jaw which rose with it before the legs supporting it folded under. Stepping over the instigator who now sat bow-legged on the concrete with his head hanging like a grotesque mannequin, he lunged wildly with an overhand right and felt it sink into a cheek before the knuckles jarred on some teeth. The group was dispersing quickly but he reached forward with his left hand and snatched a handful of the nearest collar to him. The blood had rushed to his head and he could only vaguely hear the protestations that were emitting from whoever's clothing he had a grasp of. It didn't matter who it was. With a viscous tug, he turned and threw him to the ground right in front of Rab's feet. Rab had his head up and was looking at Grant with unbridled rapture. Breathing heavily and slowly starting to feel the ache enter his hands he only managed to nod his head downwards to the prostrate figure that had scrambled to its knees and was looking pleadingly into Rab's eyes. Rab looked from the first victim who was now moaning and attempting to sit up, to the one in front of him, to Grant and then back to the kneeling figure. He wiped his snotty nose with the back of his right hand, sniffed hard, then threw a wild punch somewhere into the side of his former tormentor's head. When he looked back at Grant, his eyes were no longer so watery and he was in serious danger of smiling. Grant gave a half smile of approval and jerked a thumb down the path.

'Come on pal, let's go eat eh?'

Rab nodded and planted a sickening toe poke kick right in the face of the first boy who was now almost ready to get to his feet and caught up with his friend. He pulled a silk monogrammed handkerchief out from his pocket and gave it to Grant to stem the blood that had begun to seep from his hand. He wiped his nose and eyes with the back of his blazer sleeve and walked on in companionable silence with his head up.

Grant thought often on this first day. Even now, more than 20 years later, as he was sitting in his flat with the sunlight streaming through the sliding glass doors from his second floor balcony, he thought of it. A lot of time had passed. There had been many times he had reflected on what would have happened if he had just shrugged his shoulders and walked on. Left little Rab to his fate. He was sprawled comfortably across his black leather sofa with a bottle of beer within easy reach on the coffee table in front of him and some show he wasn't really watching droning on the big screen TV on the far wall. His left arm rested on the sofa back, flopped back towards the kitchen. The counter tops and work surfaces were spotless and the fridge and cupboards were well stocked. There was a spice rack along the back wall and each jar had a varying level inside it; this was a kitchen that was used and used often despite the fact that Grant Ferguson did not look like a man who could even boil an egg.

As he burped and reached for his beer again, the tribal tattoo running from the back of his right hand all the way up to his neck caught the light. The vest he wore had seen a few too many sunrises and spillages. Muscles rippled up his arms and down his back and his shaved head was merely the last portion of the thug image he had chosen to embrace. Lifting his legs slowly and bringing them to the ground quick he levered himself upright and carried his beer to the other part of the living room/kitchen. The cooker was on an island and the TV was clearly visible to enable the non-viewing of the show to continue uninterrupted. The gas ignited on the hob and a metal skillet landed on top with a generous knob of butter. The extractor above was brought on, drowning out the TV that no one was watching. Two sirloin steaks that had been sitting out and were now room temperature were scored in an 'X' shape by a professional chef's knife. Some salt and seasoning rubbed in; he'd read somewhere that pepper burns if it's put in prior to cooking; and then they were seared for one minute each side on the red hot pan before being set aside to finish cooking, sizzling heartily over the drone of the TV.

There had been all different sorts of fallout from his first meeting with Rab. As expected, they had returned to the school with chippie sauce greasy around their mouths to find the head of year waiting. With hands clasped behind his back and his academic robes billowing out he had put Robert Reid in mind of Count Dracula that he had seen in one of the films his father had told him not to watch. In an uncharacteristic act of defiance, he had put it on in his bedroom when the Magistrate was sleeping and spent the whole night wide awake under the covers, quivering with fear for his troubles. His pace faltered as they approached the stern looking Mr. Ackroyd and Rab found his eyes being drawn downwards towards the ground. Grant dug an elbow gently into his ribs and nodded his head up and forward gently. Rab's head came back up and his feet remained steady.

Grant looked straight at Mr. Ackroyd and had no thoughts of Dracula. He remembered a drag queen that had come on late at a holiday resort in Magaluf with his parents, done a stellar Bonnie Tyler number in a flowing evening gown and sent the room into rapturous applause as his mother slowly turned beetroot. Rab fought back tears the same way Grant fought back the peals of laughter that were building inside of him. Mr. Ackroyd addressed them as they approached with a grave air.

'Now then boys.'

Grant muttered darkly out of the corner of his mouth to Rab. 'Here we go.' It was a conspiratorial voice that no one had ever used with him before now. He basked in its embrace and felt his fear dissipate. They were in it together. That was enough for him.

In the kitchen of his flat, the two steaks still had 4 and a half minutes before they'd be fully rested. Crossing over the living room, he stepped out onto the balcony and lit up from the packet that was waiting on the handrail. This had been a big factor in buying the flat; the two bedrooms were spacious, the built in wardrobes were a generous size and the en-suite was a nice bonus on top of the normal bathroom; but when Grant had seen the kitchen/living room with its open plan feel and the glass door to the balcony, he had been sold. Sure, if you were splitting hairs it was technically in Pilton but you wouldn't have guessed it from the price tag. Sitting on the chair out here of a morning with a mug full of coffee and an open schedule was worth every penny of it.

It wasn't even noon yet and the sun was already warm in the sky. There was steak ready to be eaten in a few short minutes, coffee still hot in the French press and everything was looking rosy. The phone vibrated in his pocket and he held the cigarette in his lips as he fumbled with both hands for it. Pulling it out and squinting through the smoke, the name and number calling caused him to groan. Taking a long drag deep into his lungs and exhaling hard, he flicked the whole thing off the second floor into the path below. Pressing the button to pick up, he looked at the ashtray sitting less than a foot away from him. Why had he done that?

'Good morning Magistrate Reid. What can I do for you?'

Chapter 7

Back in his flat in Victoria Street, Luke was reclined in the window seat with his notebook in front of him and the dull pressure of a headache building in his subconscious. It was now getting towards evening and all he had to show for his day's work were a few general insights into his man and a call history on his phone consisting of the Magistrate or his secretary checking in. The pubs and the people he had spoken to had filled his head with nonsense and his belly with booze. Still, he was on the job and not many people could have the afternoon he had on the clock, far less on expenses.

The impression he had been given of Robert from the people who knew him or knew of him was a world apart from what his own father had said. This was normal of course: - it was a very rare occasion indeed when someone's parent's had a full impression of how their child was, but this was in the extreme. He was not well liked and the sort of respect he managed to garner was from people who thought it would get them a taste of his ready cash or an avenue to run up if they got themselves in trouble. Every bit as flash and arrogant as his father but without the gravitas to carry it off or any discernible justification for it. The most concrete thing that he had to go on was that he was rarely out of the company of an old school friend called Grant. He might as well take a look at the information that he had received from the office about his man and see what he could find out about his companion while he was at it.

His laptop had seen better days but served him for what he needed. The fan ran too often and too loud as it resisted the constant urge to succumb to overheating and melt altogether into a pool of solder and despair. When he had left the service and first gotten into this line of work, he was given carte blanche (literally a blank piece of paper in this case) to list what he required to do his job effectively. The flat was sufficient and the furnishings to his taste so he felt no need to splash out in that respect. He didn't drive so asking for a car was not necessary. His wardrobe was basic but his own and he objected to the idea of being dressed by someone else, even by proxy, so that was out. The sheet had been handed straight back to the company representative without a jot on it.

Slim hands had taken it back carefully and turned it over. Green eyes scanned the nothingness on both sides before a smirk twitched the cheek of his sallow face. Black hair raked back over an offensively shiny forehead, the rep had seemed impressed. His off-the-rack suit fitted awkwardly and his trouser legs were just too short. White socks with a suit and black shoes? It was the first person from the company he had seen that hadn't been immaculate and Luke liked him for it. The name-tag reading "Andy" sat askew over his right breast as he pulled a cheap pen from his pocket and scribbled a few lines on the page before he handed him back the sheet. Luke read it and made a vague gesture of acceptance as he took the offered pen. Amending "One laptop" to read "One laptop (basic)" and "One firearm" to read "Glock side-arm, 9mm, 500 rounds of ammunition and official justification for such. Gun safe with highest levels of security." It was Andy's turn to re-read the list and he laughed.

'You would be horrified by what some people ask for. And get.' He jabbed the pen towards his forehead and twisted it slowly. 'They think all their Christmases have come at once.'

This didn't surprise Luke at all. If you get used to the basics and are afforded a taste of the luxury you'd be a fool not to take it. Well then, he was a fool. His glance passed over his few possessions unpacked in the flat. They rested for a moment on his travel chess set, a folded box 20cm by 10cm, battered and bumped. Before the thought had even entered his head, Andy had started writing.

'I'm going to get you a better chess set. You're the first guy in god knows how long that's not taken liberties.' His eyes met Luke's briefly. 'Besides, it'll make you seem cultured.'

They both laughed together. Luke was relieved to meet another human in his new job and Andy seemed like a reasonable guy, the sort of guy he'd have a drink with. He wore a suit but he wasn't a suit. That was like finding a unicorn. Andy interrupted his thoughts.

'And a cafetière or French press or something. Your instant coffee is bogging.'

What a prick. They were definitely going to get on.

Most of the information that he had received about his man was uninteresting. Bordering on dull. The school records didn't indicate anything other than academic passability and minimal behavioural issues. The University of Edinburgh had awarded him second class honours in Social Sciences. There were two speeding tickets on his record and nothing else. Now that had struck Luke as being very weird. From what he had gathered, the only 'A' grades that Rab had attained in his life were the drugs he snorted, swallowed or smoked. A man involved in the acquisition and consumption of narcotics, especially an enthusiast on the level Rab was, would normally end up with at least a solitary charge for possession. They'd shake you down and threaten you with "intent to supply" in order to leverage the source. A lot of people would crack in the face of the 5-year minimum sentence. A lot more would repeat their two-word mantra over and over and over ("no comment" or the more popular one which concluded with the word "off") until they were bundled back into freedom with a court date and upcoming community service. The slap on the wrist that was the government's attempt at a war on drugs. Rab had none. Very surprising indeed, unless your father was heavily involved in the justice system. Speaking of which, it was high time that he finally returned the calls of Geoffrey Reid and his secretary. Was it Karen or something? Who knew.

On the table beside the window, his chessboard was sitting beside the phone and the coffee mug was beside the cigarettes. He often wondered why people seemed to attribute the love of chess to some form of higher intellect or why they saw it as being indicative of a greater power of deduction and a blatant symptom of an organised, systematic mind. As it happened, he fancied that he was pretty horrible at chess. The rote learning required for openings was not appealing to him. The intricate 30 move mate with bishop and knight vs lone king would take a level of interest and dedication that was well out of his grasp. He reasoned that part of it could be attributed to the many fictional characters that seemed to profess some level of proficiency in it.

Chandler's man Marlowe loved nothing more than playing through a tricky mate in four or a Capablanca 60 move epic. Sherlock emulated the Evergreen Game with Moriarty. If you ever saw a character in a movie with a chessboard in front of them, you were meant to think "this guy is smart." His reality was what they never showed - two friends who think they remember the rules trying to decide which way round the board goes. Consulting each other on where the king goes if you castle long. Most people who came round to his flat and knew the rules would play a game or two. Sure, he usually won, but it was fun. That was meant to be the point. At various point, Luke had walked back from Waterstone's with some annotated chess tome under his arm. This time he was going to study it. He would get good. The enthusiasm never lasted. The pieces would move slowly around the board and the understanding would move with it. Then, on move 8, white would push his pawn with a3?? (denoting a blunder) and the author would state that this move is so bad that the game is instantly resign-able. Who even were these people? It was a quiet move. It had no meaningful impact on the position that he could see, but sure enough, white falls apart imperceptibly, piece by piece in the wake of it. Once he'd become tired of staring at the Judas pawn and not understanding, he'd fire up his laptop and play a few 3 minute games over the internet and be happy to win anywhere near half. If the chess author could see these games he'd probably run out of question marks before the opening was evening concluded. Short games played with a mouse made for a mistake filled, fast and furious fiasco. But at least it was still fun.

The sun was making a concentrated effort to set now and the shadows were spreading wider out the window. The street lamps pooled orange light on the pavement and it was now high time to flip the script and pump the doting father for information. Picking up the phone and dialling the Magistrates office, he suddenly realised he had no idea of whether they'd even still be open at this time. It was answered quickly and the familiarly hostile voice came down the line.

'Offices of Geoffrey Reid, Claire speaking.'

Ah, Claire. Not Karen. How could he have forgotten? Such dulcet tones of thinly veiled frustration caressing his ears with all the delicacy of an ill-tempered hatchet man. The absolute minimum of candour required to maintain her position. No effort to mask the irritation at having to answer a phone, despite it being her job. Luke respected anyone who held their occupation in such a high level of contempt.

'Evening Claire, Luke Calvin returning your *many* calls.'

'Mr. Calvin, yes. The *investigator*.' - Sarcasm was clearly going to be a two-way street with her. - 'Would you like a line to Magistrate Reid or can I help you with something?'

Luke considered this a moment. In all the dealings with Reid senior up to this point, he had not been furnished with concrete assistance of any substance. If the truth had cause to embarrass or offend then it was not given. Maybe she could be the help he required at the moment: provide the morsels of truth around which he could build a real idea of what was going on.

'Actually, I think you'd be able to help me if that's OK.'

'What can I help you with?' Her tone was decidedly unhelpful. It would seemingly take a raging inferno to melt the ice queen, but he fancied the challenge.

'I've been asking around about Rab and one name seems to come up a fair bit...'

'Grant.' It was a statement, not a question.

'Yes, Grant Ferguson. Seems they went to school together or something?'

'Would you like his details?'

The chessboard in his darkening flat was sitting in front of him, the pieces having being moved through an opening he was barely conscious of having copied out of the book. The white pieces were his and his position was looking solid. The black pieces were of course also his. His position looked equally solid.

'Sure, I might drop in on him and have a chat.' The pen was in his hand and the pad rested on the table. A keyboard clicked rapidly down the line.

'OK. I have his mobile number, his address and a few other bits and pieces. What would you like?'

Luke was mindlessly overwriting and re-underlining 'GRANT FERGUSON' at the top of his page. 'All of it please.'

She dictated and he wrote. There was no offer made for repetition and none required. She paused once she'd been through everything.

'One other thing you might find useful. He works the door on a pub up the town on and off. Might be easier to see him there all the other options don't really work.'

That was actually a pretty good lead. Every man is entitled to not answer his front door but if he's bouncing at a pub the worst he can do is just not let him in. In fact, he'd probably bundle him inside to stop his questions.

'You get all that Luke? I didn't hear you typing.'

Oh, so now it was Luke? No longer Mr. Calvin? Surely the frost barrier wasn't going to come down that easily.

'I write things down.' It was his turn to pause. 'I've been told Grant's a bit of a rough character. Reckon I'll be able to handle it OK?'

'You could always hit him with your little reporter's notebook...'

A small smile crept across his face as the shadows outside lengthened even more. He could almost feel the castle looking down on him even though his back was turned. The white pawn on the board advanced one square. (8. a3??)

'I'm apparently a Traffic Warden actually. Thanks Claire.'

Chapter 8

The Bull on Leith Walk was under new management, as were many of the pubs in the area. There was a deliberate effort being made over the last few years at rejuvenating the locale and there had undeniably been changes. Whether this was for the better or the worse was down to who you chose to ask about it. Sure, you were definitely less likely to get stabbed for no reason walking around late at night, but a sense of community and an unquantifiable 'improvement' cannot be measured in lack of stab wounds alone.

Student flats were in the process of being completed at the top end of Elm Row (which now had no trees at all) with an express supermarket below it. Restaurants and Bistros were popping up in the abandoned shopfronts on the corners of the side-streets that led out onto the main drag. The main objection that a certain sort of person always used to have to this change was the upset of the status quo: - dislike of change simply because it was different. They argued that the old pubs had character, although this depended hugely on your definition of character. Some of these places were excellent, great wee establishments to go drink and have a laugh. The best banter and patter that you would get in Edinburgh. Others were just bear pits. The difficulty lay in working out which was which before you got too comfortable with your pint when both inevitably masqueraded as the other.

Grant was stood in the doorway, almost filling it, with his arms crossed across his chest and gloved hands tucked into his armpits. It didn't need to be too cold for it to become uncomfortable when you were forced to stand in it for extended periods. The reason he was here was at the request of the new owners. They had sat him down and explained their vision for the pub while he barely bothered to feign interest. He had been busy gaping at the new interior. It still had the feel of the old place but they had done a stunning job at masking almost all of the original features. A veritable whitewash.

'You see Mr. Ferguson...' (Mr. Ferguson indeed. Who was this roaster?!) 'In order for our new business to thrive we need to be attracting the correct sort of clientele.'

The two men were sat across from him in a booth to the side. They each had a sparkling water and lime in front of them and Grant was struck by the similarities between them. Both wore glasses, 'casual' suits and loafers. They most definitely shared some facial features and he had now concluded that they were brothers but not twins. He could not for the life of him remember either or their names. It had been early afternoon when they'd met to discuss the 'terms of employment' and it was only the personal recommendation they'd gotten about him that made him come along. Usually anyone who described talking about how much they were going to pay you as 'terms of employment' wasn't worth the hassle of sitting down with but they were hinting at good money for a good job and he needed both.

'This place has been attracting the wrong sort of people and we want to ensure we get off to the perfect start by carefully controlling who comes in and what goes on.'

They even had the same haircut. Same colour eyes. Maybe they were twins after all. Grant thumbed the neck of his beer bottle a few times and nodded sagely before draining it. No matter how much they tried to dress it up in business terms they were just offering him a bouncing job. Nothing more and nothing less. But it made these sorts feel better about what they were doing. He looked them both in the eyes and gestured vaguely with the empty bottle. They conferred silently before the one nearest the bar got up and brought him another. Grant toasted his thanks and took a mouthful. They seemed to be waiting on him to respond now. Clearly his mime act had only bought him so much.

'I understand what you're saying boys. It's not a hassle. If the money's right, I'm the right man for the job.' He turned his head to look slowly all around the interior again before coming back to face them both. He jabbed a thick thumb over his right shoulder. 'That used to be the bandit over there eh?'

'Yes, we opted to remove that. Although it creates some form of revenue, it isn't fitting with the way we want the bar to feel. The "ambience".'

Even his brother shot him a slight look at the use of the word 'ambience.' At least Grant wasn't the only one squirming internally. He studied the beer mat carefully then lifted his head to address them both again with a smile on his face.

'I actually got stabbed by that bandit you know?'

The first brother, who he was now calling 'Ambience' looked startled. He shot a concerned glance at his companion who seemed un-fazed.

'Is that so Grant?' His face was entirely impartial. 'Might I ask how you resolved that particular issue?'

Grant leant back with his beer. "Ambi" was nervously flattening his hair back down and avoiding his eye. The 'normal' brother, who he was now calling "Norm", had leant forward onto the table with his hands clasped in front of him. He held his gaze while Grant searched for any hint of mockery and finding none, laughed.

'I resolved it.' Both hands spread outwards and he shrugged. 'No cops were called and nothing more came of it. It was a long time ago'

Norm considered this for a moment before slowly nodding. His brother's surreptitious attempts to gain his attention were flatly ignored as he kept his eyes on the big man across the table. From his inside pocket he produced a crisp sheet of paper, folded lengthways exactly once, and unfolded it on the table.

'To keep it above board, this is the official employee agreement form.'

Another swig of beer was the only response from across the table. Writing and reading legal documents tended to confuse and irritate him as they were intended to but he had no intention of broadcasting that fact. Norm turned the page so it faced towards Grant and prodded the page at various points.

'This is legal nonsense. So is this. Health and Safety. This is about the workplace pension, don't worry about that. The rate is £25 an hour.' He paused and looked back at his new doorman. 'And we'll have a verbal agreement between us that for every day in the next fortnight that there is no trouble and the police are not called, I will give you £100 in cash at the end of the night.'

The squeaking objection that came from Ambi was ignored by the other two. Scrawling along the line, Grant pretended to read the conditions again as he asked his final question.

'What are my limitations on how I keep the peace?'

Ambi sat dejected in his seat sipping his drink. He was fully aware he had failed some sort of test that he hadn't even realised was being administered. Norm smoothed his hair his left hand and then reached his right across the table towards Grant. Rings shone on the pinkie and ring. They cost more than Grant could make minding this door for a year straight.

'If you promise not to come into my office and tell me how I should run my pubs and clubs, I can promise that I won't tell you how to do your job.' He smiled broadly. 'No cops, no trouble – no questions on our end.'

Grant's meaty paw engulfed the bejewelled hand and he was surprised by the strength of the owner's grip. 'They call that "plausible deniability don't they?'

'That's the one.'

Tonight had been relatively quiet. The first few nights had been more eventful but that was to be expected. The brothers would have probably referred to it as an "adjustment period" or some other weird term that sounded clever but meant nothing. For Grant it had meant a lot of angry drunks and an endless barrage of threats. He had decided to work the door alone but he had two of his mates in the pub drinking, right inside the door. Two or more doormen would have shown that they were expecting trouble and might have even brought some: There is no dignity in getting your pan knocked in off a solitary bouncer but if two of them chucked you onto the pavement there was always a sense that retaliation was justified. A few of the regular customers who he'd been told to keep out were actually sitting inside at the moment. When they had shown up to inspect the new layout on night one and been told the old regulars were not to be allowed, they had expressed anger only at the management and turned to walk away. Grant called them back and let them in. They were told there was a no warnings policy and they played by the rules. His hands had almost healed from the ones who had attempted to exercise their frustrations on him. Even the ones who had come back with a few of their mates had quickly learned that the sober giant at the door was worth at least three drunk pals in a fair fight and this doorman had no qualms about fighting dirty. Aside from his

50

two-man unofficial backup squad, paid in free pints from the bar, there was a foot-long crowbar propped in a cubbyhole by the door. Ostensibly it was for the crates in the cellar but in reality it had needed a surreptitious cleaning at the close of play a few times. The police had never appeared once and Norm or Ambi had greeted him with ever increasing enthusiasm night after night as the pub livened up in just the right sort of way. The extra cash in his pocket never hurt either.

It was only about half nine but the pub was full. As his hands reached for his cigarettes he began to actually think he might drop in for a drink when he wasn't working. The brothers hadn't impressed him initially but they knew how to run a pub. The barmaids were quick, polite and easy on the eye. Whichever two were on, they'd always bring him a coffee every hour or whenever they were out for a smoke. His favourites would even deposit a beer bottle discreetly in the cubbyhole by the crowbar and take the empty back inside with a subtle wink. He had told them all to feel free to tell any customer that was making them uncomfortable that he was their boyfriend. One girl in particular seemed rather keen on the ploy and he had vague intentions of pursuing something with her if he got half the chance. The lighter flicked and he took a long pull to get the cigarette to light. When he looked up there was a punter almost right beside him with a cigarette hanging from his lip.

'Borrow your lighter pal?'

Grant looked him over briefly before shrugging and extending the lighter towards him. He lit up and handed it back as Grant quickly sized him up; slightly taller, longer reach, a lot lighter but looked fit. He was not worried. His friend leaned against the doorway of the pub and looked up and down the road, watching the cars honking and speeding by. His hair was an untidy mess of curls, extending over his collar on his neck and threatening to drop into his eyes at any minute. They smoked in companionable silence briefly before the punter spoke again.

'Busy the night pal?'

Grant kept scanning the street absent-mindedly. There weren't many other folk about and he didn't mind killing some time with inane chit chat. Came with the territory; helped him to get a handle on how drunk someone was or if they'd be any trouble.

51

'Aye man. Fair bouncing in there. Not a bad wee place nowadays or so they tell me. Hard to tell from out here.' He glanced at the taller man leaning back on his doorway. 'You ever in here before it got redone?'

Nodding slowly, the punter exhaled fully out of his nose before replying. 'Long time ago. I'd have been 19. Maybe 20.' He ashed carefully and replaced the cigarette in his mouth and looked at the bouncer. 'Used to be a bit rough around the edges as I recall.'

Grant laughed and nodded emphatically in response. 'Aye man. Aye. You could say that'

The punter finished his smoke and crushed it on the lid of the ashtray before slotting it in. Grant moved slightly to the side to open the door but his new friend put his hands back in his pockets and leaned against the wall again. The blue eyes were fixed on exactly nothing across the street and he didn't seem to be struggling with the cold even though he wore only a light jumper. Most people so inadequately dressed would have been hurrying into the warmth and noise, not loitering for no reason. Grant gave him another once over, checking for any tell-tale bulges of weapons. Seeing none and reaffirming that he had at least three stone on the punter he resumed his position squarely in the door. Never hurt to be careful, but the punter's next question threw him.

'Is Rab about?' He hadn't even turned to face him, far less come away from the wall. His tone remained casual. 'I haven't seen him in a wee bit.'

'Rab who?' The bouncer's feigned ignorance was all but transparent and he knew it.

'Rab Reid. I knew him way back. Can't get a hold of him all of a sudden.'

'Couldn't tell you.' Grant sniffed quickly. 'Wouldn't mind clapping eyes on him myself as it goes.

'Oh aye?' The punter had rotated 90 degrees and was now leaning sideways on the wall looking at him. 'Any idea where I could look? Kind of hitting a dead end the now.'

The bouncer turned so that they were facing each other and shrugged.

'If only I knew bud. His old man's been blowing up my phone trying to speak to him.' The punter didn't look surprised in the least that a Magistrate would have a bouncer's mobile number to hand. It probably wasn't the best plan, but Grant felt like talking about it might help somehow. 'We went to the same school, kind of got in tow together. Now we're in our 30's and I'm still having to look out for him.' His hand ran over his shaved head as he looked up into the sky. 'It's no the best gig in the world.'

Nodding slowly, the punter extended his hand. Inside it was a business card with a name and a number. Grant took it carefully, as if it were made of glass and turned it this way and that.

'My name's Luke. If you find anything out give me a shout. There could be something for you in it.'

'What's your deal then?' The bouncer's eyes narrowed suspiciously. 'He doesn't owe you money does he?'

Luke Calvin took his hands out of his pockets and placed them squarely at his side, palms out. Completing a deliberate and slow spin, he smiled at Grant. 'Do I look like a loan shark, man? Or a drug dealer? Or an enforcer?'

Grant took in the messy curls that framed his face, the slender neck and the lightly muscled body. He was long and rangy but aside from the coolness behind the eyes, there wasn't a single thing about him that was physically intimidating. Grant actually laughed and took his hand away from the cubbyhole and his steel insurance policy.

'Fair enough. Why do you need to find him so bad anyway? Why should I help?'

'His dad asked me to find him.' Seeing the disgust in his eyes, he quickly continued. 'Look, I don't like him much either. Bit up himself. But a job's a job.' He glanced at Grant's almost-healed knuckles. 'I'm sure you can appreciate that.'

'Sure man.' He itched the back of his neck with the corner of the card before stepping aside and holding the door open. 'Nice to meet you Luke, if I hear anything I might just hit you up.'

Luke smiled briefly went to walk in. He paused with one hand on the open door and faced Grant in the doorway.

'You sure you're not gonna tune me up with your bar there?' He nodded towards the shadowy cubbyhole. Seeing the two big men inside the door stand up, he nodded towards the pub. 'Or set your pals on me?'

Grant continued smiling. Maybe he was a little handier than he looked, but he could appreciate a man who just came out with the truth instead of burying it under layers of nonsense.

'I'm thinking about it big man.' His shaved head inclined ever so slightly towards the pub. 'Get yourself in before I change my mind'.

Luke complied, smiling broadly at the two unofficial doormen who glanced over his shoulder before sitting back down with a disappointed air. Luke clapped one on the shoulder jovially. 'Maybe next time pal.'

Crossing to the bar, he ordered a pint and a beautiful girl with crimson hair and sparkling eyes poured it for him with a smile. She leaned across with the pint. The smile on her face was dangerous; he could all but see the hundreds of men who had wrecked themselves on the rocks of its implied promises. Sipping his lager, he found himself hoping Grant wasn't one.

Chapter 9

The sun was rising lazily over Edinburgh's old town, creating shadows and casting them long over the sleepy commuters. All along the mile-long stretch from the West End, the dark was being slowly but surely swept up in the light as it probed here and there, reaching into the corners and sliding slowly up the walls. Trains had begun to move slowly across the foot of the Gardens, pulling in and out with steady precision as the busses and trams ambled up and down at street level. Foot traffic was lighter than it would be later; only a steady stream at the moment instead of the raging torrent that it would be in an hour or so. Schoolchildren, businessmen and the last few stragglers from whatever festivities they had enjoyed last night were the only participants in the early morning exodus where no one wanted to be out in public and they were silently bonded by their mutual hatred of the fact they were forced to be.

The Scott Monument in Princes Street gardens, just off the main drag itself, stood high and proud, a black monolith tapering to an imposing peak. Edges, ledges and precipices jutted out from every angle all the way to the top giving it a Gothic look that brought admiration from many and seemed to bring out the morbid thoughts in an unfortunate few who were looking to leave the gig early. Between the North Bridge, high above Waverley Station and the monument which was visible from it, there had been countless threats of suicides and a sad amount of successful attempts. If the street was ever closed off for an 'incident' it was assumed by the locals that someone had reached their breaking point and taken extreme action. It was assumed by the tourists that some form of maintenance was being carried out. And it was assumed by the despicable few that a man or woman's moment of deepest despair was an acceptable occasion to break out the camera phone in the hopes of immortalising whatever was about to happen on film.

In order to access the higher levels of the monument, it was necessary to purchase admission at the entrance in the gardens and then climb the claustrophobic tight twisting stairs, slowly rising upwards right to the top. The observation level gave a panoramic view over as far as Arthur's Seat, all the way up and down the street, over the Gardens to the Castle and was always popular with anyone who visited the city.

The monument had yet to open its doors to the public this morning but there was a solitary figure standing on the deck, silhouetted against the sun. Hands stuffed deep into the pockets of a parka, breath emanated in long slow clouds of condensation from inside the fur lined hood. Facing the Mound, they appeared deep in thought, oblivious to the sounds of the waking city that had begun to emanate upwards to the observation level. On top of the Mound stood the Free Church College, offices of the courts and the court itself. The hood of the parka was fixed firmly in this direction as if expecting to see something but the buildings remained impassive as ever. The Castle sat proudly above all; older than the College and more historic than the court; and watched as the figure on the monument breathed a final sigh and was gone back through the small wooden door and into the stairway before the parting cloud of breath had even fully dissipated.

The paths and pavements that circled around Arthur's Seat were numerous and surprisingly well used. A firm favourite of joggers and dog walkers, they passed each other regularly enough to briefly raise a hand in salutation or participate in the mutual upwards head bob of recognition. Today was no different. On the uphill portion of the path, a young man in lycra had just sped past, narrowly avoiding a Yorkie puppy that had become too excited at being let off the lead. Hustling after it in vain was an older woman whose face was beetroot with exertion and embarrassment at her suddenly nuisance dog. She moved as quickly as her legs would carry her girth but knew full well that she'd only catch the dog when it became distracted by something and chose to stop. Her attempt at a breathless apology was waved off by the jogger with a smile: poor woman. Just as the puppy rounded the bend and threatened to disappear from view, it veered off hard to the left like a fur clad stinger missile, yapping shrilly the whole time. The owner rested her hands on aching knees and took a moment to try to catch her breath and collect her thoughts.

'" Get a dog" he'd said. "Do you good to get out of the house" he'd said. "Keep you young." he'd said.'

Right about now she felt every one of her 59 years. What hurt more than her chest and hips was the thought of losing her puppy: - despite all of her complaints she had become quite fond of little Eva. Hauling in a half lungful of air she resumed her pursuit, albeit more slowly, following the steady yaps that seemed to echo for miles around the slopes and over towards the city. Such noise from such a tiny thing. She followed the sound away from the roadside and off the path towards the shrubbery at the start of the incline. Sweat had already plastered hair to her forehead and she had no doubt that she probably looked ridiculous. It was of no concern at the moment. She gripped the lead firmer in her hand and continued her trek through the muddy grass. Another few paces brought her to the source of the ungodly noise: Eva, all 8 inches of her, was staring intently at the bush nearest them both. Scratching furiously with her tiny forelegs and burying her nose then standing straight and yelping.

'Come here you.'

She advanced on her companion with relief and scooped up the wriggling puppy into her arms. Eva stopped squirming and happily began to lick her owner's face with her rough tongue. All was clearly forgiven on both sides. The lead was attached back to the collar and the puppy lowered carefully back to the muddy ground. Her coat was already filthy; no point in carrying her to keep her clean. That ship had already sailed. Eva strained at her leash in an attempt to get herself fully under the bush. The owner was too indulgent of her little ball of energy.

'What is it then Eva?' She braced her hands on her knees again and used the positive voice she'd read about in the puppy training books. 'Show mummy what's so interesting.'

Might as well let her have a little more excitement before she had to administer the ultimate betrayal of giving her a bath at home. The scratching and digging ceased for a moment and the puppy began tugging at something underneath the undergrowth. Snarling and twisting her head, she came away with the remnants of some sort of shirt. Now the owner was aghast.

'No Eva! Put it down. God knows who wore that last or what they did with it.'

She moved to collect her up again but paused. It wasn't visible until she was almost on top of it but the soil underneath the low lying scrub was freshly turned and there looked to be more clothes semi-buried under there. Holding Eva over her shoulder and unconsciously shielding her from the view, she prodded at something solid with her trainer. Now it was her turn to yelp; a bone was sticking out from whatever chequered rag her dog had been attempting to eat. Eva's bath would have to wait. She reached for her mobile with her free hand and dialled the non-emergency number – she wasn't about to waste the police's time if it turned out to be nothing. A deep sniff seemed to compose her as the ring was answered and the puppy happily licked her face as she explained what she had seen.

At the police station, they took the information to be a little more serious than the dog walker had portrayed it. Dispatching officers immediately, the operator asked the dog walker to remain where she was until the officers arrived and not to disturb the scene any more than was necessary. Once the call had ended, the operator leaned back in her chair and thought for a moment. She was in her early twenties, and her blonde hair was tied back underneath her headset. It took her the best part of 30 minutes of careful application each morning to achieve her "no make-up" look. Her eyebrows furrowed slightly over pale blue eyes as she thought and her pen went from twirling absent-mindedly to being inserted carefully between her lips. The find could be nothing but she had been asked to keep him informed on anything that could be pertinent. The dilemma as always was to disclose irrelevant information and lose credibility or to not disclose information that later turned out to be key and lose all credibility entirely. Snapping out of her thoughts she realised she had been staring across the table at another operator who was holding her gaze with a confused smile. She returned the smile, carefully removed the pen and pretended to focus on the monitor in front of her. There was really no option. The mouse found the official contact list folder and meandered slowly down the list. Expanding the "other" tab, she selected "personal" and selected the only number there. The auto dialler began to do its thing as she found herself hoping and praying in a macabre fashion that it was indeed a corpse under the bush on the hill.

The patrol car had arrived and the first men on the scene had spoken to her briefly. She gave her details to the polite young officer who was all smiles and reassurances while his more severe looking colleague had gone to inspect the area. The younger officer closed his notebook and looked her over.

'Now Maureen...' The yapping from Eva caused him to pause a moment. Ignoring the shushing, he reached across and began scratching the happy puppy behind her ears. 'And Eva of course. We are happy that we have your details and can get in touch if we need anything else. Thank you for letting us know and I don't think we need to delay you any longer.'

Filled with the enthusiasm and vigour that only carried most through training and not long beyond that, the policeman was every bit the friendly face of policing with his immaculate uniform and the much practiced smile that emanated from his honest face. His eyes flicked behind her to his returning colleague and the smile briefly faltered. Regaining his composure, he continued.

'Would you like a lift home? We aren't really supposed to allow animals but I think an exception can be made.'

Maureen shuffled her furry burden to the opposite arm and returned the officer's smile.

'That won't be necessary. Although we both appreciate the offer.' The other officer was at the car and reaching for the in vehicle radio. 'We're just five minutes away and someone needs a bath.' She looked briefly behind her at the shirt in the earth. 'Do let me know if anything comes of this. Say goodbye Eva'

She turned to leave with a cheerful wave and Eva trotting merrily alongside. The radio on the young officer's vest squawked, relaying the transmission being made from the car.

'Yeah, it's a body. Send everyone to our position. We'll start setting up.'

The young officer's smile was totally gone now as he watched the charming Maureen saunter off towards her home. He sincerely hoped he'd succeeded in convincing her it was nothing before "Officer Tactful" had broadcast the fact that it was a body. He sighed and started back towards the car.

'Steve?' His partner flatly ignored him as he popped the boot and began to rummage. 'Steve?'

Steve straightened up and turned. If that guy had ever smiled, he was sure it was by accident. 'What?'

'You know you aren't meant to say "body" on the radio right? Especially not when your partner is still speaking to the witness who discovered it.'

The only response was a grunt and a shrug. He resumed his search and came up with two rolls of tape emblazoned with "POLICE LINE DO NOT CROSS" over and over and over. He threw one across a little too hard and it bounced off the younger man's vest before he managed to juggle it under control.

'Well Dave, you keep chatting up the old biddies and petting the dugs and I'll keep on doing actual police stuff eh? How's that for a deal? Start barriering off and stop giving me grief.'

Dave clicked his heels together and stood ramrod straight, administering a sarcastic salute. 'Sir yes Sir.' Steve looked on impassive. 'No more being polite to the public Sir. I promise to kick all dogs and take sweets from all the kids and...'

He was cut off by the second roll of tape clouting him in the chest and falling to the ground. Steve still had a hold of the loose end.

'I take your point. Stop messing about and help.''

Together they began to stretch out a cordon and wait for the cavalry.

Chapter 10

The flat buzzer broke through into a particularly pleasant dream that Luke Calvin had been enjoying and as he jerked into consciousness the details of the dream were already slipping away through his fingers as though he was trying to keep hold of a fistful of sand. The watch face on his wrist indicated it wasn't quite 8am and as he levered himself upright to put his feet on the ground and leave the security of his bed, there was a sleepy moan of protestation from the other side of the pillow. He glanced over his shoulder at the red hair fanned out over the pillowcase as the barmaid from the Bull turned over and nestled down further under the covers. Finding a pair of jogging bottoms with his bare feet, he pulled them on as he stood up and padded out into the hall bare chested. Yawning and stretching, he crossed to the receiver and looked in confusion at the screen that showed an unknown woman standing by the main entrance.

'Yes?' His voice was thick with sleep and his throat felt raw. 'Who is it?'

'My name is Claire, Mr. Calvin. We spoke on the phone several times?'

The Magistrate's secretary; the ice queen. What an unexpected surprise. He wondered what sort of bad news she was bringing him at this time in the morning. Without even bothering to tell her which flat was his, he depressed the buzzer and watched her walk in. The Magistrate had doubtless given his address to her. He'd probably posted it on every lamppost in the greater Lothian area. Great. Undoing the locks on the door and leaving the Yale off the snip, he crossed to the kitchen and busied himself with getting the coffee on. Once that was underway, he extracted a cigarette from the crumpled packet on his favourite table by the window and lit up just as a hesitant knock came at the door.

'It's open.' The smoke pooled in his lungs briefly before he blew a jet towards the ceiling and returned to the coffee, 'Come on in. I'm in the kitchen.'

The door opened and he heard the Yale lock being clicked back in place. In the kitchen, he took two mugs out and sat them ready. Pouring his own first, he filled it up and replaced the pot. Without turning around, he was aware of her presence behind him in the doorway.

'Good morning Mr. Calvin.' She sounded almost apologetic. 'I hope you don't mind the early visit.'

Her question was flatly ignored. 'How do you take your coffee?'

She paused for a moment before replying. 'Black as you can get it.'

Pouring out the second mug, he nodded towards the living room and heard her footfall quieten as she went through ahead of him. Entering with the two mugs held carefully he saw her for the first time, perched on the very edge of the sofa. Her hair was dark and worn loose, reaching well below her shoulders. She was wearing some sort of Lycra leggings and bright white trainers with a hoody that seemed to swamp her torso. As he placed the mug within easy reach of her on the table, she met his eyes for the first time and they were every bit as dark and fierce as she was. Luke was suddenly very aware that he was half dressed. Leaving her coffee on the table between them, he retrieved his burning cigarette from the ashtray in the kitchen and sat down opposite her with his mug cradled in one hand. She took a sip of her steaming mug and smiled at him.

'Good coffee.' Placing it back on the table, she gestured towards her legs. 'Excuse the get up, I was on my way to the gym.'

Luke's response was to glimpse briefly at his own exposed torso and smile back. 'I can safely say this isn't my usual attire for business meetings either.' He took a long drag and exhaled slowly. As usual, it was making him feel slightly more human. 'I'm assuming that's what this is.'

She had the mug in both hands drinking and seemed to nod her whole upper body in confirmation. There was something strangely innocent about her that she clearly worked very hard to cover up. Her eyes met his through the steam.

'What?'

Putting his mug down on the table, he leaned forward and pointed his right hand towards her. Making a circular motion that traced her outline in smoke, he looked confused.

'You don't look anything like I thought you would.' The cigarette jabbed in an accusatory manner before returning to his lip as he leaned back. 'You sounded very severe. Very imposing.'

She laughed and helped herself to a smoke from the packet. Extracting the lighter from beside it, she placed it between her lips and paused before sparking it and looking at him with a glint in her eye.

'You should see me in my glasses and skirt suit.'

Luke was sure he probably should. He waited for her to get her smoke going before he carried on. 'As enjoyable as this is, is there a particular reason you're dropping in on me first thing in the morning or were you just hoping for a free breakfast?'

'Magistrate Reid called me.' She let a thin trail of smoke trickle from her lips. Apparently someone found some remains on Arthur's Seat this morning.' Luke found a notebook and pen and motioned for her to continue. 'Some old dear walking her puppy this morning about seven. Not many details yet but he thought you should check it out before it turns into a circus.' She took another pull and washed it down with a swig of coffee. 'Might be nothing but he is understandably concerned.'

Luke wrote only a couple of lines before he set the book down. Crushing his cigarette out in the ashtray, he tucked his legs underneath him and reached for his cup.

'How is your boss finding out things like this so quickly?'

She shrugged again and continued drinking with one hand and smoking with the other. Luke assumed a man of Geoffrey's standing had plenty of unofficial contacts through the police force and beyond. Men like that always knew before the rest of the public, but this was truly an early notice. The reach of the Magistrate evidently extended further than he had initially given it credit for. The direct lines to the higher ups sort of came with the territory but he must have people in at the ground level to get this sort of access. His questioning continued:

'And why are you being dragged out of your personal time to pay a visit to some random investigator with this news?' His gaze shifted to the window and he stretched again, trying to see the outline of the castle. 'It must drive your boyfriend mad.'

Claire reached up and pulled a stray strand of hair from her fringe out in front of her face and studied it closely. Her hands had no ring.

'I don't have a boyfriend at the moment as it goes. Not much free time with Mr. Reid.'

Her brown eyes took in the sparse decoration in the living room and the awkwardly tall frame of the man who sat in nothing but joggers on the chair opposite. His hair was hugely untidy, piled up in bunches here and there from sleep and his lean torso had several prominent scars; one that exploded out in a star shape from a circle on the right hand side of his ribcage and the other a straight slash diagonally down across the abdomen. The light blue eyes that were fixed on nothing out the window were still slightly sticky from waking up and a couple of days' growth were visible on his chin. She safely assumed there was no feminine hand permanently on the tiller here. He turned his head from the window to address her again.

'I don't imagine either of our jobs keep normal office hours then.' Draining the dregs from the mug, he placed it on the table. 'Another thing we have in common.'

Her nose twitched slightly and she crushed her stub on the edge of the ashtray. She scanned the table in a futile search for a coaster before putting her cup down anyway. 'What else do we have in common then?'

There was a twinkle behind her eyes now and a smirk on her face. He clasped his hands together behind his head and stretched them upwards, barely stifling a yawn.

'Neither of us like your boss that much.' He finished his stretch and covered his mouth after he had finished yawning. 'Excuse me, I was round the Bull last night seeing Grant. Ended up staying until after closing.' Trying and failing to flatten a particularly rebellious clump of hair, he held his hand hard over it for a moment before it sprang immediately back up. There was little reaction from the other side of the table.

'Did you find out anything worthwhile? If anyone knew about Rab it would have been Grant.' She leaned forward and pretended to study his face closely. 'I can see you didn't annoy him in any way at least. Still got all your teeth?'

64

'All the ones I turned up with anyway.' Grinning wide and long, he tilted his head from side to side as if to prove his point. 'Strikes me as a nice guy if you stay on the right side of him. I'm sure he's a menace once he starts swinging though.'

'Yeah, I like Grant.' She looked downwards quickly as if she'd misspoken and there was the start of a blush on her cheeks. 'I don't know him that well or anything, he's just always been nice to me.'

'I can believe that.' Luke scratched his cheek and felt the prickly hair thoughtfully. 'Reckon I should jump in the shower and head round to see what the script is on Arthur's Seat eh? Can't sit and speak to pretty girls while I'm half naked all day now can I?'

'Aww, why not?' came the pouty reply from the hallway. They both turned.

The barmaid from the Bull had appeared in the doorway clad in one of his basketball tops and nothing else. She too was trying unsuccessfully to flatten her shock of red hair with her hands. It hung in tight little ringlets that fell all around her bare shoulders and cascaded down her back. A tiny little thing to begin with, she seemed even smaller in the long, loose top as she crossed to the table and helped herself to a smoke from Luke's pack before sitting down on the couch beside Claire and lighting up. Luke laughed.

'Claire, this is Jen. She works at the Bull. Jen, this is Claire, she works for the guy I work for. Apparently neither of you are capable of buying your own tobacco so you should get on fine.'

The two women shared a look of mutual disdain for their ungracious host before they shook hands briefly and awkwardly. Luke was collecting up the two empty mugs and gestured with one towards Jen. She shook her head.

'None for me thanks, I've got to go.' She blew smoke upwards in an attempt to get a particularly persistent ringlet out of her face. 'Better get home and sorted.'

Claire stood up and took the mugs out of Luke's hands. She carried them through to the kitchen before he could protest and returned with a business card in her hand.

'I'd better be off too. That's my number if you find anything out.'

He took it from her and placed it on the table. Jen reached forward and took the card and his pen from on top of the notebook. They both watched her scribble on it briefly before returning it.

65

'And there's mine just in case you forget where the pub is.' She winked at him from behind Claire's back. 'You usually in the habit of getting two women's numbers before 9am?'

Luke smiled broadly at them both and held up his hands in an apologetic gesture. 'We all have our slow days I guess....'

Claire thumped him in on the shoulder. 'That's from both of us.' He thought she looked genuinely amused despite the violence. 'Now try and be a gentleman for ten seconds and show me out if you think you can muster the decorum.'

Jen rose from the couch and rushed past them both towards the bedroom.

'Wait a minute and I'll come out with you.' She thumped his other shoulder on the way past. 'I doubt he has two bouts of manners in him.'

'Abused in my own home by two strangers.' His head shook slowly. 'What is the world coming to?'

Jen reappeared shortly, dressed and hopping as she got her second shoe on. He held the door open and bowed deeply from the waist with his arm across his body. Jen went out first and pecked him on the cheek as she passed.

'See you later, your idiot.'

Claire was hot on her heels and stooped down to kiss his other cheek so as not to appear rude. And maybe just a little bit to noise him up.

'I agree. You are an idiot.'

He watched them disappear down the first flight of stairs, laughing together. Women made absolutely no sense to him. Shutting the door, he flicked the switch for the shower and crossed to the living room where Jen's cigarette was sat smouldering in the ashtray. Finishing it off, he put it out and went to the bathroom. Turning on the water and undressing he stepped under and let the heat wash over him. There would be time to think once he was clean and dressed.

The phone rang just as he was doing up his shoelaces sat on the edge of the bed. Dark jeans, a white t shirt and a woollen style jumper were his fashion choice of the day from his sparse selection.

Answering the call from the "office" he straightened and left the bedroom, picking up his house keys from a hook in the hallway.

'Luke's Antiques and Curio Emporium. How may I help?'

Laura did not sound too impressed. It was a seemingly endless battle to get her to lighten up; she took her very serious job very seriously and Luke didn't seem to have it in him to respect that.

'Good morning Mr. Calvin. We've received information regarding remains found...'

The phone was cradled between his left shoulder and the side of his head as he struggled to exit his flat and double lock the door. 'Yeah, I know. Arthur's Seat.' The lock finally clicked home. 'A day late and a dollar short as ever dear.'

'Who have you been talking to this early?'

Taking the phone and switching it to the opposite shoulder he began to descend the staircase. 'Just attractive women who won't stop stumbling into my life.'

'I see. Sounds like a rough existence to lead.'

Her voice sounded tight: she was apparently in no mood for their usual back and forth. He pictured her at her desk in moccasins and a home knitted sweater, surrounded by pictures of her many *many* cats.

'I'm just going to jump a taxi the now and see what's what.' Reaching the ground floor and exiting into the street, he saw a cab passing and hailed it. 'I'll call you with what I know as soon as I know it.'

Clambering into the back seat before it had barely stopped he held a hand to the receiver and asked the driver to get him as close to the cordon on Arthur's Seat as he could. Clearly confused, the driver was about to ask which police cordon but Luke had returned to his phone and was talking once more.

'Everyone's slow off the mark now and then. Don't beat yourself up.'

'I'm not beating myself up.' was the instant reply, in a tone that deeply suggested the very opposite. She paused a second. 'Did an attractive woman really drop in on you with this news?'

'Yup. And scared off the other one that was already round.'

It was clear she didn't believe him and her tone was slowly adjusting to become as playful as his.

67

'I'm sure you're keeping quite the collection. And your wallet is too small for your £50's. Poor Luke Calvin.'

'Jealousy does not become you Laura. You know you're the only woman in my life.'

The driver made brief eye contact in the rear view. Luke moved the mouthpiece slightly away and pointed at it with his free hand while executing a loud whisper -

'The wife. What can you do?'

Instant anger down the phone: - 'I am not your wife! Don't tell people that, it isn't funny...'

Widening his eyes in mock exasperation, he received a sympathetic and knowing glance in return from the driver.

'OK dear, see you at home tonight.'

'I've told you, I'm not...'

'No, I love YOU more.'

'LUKE'

'Goodbye love.'

Hanging up the phone and watching the buildings pass, he replaced it in his pocket beside his trusty notebook and pen. There'd be hell on when he phoned her back. He found himself imagining her in an apron in his kitchen with dinner for them both on the table. Sitting on his sofa watching a film that she liked and he hated. Sleeping on opposite sides of the same bed. Shaking his head quickly to dislodge the offensive imagery, there was only one conclusion that a reasonable man could draw - Yup; he was definitely going soft.

Chapter 11

Claire Davidson had left Luke's flat and despite strict instructions to the contrary, had gone to the gym after all. It wasn't more than a five-minute walk from where she stayed and maintaining some form of routine was the only thing that kept her vaguely on an even keel. Depositing her gear in the locker, she plugged in her headphones and jumped on the treadmill. Setting the speed and incline, her legs began to rise and fall faster and faster until it reached its desired pace and she settled into a rhythm.

The music in her ears pounded in time with her feet as she ran and she could feel the disconnect from reality that she craved. Slowly, the sweat began to seep out from her pores as her heart-rate peaked then settled. Her breathing became briefly ragged before that too settled out: in, out, in – in out: over and over. Every time she became too comfortable with the pace she increased the speed slightly until she was at the most she could manage where she rode it out as long as she was able. The burning in her lungs and the lactic acid building in her thighs and calves were beginning to become excruciating – the last five minutes of her half hour run were the only time she was ever mentally in the moment. A million excuses to hit the "cool down" button and just call it a day ran through her mind and were each dismissed in turn as the counter ran up and up until it hit 30:00 and she slapped the control panel in the general vicinity of the button. Obediently slowing down to half speed and reducing the incline, the machine began the 5-minute cool down period which she skipped by hitting the stop. The belt beneath her trainers wound down to a complete stop and she stepped off, dripping with perspiration and attempting to get her breath back.

Wiping her face with the towel, then the machine she went straight back to the empty changing room and stripped down naked. Glimpsing herself in the mirror, she turned to her left, then to her right, inspecting carefully from every angle. Her stomach was flat and toned and the running had left her legs lean rather than muscular. Turning her back to the mirror and looking over her shoulder, she found no signs of cellulite: the squats she was doing every other day were definitely paying off. Facing to the front again, she cupped her breasts with her hands and lifted them up. Letting them drop she was satisfied enough that there was still enough bounce for someone her age. OK, so her face was bright red and strands of hair were stuck to her face with sweat but she was happy with the overall look. She entered the shower stall and turned on the water. Standing under the powerful stream with eyes closed and both hands braced against the wall, she felt the sweat of her daily penance being washed away and felt a million times more human.

By the time she was dressed and leaving, it was approaching 10am. There were no missed calls from Magistrate Reid so she could only assume that his early morning call demanding her to make a visit in person to the Victoria Street flat came with a certain amount of leeway in terms of her normal work day. She began the walk upwards to the top of the Mound up the Royal Mile enjoying the crowds of people and the mid-morning sun that still somehow felt cold.

Arriving at the offices, she entered the so-called "ante chamber" where her desk sat. It was less grand than the Magistrate's by a long way but sufficiently elegant that people would still be impressed with it. That was Geoffrey all over – appearance above substance and above all else. She had dressed in a simple white blouse and tied her hair back with a small black bow. Once you added in the flat black shoes and the light grey skirt, even her solid black rimmed glasses couldn't pull this ensemble back from looking demure. She was secretly happy with it – this did not feel like a day for going to war with everyone. No sooner had she settled herself in behind the desk than the mobile rang inside her handbag. Looking at the screen, she sighed audibly and slouched back into the seat before answering.

'Magistrate Reid. What can I do for you?'

Despite the heavy door that separated them she could hear him pacing up and down on the wooden floor. There was a bizarre echo and delay response between the phone and the real source ten feet behind her which was unsettling.

'Claire. Did you see him? What did he say? Has he gone up there?'

This was new: he sounded almost frantic and that made very little sense to her.

'Yes sir, I went as soon as you called and updated him with the new information.' Pre-empting the next question, she continued. 'And he left to go up to see for himself just as soon as I left.'

'That's good. That's good. Did you actually see him go? When is he going to call in? Did you tell him that I wanted to kept up to date?'

She reeled off the answers to his stream of questions in order and counted them down on her fingers with a bored air. 'It is good. Yes. When he knows something. And Yes.'

Mercifully there was a silence on the other end of the line. The sound of endless pacing had disappeared from both the phone and the room opposite. The way his mind was wired it wasn't just that you could hear the cogs turning – you could actually hear the fuses blowing. When he finally did speak again it was back to the cool and measured tones which he used both for giving his lunch order and for describing heinous crimes in extreme detail.

'OK Claire. Thanks for that.' There was another pause. 'I know it probably isn't anything to do with Rab but you can't stop yourself thinking.'

She was busy smoothing her skirt over her knees with her free hand and couldn't really think of an appropriate response to this sort of personal revelation. This was not how their interactions usually went. He spoke again.

'Thinking about it, I've disturbed your morning. I don't think I need you to come in today.' It sounded like he was attempting to be nice. 'Maybe take the rest of the day off. There is one more visit I'd like you to make on my behalf though.'

She stopped smoothing her skirt. In all the late night and early morning demanding phone-calls, she had never once elicited an apology from Geoffrey Reid. No doubt this little favour he wanted would be for her to call on his elderly aunt in Outer Mongolia to drop off a pint of milk and a loaf.

71

'Go and see Grant for me. Just let him know about the developments and remind him how much any information is worth to me. Let me know what he says and how he reacts.'

Subconsciously, she had reached up and felt her little bow to make sure it was straight. She was glad she wasn't in her full business attire for some reason. All her anger at the disturbed morning seemed to have disappeared.

'Certainly sir. I'll be in touch.'

He hung up without saying goodbye but that was no surprise. Resisting the temptation to press the intercom just to let him know that she had already been in at work, she gathered her things and made for the door. Her flat shoes were ninja-like in their silence compared to the heels and she thanked whatever ridiculous notion caused her to alter her usual dress this morning. For a disaster of a day, it was actually threatening to go rather well.

The police had closed the road around the sight of the find and placed a barrier to keep the public at least 100 feet away at all times. Steve and Dave, the two first responding officers had handed over what they knew to the forensics' guys when they arrived then promptly been relegated to standing at the border of the tape barrier to keep people away. Even though they both expected it, it wasn't ever easy to just roll over for the self-proclaimed big boys of policing. The younger man, Dave, stood straight with his arms clasped behind his back and his head forward. Not yet 25, he was still at the stage of being in love with the force and its ideals. His partner was past 40 and was probably born with a cynical smirk on his face: – he was facing inwards towards the crime scene and his grey eyes were fixed on the men in slicker suits and face-masks struggling to erect the plastic tent that they used to preserve the scene.

'Look Dave, the clowns are getting the high-top all set up.'

The younger man ignored him and only attempted to stand straighter. Steve sighed and turned back around to retake his position beside his partner. Dave had wisps of blonde hair peeking out from underneath his cap and was clean shaven. He shined his shoes every single morning without fail, even if they were just going to sit in the car all day. When they were on a quiet patrol, Steve would ask him about obscure crimes both real and fictional to "test" his knowledge and to his credit he never failed to reel off the correct handbook response or state with definite assurance that "wearing purple on a Tuesday" was not technically against any laws of the land.

Steve had initially resented their pairing, not because he was keen or tried too hard, but because it felt like he was being plonked firmly into the role of "veteran". That had stung and his bitterness had been projected onto the young man who had all but bounced into the break room in his perfect uniform and shaken his hand so hard he practically got nerve damage. Despite himself, he had found himself warming to his new partner and even beginning to enjoy his company. Sure, he was a jobsworth but he was funny and seeing someone actually care about the job that he used to love himself was bizarrely refreshing. Once the initial phase had completed it was Steve's turn to be surprised when he was informed by the Sergeant that he had received a request from Dave to continue their partnership.

He had fully expected a reaming for smoking on duty, napping in the patrol car or generally winding up the younger man but instead he received a vote of confidence. The unlikely duo continued in their unlikely friendship. Looking down at his own scuffed, muddy boots and the shirt he had worn yesterday he wondered if he could put the same effort into improving himself instead of trying to drag Dave down to his level. When he looked up again, there was a familiar man approaching the cordon with a cigarette in his lip and his hands stuffed in his jean pockets.

'Morning Officers. How's it going?"

Dave looked him over and made estimations for any report that might be necessary as was his habit. Male, Caucasian, early/mid 30's, 6ft 2, 12 and a half stone. Eyes blue, hair black. Medium length, untidy. Last seen wearing dark jeans and a dark top. No wonder they never picked up the right guys with these sorts of descriptions.

'Fine thanks.'

He was deliberately evasive. Rather than his usual willingness to interact with the public he maintained a professional and cold distance when it came to matters like this. After all, these were remains that they had found. This was serious business and confidentiality could be key with regards to any forthcoming investigations. Then again, you could always rely on Steve to choose the most inopportune moment to practice his public relations.

'Found a body.'

Ignoring the death stare that he was probably getting, Steve looked steadily at the man and saw no reaction. Only a careful nod. Finally acknowledging his partner's glare, Steve attempted an innocent shrug to accompany his explanation.

'I know him. Trust me, it's OK.'

Extracting the cigarette form between his lips with his left hand, the man extended his right towards Dave with a grin on his face.

'Luke Calvin. I knew your partner a lifetime ago.' The handshake was tentatively taken. 'He was about a stone lighter then but still just as happy.'

Placing the cigarette back in his mouth, he fumbled in both pockets at once and came up with a business card for the young officer and the packet and lighter for his old friend. Both were taken readily and inspected. As Steve lit up, Dave was too distracted by the card to even tell deliver his customary withering glance. Pocketing it finally, he seemed satisfied and addressed his new friend.

'A friend of Steve's then? You must be ex-forces.' Now he took the time to look disapprovingly at the older man who was facing away toward the city, smoking peacefully. 'He never really talks about it to be honest.'

Luke thought about it for a second before responding. No one who ever actually saw any serious action or was involved in anything heavy would ever want to relive it again. Trading war stories was for blowhards and plastic soldiers.

'Most of us just do our time and get out. I don't talk about it either too much.' He clapped a hand on the flawless lapel of Dave's jacket. 'Don't take anything he says to you to heart man, because now you have my number and I'll give you some ammo for a counter attack if he's ever over stepping the line.' He finished with a conspiratorial wink and removed his hand.

Steve was now facing them both with a smile that made the lit smoke stick up towards his eye.

'Still stirring Calvin eh? After all these years?'

Luke said nothing and Dave was too distracted by the fact he was seeing Steve smile to register anything else. It was wildly unnatural; like seeing a giraffe riding a tricycle. Luke returned the smile then indicated the younger man questioningly with his eyes. Steve made no response and that was as good a recommendation as a man could get. Luke beckoned them both towards him.

'OK then boys. I need to know as much as possible about what these idiots find up here. Off the record though – personal phones and that sort of thing. I know it's not protocol but I would appreciate the head start. I'm looking for this guy.' He produced another slip of paper from his back pocket with Rab's details and a copy of his photo. 'It's been put out on all the official networks but I could do with any unofficial info you can get me.'

To their surprise, it was Dave who's hand extended and received the paper willingly. He placed it beside the business card in an inside pocket and nodded. Steve spoke up.

'I didn't think you'd go for this sort of thing Dave?' For Luke's benefit he placed a hand by his mouth and pretended to whisper in a voice loud enough to be heard half a mile away. 'Bit of a "Rulebook Jones" this one.'

'I haven't agreed to anything. No law against taking details and a photo is there?'

Luke nodded his approval and waved a hand briefly before turning on his heel and beginning the walk back downhill. The two officers stood and watched him go. Steve scratched the stubble on his neck and elbowed his partner gently.

'What did you think of him then?'

'Nice guy.' was the non-committal response.

Steve was in agreement. Luke Calvin had been the nicest officer he had served under. He also happened to be the most ruthlessly efficient killing machine that he had ever known. As Dave took the pieces of paper out of his pocket to re-examine them, Steve thought it prudent not to disclose any information of that ilk. Trading war stories was for blowhards and plastic soldiers anyway.

Chapter 12

Grant snapped into consciousness and propped himself up on one arm in the bed. His mouth felt like a junkie's carpet and the headache that was pounding around inside his skull had moved onto the quick cycle with the sudden movement. Gradually, he realised it was his own bedroom. He let rip with a burp that brought the taste of vomit into his mouth and he had to swallow hard while he talked himself out of spewing. Moving slowly over to the far side of the bed and reaching for the curtains he found they lay just out of his reach from the bed. Placing his feet on the floor and his head in his hands he paused to take stock and slow his breathing. Why had he drunk so much last night?

Trying to piece it all together was difficult: once the Bull had settled down he'd headed up town with his two pals and the lager had started flowing in earnest. The memories from midnight became patchy and ended entirely when he was waiting on a taxi, swaying dangerously with a chippy in his hand. On the bedside table there was a glass full of clear liquid which he sniffed before downing as quickly as he could – no point in playing water/vodka roulette in the state he was in this morning.

Rising cautiously, he stumbled around the bed towards the bedroom door, finding his t shirt on the carpet (not stained by some miracle) and his jeans lying half in and out of the hallway. His shoes were haphazardly kicked off just inside the door which he had mercifully locked behind him when he arrived. Kneeling beside the jeans he rifled through the pockets – Keys, Wallet.... no phone. The panic rose inside him as he rechecked each pocket, turning them inside out as he went. A vibration from beside the bed caught his attention – his phone was not only there but plugged into the charger. Thanking his lucky stars, he pulled on the nearest pair of shorts and a grubby vest before picking up the phone. The only message was from one of his pals apologising that the two of them had ducked out early because they were too gone to make any of the clubs. A surge of relief ran through Grant once more – no fall outs either. Exiting towards the kitchen and living room, he tapped away on his phone:

"No worries man. Cracking night eh? Give me a buzz when you're free."

The hangover hunger had not hit quite yet; the thought of food made him feel ill at the moment; but despite his fragile state and the dryness in his mouth he knew he could not put off his morning smoke any longer. Running the water from the sink into another pint glass, he downed it while the water continued to run and topped it up again before heading out to the balcony, cigarettes in tow. Thankfully the day was beginning to warm up as he flopped into his chair and flicked the lighter. No work – the whole day stretched out in front of him, full of possibilities. Sure, the most likely possibility in the immediate future was gouching on the sofa with water and energy juice within easy reach watching the box until he felt like he could face the rest of humanity, but it was always good to feel like you had the option of doing something productive if you were that way inclined. The flat could do with a tidy and there probably wasn't a huge amount in the fridge but aside from that he was prepared for a day of doing nothing and thoroughly enjoying it.

Once he had finished his smoke and washed down a couple of painkillers with another pint of water, Grant brushed his teeth furiously in an attempt to disperse some of the taste that a heavy night always left him with. Returning to his bedroom to use the en-suite all he had been able to smell was booze. It was funny how you never noticed until you left and came back. Pulling the curtains fully open and cracking both windows he picked up the obviously dirty clothes to wash and collected the glasses and mugs that had begun to accumulate within reach of the bed. In the kitchen the clothes were put straight in the machine and the dishes loaded with the rest in the dishwasher. As soon as he'd turned both on he found a dirty plate in the living room and a hoody he wanted clean: - typical. Having made what he considered to be a significant dent in the objective of tidying the flat up, he opened the kitchen blinds and the massive curtains that covered the balcony windows before dropping into his favourite seat on the couch and reaching for the remote. As the TV came on, the music that blasted out of it felt like it was vibrating his brain and rattling the windows. Holding his thumb hard over the volume down button he reduced it to a bearable level, making a mental note to adjust the noise level prior to going out in future.

With the worst of his suffering satiated by the recovery of his key items and his immediate physical discomfort lessened by the water and painkillers, Grant was confident that if he waited a few hours he could weather the storm and maybe even leave the flat if required. The repeating single tone of the door entry intercom pierced his ears and his heart raced from the surprise and the jump to his feet that he had made without even realising. As he had aged past twenty, then twenty-five, then thirty he had come to find that the physical side of a hangover was definitely becoming more painful but worse by far was the mental anguish; the "Fear"; the paranoia and depression that could lurk for a day or more. Instantly assuming the worst about every situation and sitting constantly on edge. All that went through his mind as he went to the buzzer was the missing segment at the end of the night. He sincerely hoped that he hadn't jumped the taxi or worse. Surely he'd remember that. Surely.

'Hello?'

'Morning Grant.' Definitely a female. First name as well, so no cops. 'It's Claire. Claire Davidson. Can I come up for a minute?'

The sigh that came out from him was one of unbridled relief. He felt the tension in his body ease off then disappear and the whiteness of his knuckles lessened as he relaxed a death grip he'd unconsciously applied to the receiver.

'Second floor. Lift usually works.'

Depressing the entry button before she had a chance to reply, he removed the chain from the door and opened the locks. Putting his shoes into a random cupboard they happened to be near, he quickly looked over the hallway. The bedroom was a bomb site and there was no way he could tidy it in time – instead, he went for the oldest trick in the male handbook of housekeeping by closing the door. If you can't see the mess it doesn't exist. The living room/kitchen actually looked pretty presentable from his quick scan of it; sure it was a little lived in but Grant was sure she probably expected used needles and bloodstains up the wall. It was only when the knock came at the door that he even realised how strange it was that he'd been caring so much about how his place looked. Walking up the hallway, he opened the door and smiled at Claire.

'Come in.'

He almost fancied that she looked happy to see him as she walked past and into the living room at the end of the hall. A trail of perfume left a subtle path for him to follow and he ran one hand roughly several times over his prickly head before heading there himself. She was sitting in his spot leaning all the way back with her head on the top of the couch and her eyes shut. He loitered awkwardly in the doorway and took her in – she looked more dressed down than every other time he'd seen her and it was definitely a more attractive look.

The first time he'd been admitted to the Magistrate's office she had been sitting straight in her chair with a serious look on her face and shot him looks from over the top of her glasses as she typed furiously on the keyboard. Her heels had clicked as she went in front of him to open the door and she had barely given him a second glance as he entered. He had responded only with friendly remarks and smiles. Every time after that he had been chipping away, getting less dirty looks and occasionally even eliciting a reply that wasn't dripping with venom. The last time he had seen her they had both listened to Magistrate Reid screaming down the phone at someone through the door in silence. She returned to the keyboard quickly but there had been the briefest flash of fear in her eyes which had brought up a feeling of anger in Grant that he couldn't quite justify. Catching her eye over the barrage of noise he had indicated towards the door with a nod then smashed one gnarled fist into the palm of the other hand with a smile. She had actually returned his smile and struck a camp "thinking" pose before shaking her head with a disappointed air. He shrugged as if he wasn't bothered and clasped her shoulder briefly on the way past into the office.

'The offer stands if he ever gets too much.' She hadn't flinched when he touched her but he removed his hand anyway in case it was too much. She had stopped typing. 'Your new glasses look nice by the way. Chin up Claire.'

That was no more than a month ago but he felt it had bought him some leeway. Coming back to his senses in the doorway of his living room he realised two things at once: - he had been staring and she had opened her eyes and was staring back. Shifting his eyes to the television then to the kitchen his hand rose again and rubbed over his shaved head and then settled on his neck.

'You wanting some coffee or something? Sorry the place is a tip, I'm a wee but rough this morning.'

She was looking at him upside down with the tilt of her head but she could tell he seemed a little sheepish. Without waiting for her answer he had begun to potter around in the kitchen opening one cupboard after the other and generally trying to make himself busy. She reverted her head to a more normal angle and faced the TV full on. Her hands worked in tandem trying to smooth her skirt down before reaching up to make sure she hadn't crushed her bow against the seat. Pausing briefly, she removed her glasses carefully and set them down on the table beside the pint of water.

'A black coffee would be lovely thanks. Or just whatever's easiest.'

There was no response other than the continued opening of drawers interspersed with running water and the occasional mumbled expletive. On the screen there was a group of young guys singing a song about loving some girl forever. None of them looked older than 20. The commotion in the kitchen had stopped and Grant was waiting for the kettle to boil, facing forwards over the island towards the screen. He exhaled slowly through his mouth:

'Change the channel if you want. I just keep the music videos on as a bit of background noise.'

'I hadn't pegged you as the boy band sort to be honest Grant.' Her tone was mocking but she kept her eyes forward. He protested to the back of her head anyway.

'I'm not. I hate they guys.' For some reason he continued explaining despite the awareness that he had just bitten and the wind up was deliberate. 'I can't control what comes on can I?'

'You can if you keep phoning in and requesting the songs......'

'I don't......' he paused for a moment. 'I'm no biting.'

She turned again in her seat, beaming at him. Her glasses were sitting on the table in front of her and he realised it was the first time he'd seen her without them on. The irritation seeped out of his body and he laughed. She turned to face the front once more.

'Sure seemed like a nibble at least.'

He let that one hang as the kettle clicked off and he poured two cups of instant coffee which he carefully carried round. Considering only a second he chose to ignore the empty couch that ran along the balcony window adjacent to his usual spot and sat next to her. Taking a hearty gulp, he immediately realised he'd burnt his mouth but swallowed anyway. "Smooth, man. Real smooth." Changing the channel one up to a mix of dance tracks he sank back in the sofa as he felt his liquid fire scorch his throat all the way down to his belly.

'So what do you want to see me for then?'

Surprised at how difficult he found it to keep his tone casual, he concentrated on the flickering images and tried not to think about how close she was to him. She too seemed overly interested in the generic video accompanying the music as she addressed her reply to the screen rather than him.

'The Magistrate wanted me to tell you the cops found a body this morning. On Arthur's Seat.'

Her eyes flicked briefly to his impassive profile then back ahead. If he'd reacted in any way, then it had gone unnoticed. Even though he had left a gap between them, she could feel the warmth emanating from his body.

'And?'

'It seemed very important to him that I told you.'

Claire turned to face him fully, extending her left arm across the back of the seat about half an inch away from his neck. She had expected this news to get some sort of response that would explain to her why she had been send to deliver this mundane news in person rather than over the phone. Instead of that he seemed entirely unphased by it and it was only when she'd spoken it out loud that the true hollowness of the statement sank home to her. The back of his neck was muscular and there was a fleck of ash on it that had been transferred there by his hand. She struggled to resist the urge to wipe it off for some reason before he responded.

'I guess he reckons it might be Rab?' Shaking his head slowly and finding it brushed lightly against her fingertips, he continued. 'He wouldn't go out like that.'

'It doesn't look like a suicide. More like a shallow grave.'

Grant also turned so they were facing each other. His arm sat over the top of hers on the back of the couch not quite touching. His right

81

knee was on the cushion against her left and he looked straight at her.

'He wouldn't go out like that either. I know he's not got a lot of mates the way he goes on and the stuff he gets up to but no one's just going to take him out and dump him in the middle of Edinburgh.'

She could sense the intensity building inside him as she took in the broadness of his chest and the biceps bulging above the vascular forearms that could crush her in a second. There was a strong feeling building inside her also but it wasn't the fear she expected. She couldn't think of a response but it made no odds because he seemed to be building up a head of steam:

'There's no gain for anyone in killing him. Far less without at least trying to squeeze some cash out of his fat idiot dad first.' He felt like a runaway train pulling away from himself. Every sentence made it more certain than the last that he was getting overly angry. 'Besides.' He found his arm had come away from the sofa and was pointing at her face. 'No one is gonna get their grubby mitts on him without coming through me first or seeing me after. Everyone knows that. No one's that stupid. No one.'

She placed her hand onto his wrist behind the accusatory finger calmly. His skin was hot underneath the ink that ran from the right hand all the way up to his neck and below his vest. She saw in his eyes that he became instantly ashamed of losing his temper and went to withdraw his hand. She kept a grip that he could have broken without even trying but he didn't want to. They faced each other as his anger abated and he began to stammer an apology. She cut him off.

'No one thinks you'd let him be hurt Grant. Far less...' She left the thought unfinished. 'I'll let you know as soon as we get any other news.'

Grant nodded sheepishly and allowed his arm to lower to the seat with her hand still maintaining a grip that barely reached halfway around it. Picking at a bit of fluff on his shorts with his free hand he spoke again, seeming to address his own kneecaps.

'I've got the day off. I'll ask a few questions.' In his head he was running through a veritable who's who of the scumbags in Pilton. 'Your boss's guy came to the boozer last night, gave me a card.

Weighed as much as a photo of himself but seemed handy. I'll hit him up, see if we can help each other out.'

Her thumb was making small circles on the inside of his wrist as she thought. Suddenly, she dropped his arm and snatched his phone up from the table. There was no protest as she put her glasses back on, tapped at keys for a while and then stood up and offered him his own phone as if she were doing him a favour.

'I've put my number in there now. You can keep me posted. I need to head back out.'

He took the phone and dropped it back into his pocket as he stood himself, stretching above her. Leading the way to the door, he opened it and she lingered in the doorway. Neither was sure what to do but both decided to take the initiative at once: Grant attempting a firm handshake just as she reached up to put her arms around his shoulders. Trapped in the hug with his arm jammed between them against her stomach, he still enjoyed it. She released him and they both were at a loss again as to how to proceed. He wanted to tell her that he liked her without the glasses even more than he had liked the new ones. That her bow was cute. That her dressed-down look was far better than her office one. He wanted to ask if he could use the number for social calls. If she wanted to hear from him with regards to things not to do with work. Instead, he only spoke two words.

'Bye then.'

'Bye.'

He closed the door and sighed deeply then went back to the living room, downed his own coffee and carried her untouched one to the balcony where he sat and smoked three cigarettes one after the other without knowing why.

Chapter 13

If you were to ask people what sprang to mind when the city of Edinburgh was mentioned, you would get an extremely varied array of responses. Most know that it is the capital; full of historic buildings, tourist trap shops and the occasional festival that is famous worldwide and nothing but an inconvenience for the locals. Sports fans would talk about the Hibs and Hearts rivalry : – never quite viewed as being on the same level as the hatred and bile that flows around Glasgow on Old Firm days and rightly so. If you had an interest in linguistics you could mention the commonly held opinion that there is no "Edinburgh accent" or dialect on the same level as Glasgow. Arguably untrue since it seems to be based only on the weegies with the strongest accents against those in the capital who speak well.

Transport, Education, Law, Art, Music, Culture – these are all facets to the city's history that are touted by all who love it. Drugs, Violence, Poverty, Alcoholism – these too are defining aspects of life that are less readily admitted. You can cherry pick the statistics and the facts to make anywhere in Scotland look any way you want but the overall character of the country cannot be denied. The ease with which many manage to do so is by being so far removed from these issues that it has no impact, meaningful or otherwise, on their day to day existence. You aren't driving your two little terrors to private school in a 4x4 that is impractical and unnecessary in any city and being concerned that someone will try and sell them drugs at the gates. You don't sip cocktails at £12 a pop while concerning if your last tenner should go to keeping the lights on until Giro day or getting some food in the fridge and hoping it doesn't spoil when the power is cut. There is a divide and a disconnect between the people who see the city one way and those who see it the other but they walk the same streets. They use the same supermarkets. They exist together yet they exist in separate worlds.

Luke Calvin was sat in a cafe on Rose Street – the lane that runs between Princes Street and George Street – with his notebook out, thinking these thoughts about Edinburgh and watching the world going by. Coming back from the crime scene he had decided to stay in the town centre for a bit and sort out his plans instead of going back to his flat. Tucking into the fancy looking toastie that he'd pointed at through the glass and having been curtly informed that it was a "Croque Monsieur" by the employee, he was sat on a high stool at the window eating off a ledge that masqueraded as a table. Poor show when you're getting called uncultured by someone selling you sandwiches. On the way down he had been in contact with the office and Laura had very graciously decided to get over "wife-gate" and got him more detail on the employment history of the missing man.

It was actually surprisingly extensive: The Magistrate was clearly trying to instil a decent work ethic in his offspring if nothing else. There were no jobs directly with his father or even in a related field. It seemed that Geoffrey's shame held him back from being seen to help too blatantly in that respect. The majority seemed to have some sort of relation, even if only a passing one, to the tourist industry. In fact, he'd worked at no less than five locations or venues where the public went to gain some historic experience of the city. Sometimes for periods of up to a year. Luke had fully expected to find a CV full of gaps and holes to indicate tardiness, poor attitude or general unwillingness to work. Instead it seemed that there was something else other than money and hard drugs that held Rab's interest at one point. As tempting as it was to zip around town to each place after the other, start shooting questions at employees who didn't care and get nowhere, he knew he needed a little outside assistance. The obvious option was Grant, but given that it wasn't quite midday yet he didn't reckon that he'd have surfaced. Besides, in a perfect world he wanted the big man to reach out to him and ideally, he wanted to have something of substance to give to him when he did. Some direction to be headed in or a new discovery that he could hang his hat on – prove his investigative chops.

For the moment he was content to investigate the rest of his lunch and watch the strangers passing by outside the window. The sun had come out for the second day running and as he chewed he tried to remember if two days of sunshine in Edinburgh was one of the seven signs of the Apocalypse. He was pretty sure it was. Soon the sky would turn black and the four horsemen would appear – Death, Pestilence, The Horseman of Coupon Busting Dead Certs and The Rider of Minging Lager In An Overpriced Nightclub. Luke sipped his Latte and waited for the end of days with a casual indifference. Surely the world couldn't end when he was learning so much about sandwiches every day?

There was an interesting scene unfolding beneath the canopy on Arthur's Seat. One of the junior technicians had begun to photograph the skeletal remains that they had unearthed and was meticulously itemising every aspect of the scene. The rags that were draped around it were charred and burnt and the bones that were easily visible without interfering too much seemed blackened by smoke, yet there was something very curious about it. He sidled up to the commanding officer – not an easy task when everyone wore the exact same protective clothing and had only their eyes visible – and voiced his concern. The clothes were burnt but not rotten, yet the body was reduced to a skeleton. There was no smell of decay or putrefaction. There was no real overpowering scent of death and no visible flesh whatsoever. The reply was brief and final and he sheepishly returned to continue taking photographs and cataloguing all the evidence he could. He did notice that his superior had come over beside him and was looking with renewed interest at what he'd pointed out. Just as he pressed down to take another snapshot of the grim scene a gloved hand clapped his shoulder twice and he was again alone. The shame disappeared and he glowed inside as he retook the picture of the corpse just in case the apologetic tap had knocked it out of focus.

Emerging from the tent and going through the decontamination process, the Sergeant got clear of the exclusion zone and stripped off the suit and mask. It was just before 2pm and the shift change was taking place at the scene for the two cops that were standing by. The younger one (Daniel or something. Maybe David?) looked as if he was conducting an entirely too thorough briefing of the two uninterested officers who had showed up to begin their stint of standing around. Steve stood a little way away smoking with his hat held at his side, squinting at the sun. They had joined at the same time, both ex-forces and had maintained what could maybe pass for a friendship for the years in-between. Replacing his own cap on his head, he walked towards all four officers and Steve seeing his approach came towards him, tucking his hat under his smoking arm so his other was free for a handshake. Clasping hands, Steve greeted him with his favourite sarcastic cliché.

'Never gets any easier.' The cigarette was bouncing slowly with every word and the Sergeant smiled appreciatively into the cynical face.

'Cut the routine man. I've got something you might be interested in. One of the boys told me your old buddy was around earlier. Showed up before even they did.'

'I know blind dogs with no legs that could show up before your boys.'

'Very good. You wanting to hear this or no?'

Steve shrugged and ashed his cigarette. That was about as much enthusiasm as you could reasonably expect from him. He was off shift. He was tired. He was hungry. But if he could help Luke out in any way he was going to do it. He owed him that much.

Round Grant's flat in Pilton the washing machine and dishwasher had finished at the same time and he swung himself up off the sofa to empty them. The worst of the hangover had passed and a long shower he had taken in the interim seemed to rejuvenate him. After drying himself, he had pulled on a clean pair of jeans and a black t shirt before looking out a clean hoody and his boots to wear later when he left. The music channels were still cycling through their flashing images over noise and he was even less connected to it than usual. As he methodically started shaking each damp item then draping them over the clothes horse to finish drying he ran over the early morning visit for the hundredth time. It made no sense for Claire to have been asked to come round in person when a phone call would have done. He was happy to have seen her, but there was definitely something off about the whole thing. The only solution he could come up with was the same one he had arrived at every other time before putting it off or dismissing it: he was going to have to call the Magistrate and find out what was going on.

Once the dishes were all stacked back in the cupboards and the clothes laid out as well as he could be bothered, there was nothing more to stop him from making his call. Proceeding to the balcony with a certain amount of foreboding he had his phone in one hand and his cigarettes in the other. He was certain he'd need them. Dialling the number before he had a chance to change his mind he lowered himself into the sunlit seat and lit up. It was picked up with the usual punctuality.

'Hello? Yes? Who is it?

Geoffrey Reid sounded well and truly rattled. This was not an everyday occurrence nor was it an opportunity to be passed up. His defences would be lowered in this frantic state and if there was one thing Grant needed it was honest answers.

'It's your favourite meathead.' Grant surprised himself with the coolness of his voice. 'Just calling to see how you are. What you're up to. Why you're sending your secretary round my flat. The usual.'

Through the phone the voice sounded tinny but the lack of quality couldn't mask the obvious deceit in the Magistrate's tone.

'Claire was just telling you about what the police found.' He sounded too huffy: too flustered. The statement hadn't merited the defensiveness that the answer was wrapped in. 'Thought you might be interested. That's all.'

Grant licked his bottom lip carefully and took a draw. He exhaled as he spoke. 'Why don't you just ask me what you want to ask me like a man?'

There was barely a pause before the Magistrate responded.

'I don't know what you're talking about...'

The defence was paper thin now. He had him on the ropes and was just toying with him, bobbing and feinting.

'You want to ask if I knew anything about it. If it was my doing. If I'd taken your request a bit too literally and caused you more problems.'

'I have no idea what...'

Grant cut him off. Once again he could feel his temper fraying. This fat old fool was playing games with him again and didn't even have the common decency to just come out with a question or the guts to lay an accusation on him.

'You wanted to know if I'd topped your boy and stuck him in a shallow grave.'

Silence from the other end of the phone gave Grant a second to consider, for the first time, that discussing being accused of murder was perhaps not a conversation to have in the early afternoon on his balcony at full volume.

'Well did you?'

There it was. The only reason he'd sent Claire round. To see if he was spooked. Gauge his reaction. He hoped with all his heart that she was unaware of her role in this because he knew he'd have to try very hard to hate her. Taking a long indulgent pull, he let the Magistrate sweat before he replied.

'No, Geoffrey. I didn't. When you made me your offer to encourage him to "disappear" I told you exactly where you could shove it and I'm a man of my word.'

'I didn't really.... I was just.... I meant relocate elsewhere.... You know that....'

'I didn't tell him what you said either, even though I should have, because my word means something. Unlike yours. I will bet any amount of money you like that the body they found wasn't Rab. And once you find that out for sure you can call me to let me know.' He had begun to point accusingly with his smoke again despite the fact there was no way of Geoffrey seeing it. 'I'm going to head out and find out what I can. If you have any information that will help me, you get it to me immediately and I might consider not pummelling you.'

Geoffrey made an effort to compose himself before he made his reply. The assertion that his son was not the corpse seemed so definite that even without the proof he believed it. In retrospect, accusing a long term associate of killing his son might not have been his slickest manoeuvre. He needed time to think.

'OK Grant. OK OK OK. I'm sorry. My head's totally gone with all this. I didn't really think.... Anyway. If you can keep me posted I'll be much obliged and return the favour. There will obviously be a substantial financial consideration for any help you can give.'

Hitting the hang up button, Grant relaxed in his seat. All the adrenaline left his body at once and he felt drained. Then again, it's not every day you get called a murderer to your face. He squinted at the sun as he decided his next move – the guy from the pub seemed decent enough and he was meant to be a pro. Might be worth getting their heads together and working it out. Heading back inside, he found the card crumpled up on the living room table and dialled the number. Grabbing a beer out of the fridge he only just managed to get the lid open before it was answered.

'Luke? Yeah. It's Grant Ferguson, bouncer from the Bull? Aye man, aye. Went out after, feel like a truck ran through my head. You up for some hair of the dog? My brain's a shambles with all the stuff that's happened today. Need a hand straightening some of it out. You know "The Fluke"? Foot of Pilton Drive? Sound. Call it five. Right man, catch.'

Drinking deeply from the can, he wondered why all his other conversations today had seemed so hard. Sitting back on the sofa he sat and thought. There was no logical reason he could give that would explain why he knew Rab wasn't dead but it wasn't even up for debate. What mattered now was how to get his hands on him and he couldn't be sure if he was wanting to hug him or lamp him out. Both seemed tempting at the moment.

Chapter 14

Derek Robertson was sat in his flat in Craigmillar with the telly on for company. Lying along his stained couch, he was trying his best to get motivated to do something – anything – to get out of the flat for a bit. Staring at these four walls was driving him crazy but then again he had his customers to think of. The flat was a bit pokey with peeling wallpaper and a kitchen that needed an upgrade in a hurry but it served his requirements fine. There was beer in the fridge, a kilo of hash in the spare bedroom and four locks on the door. For once it seemed the career officer at school had made a correct prediction all these years ago when she told him he'd end up dealing drugs or going to prison. Two out of two. That was pretty good shooting even for a crackpot trying to help kids pick what they want to do for a living when they're still 15 and younger.

His face was pale, drawn and slightly elongated. A particularly unkind observer would remark that he looked like an unwell horse. The long limbs that sprawled in four different directions over, on and around the couch were stick thin, feeding back to an unnaturally long torso. The stained joggers with burn marks through them were straight from the catwalks of Milan and the hair that sprouted in patches around his angular jaw was going to be the next "in" look. Sniffing deeply, he reached one spidery hand to the ashtray to retrieve the joint that he'd left smouldering there two minutes or two seconds ago: he wasn't sure which. Just then, there was a banging at the door. Something rushed over him, either paranoia or an adrenaline dump and he froze leaning half off the sofa staring at the door as if it's vision was based on movement. If he knew what time it was he'd have an idea about whether he was expecting someone or not but he was too stoned to keep track of such an abstract concept and just kept his eyes on the door.

'Deek? Deek? Open the door you roaster.'

He must be expecting someone after all. What Deek had forgotten was that his flatmate had nipped to the shops for a bit of grub somewhere between five minutes and five hours ago. He'd quadruple locked the door as soon as he left and promptly forgotten he'd ever existed. Posting the unlit joint in the corner of his lip he unravelled himself from the couch and went to start unlocking the door. The chain slid out of its flimsy runner easily enough and the deadbolt retracted in two movements as he rotated the lock clockwise. When he did the Yale lock though, the door wouldn't budge from its frame. Maybe it was a push door? Tentatively leaning against it yielded no different result. Releasing the Yale, he took a step back and looked at the door the way an astrophysicist would look at a whiteboard covered in equations that just wouldn't balance out. To his surprise the door spoke again.

'Have you done that bolt at the bottom man? My arms are getting tired.'

Eureka – There was a backup deadbolt located about half a foot below the first. As he stooped to release it he first wagged his finger at it, to let it know it had fooled him this time but no more. Retrying the Yale, the door exploded inwards in a burst of light, thumping off his face which was all but leaning against it and sending him sprawling in the hallway. The jig was up. He was getting raided. He'd been betrayed by his own door. The shame. The ignominy. Looking up from his back he saw a messianic figure silhouetted in the light carrying bags of shopping - Mark had returned with the food. The sound of the door closing and each lock being reapplied was accompanied by a deep sighing.

'Get up you tube. How much have you had?'

Deek felt arms looping under his armpits and hoisting him roughly to his feet. He was assisted back to the couch where he resumed his sprawl with the satisfaction of a man who'd undertaken a massive journey and was relieved to be back home. Mark brought the shopping bags through to the kitchen and returned with various snacks which he threw onto his friend. Deek puffed twice on the joint that had remained in his mouth throughout his ordeal and offered it to Mark who had sat down on the chair beside him.

'That's not even lit man. I was only gone like an hour and half.'

Mark was the same age as Derek and was equally culpable in their ongoing business venture. However, he made an effort to not be so heavily involved in the testing of their product as the pool of skin and worry on the sofa, who was now studying the unlit joint carefully as if trying to find an on switch. Mark sighed and found his lighter. Leaning across, the spark startled Deek who recoiled before carefully pouting his lips and edging his face towards the flame until it barely grazed the tip and lit once more. Leaning back again he stared at the TV but saw nothing. Mark considered only a minute before shrugging for the benefit of no one in particular and begun skinning up himself.

He was shorter than Deek but then again so was everyone. They both had brown hair although he wore his long, down to his shoulders and made a half-hearted effort to keep it controlled by a bandanna. The earring in his left ear was just a gold stud but with the plaid shirts and skate shoes he came across as a student to most. Derek was never out of his joggers and loved nothing more than offensively white trainers and the occasional polo shirt with his chain hung outside. Tale as old as time - The Ned and the Baggy. They were an unlikely double act but they had been friends for too long now to ever be any different way. Mark finished rolling and sparked up himself.

'I nipped into the "Boat" for a quick pint on my way to the shops. Just a quick one and a few goes on the bandit ken?' Checking if his lanky pal was listening he saw nothing to indicate positively in either direction. The meticulously maintained sprawl made it look like he was glued to the leather on the sofa and Mark was put in mind of a long sloth. 'Oi! Cloth Ears! I'm speaking here.'

'I heard man, I heard. Stop stressing Jackanory.' His glazed eyes were still facing the telly. The joint rotated slowly in his hand in front of him. 'Carry on with your rubbish story and I'll carry on pretending I'm interested.'

Highly amused at his own razor sharp wit Deek dissolved into a fit of the giggles that bounced his slender rib cage and creased his face inwards. Mark watched him until they had died off to the occasional titter.

'You listening?'

'Aye man. I'm listening. You was in the Boat getting your breeks pulled down by the puggie as per usual. Losing your shirt to the bright lights and noises. Pumping it full of money for the next radge.' His long neck craned and twisted to fix his eyes on Mark. 'It's a great story so far man. Real edge of my seat stuff like.'

Mark was not fond of his habitual gambling losses being mocked. Puffing away, his retort was far snottier than he expected.

'I won £12 as it goes.'

'When are we moving to the Bahamas then mate? Retiring on your winnings?'

Fingering the stud in his ear was always the tell-tale sign that Mark was making a great effort to pretend like he was totally calm. Deek watched him reach towards it then stop, placing it in his pocket instead. Almost there. Almost. Deek took another toke and asked as casually as he could:

'How much did you put into it before you pulled out that life changing £12 then?

'Two quid. Maybe three.'

It had actually been closer to twenty.

'And how much of it did you put back in?'

'None.'

It had all gone back in and he'd even broken a ten at the bar to have another pop. No one who played a bandit thought about these things properly or answered these questions honestly, mainly due to the fact that the output outstripped the winnings so badly that it made them confront the stupidity of continuing to play. Mark was well and truly in the huff now and the shine had been taken off his win.

'None? Pffft. You sure it wasn't dropped in there against your will by the flying pigs that were going about as soon as you walked away from the bandit with winnings?'

The only response was silence and Mark casually massaging his ear lobe. He'd got his man. Satisfied in his victory he made an abortive attempt to sit up and abandoned it after two seconds of effort. The only tangible result of his effort was that he was now further on his side facing his pal.

'Right man. What were you trying to tell me anyway?'

The massaging stopped and Mark reclined back into his seat, looking at the telly instead of Deek. His intention to make him ask again for the story before he told it was thwarted by the fact that Deek was so stoned he'd probably lie there staring at him for a full hour and as long as he didn't move too much the assumption would be that he had started immediately anyway. The joint was starting to mellow him out anyway, topping up the drinks he'd had. He took another few short puffs and started again.

'Right. So I'm in the Boat...'

'Yup. In the Boat.'

'Aye. Like I said. I'm in the Boat having a pint....'

'And playing the bandit Mark. Mind you won £12?'

Despite himself he burst out laughing. The look of innocence on his friends face also dissolved into laughter as he placed his head down onto the arm of the sofa and his body was wracked by big gulping sniggers. Once it had abated again in both camps, Mark held both hands palm down and lowered them slightly towards the carpet in an attempt to induce calm.

'Right man. Right. I'm in the Boat having a pint...' Deek had raised his hand to interject but was pre-empted 'AND playing the bandit. OK, Happy? Good. Now. Seen they two coppers in that drink in there sometimes. You know? One's older and one's younger?'

"Great powers of description Mark" he thought, aware that he was making an absolute meal of this story but it seemed to be capturing the attention of his audience who was actually participating.

'Aye, one's called Steve. He's sound as anything for being filth.' Deek considered a moment before continuing. 'The other one takes himself a bit serious but he's an OK guy too."

'Aye. The other one's David something. Anyway. They're yapping away about something to do with the job and usually I'm no bothered about what sort of nonsense their wasting time on but I caught a bit here and there.'

Mark glanced to make sure that he was still holding the interest of his friend and was pleased to see he was staring with rapt attention. Taking another hit, he relaxed further into the seat and continued.

'They were on about something they were called to this morning. I didn't catch what it was about but that Steve boy was on about phoning an old mate of his to give him some information and that

Dave guy was a bit unhappy with it. Talking about protocol and stuff like that eh?'

'Aye. Protocol. Sure man. I love a bit of protocol, me. Then what happened?'

Mark was a bit surprised at his friend's indifference.

'What do you mean "what else"? That was it.'

'That was it?'

'Aye. I find out that there's a bent copper in the local and you're no bothered?'

Derek studied the end of his joint which was burnt down almost to the roach and thought carefully before replying.

'Mark, you can't call them that any more. You shouldn't care what he's into. It's meant to be a modern world.' He puffed carefully. 'Acceptance and that. Besides, I'm sure he has a wife and kids.'

Mark was now thoroughly confused. 'Aye he's married. And what?'

'I just don't think you should be running in here telling me about how he fancies dudes as if it's any of either of our business...'

The laugh that came from Mark was loud, long and entirely genuine. He rocked forward in his seat with tears streaming down his face before composing himself to look at Deek who was looking as hurt as a kicked kitten. Mark held up a hand towards him in apology.

'Sorry man. Sorry.' He snorted and covered his face with his hand. 'I meant bent as in on the take. Giving out confidential information to folk, usually for money. No the way you were thinking.'

It took a second but the penny dropped and Derek's face softened. He smirked a little but Mark was worried he might have offended him now. He had turned away on the sofa.

'Here Mark?'

'Aye?'

'How'd you manage to hear them over the bandit dropping that fortune you won all over the pub?'

They laughed together for longer than was necessary and the telly that no one was watching continued to blast over the top of it all.

Steve and Dave had finished their shift and headed back to the station to change. Standing at the entrance in their civvies, they both paused. Tomorrow was a day off and it was barely 3pm now - surely there was time for a pint before home? Neither wanted to be the one to suggest it. Steve looked older than his compatriot by an additional measure when they were wearing their street clothes: it had been well over a decade before he'd even given a thought to the fickle winds of fashion. Dave told anyone who would listen that he didn't care about how he looked while meticulously planning and executing every detail of each outfit with military precision. Why on earth garishly coloured chinos ever became the next big thing was the sort of question that kept Steve up at night. They both lived up past the Commonwealth Pool in Craigmillar and Niddire respectively. As they jumped into Dave's car and started the drive back they chatted amiably over the radio, along Fettes Avenue and up to Queensferry Road. It was only when they were nearing their destination a quarter of an hour later that Steve finally asked the question they'd both been waiting for.

'Pub?'

Dave nodded as he accelerated past his flat and onwards to the Boat.

'Just the one mind, I'm driving.'

Steve stared out the window absently: his mood was always at its best when the beer came so close he could almost taste it.

'See how we go. You can leave the car if you fancy a few more.'

No matter which one of them was driving that day, they invariably ended up leaving the car and getting a taxi or lift round to collect it the next day, after the effects had worn off. Most of the coppers they both knew seemed to drink in places like "The Ox" but neither was the sort of man to forgo a local within stumbling distance to spend more time with people of their own profession. Dave was taking it slow, not rushing, savouring the promise of beer to come. Turning the radio down slightly he kept his eyes ahead while he posed his question.

'How did you know that guy from earlier anyway. Were you in the army together or something?'

Steve shrugged and didn't turn his head away from the passenger window. As well as he got on with the younger man, there were limits to what he was happy to discuss. It wasn't worth falling out over but he supposed his hesitancy and silence would be enough to stop any follow up questions. The sound from the radio increased

97

slightly back to its previous level and he was happy to be proven right again. Presently they arrived at the pub and parked the car behind it. The paint on the sign was peeling and the wood underneath rotten but it was the sort of thing that you could try to pass off as "rustic charm" if you really stretched. Through the door at the front, they entered into an almost deserted lounge occupied by only two or three people who all looked up, nodded in recognition then returned to their papers. Dave had driven so Steve went to get the first round in while the younger man approached the jukebox and dropped a pound in it. Before the pints were fully poured the sounds of Iggy Pop had filled the silence. The pints were carried carefully to their usual seat near the window which you couldn't see out of but which gave a stellar view of the TV, the door and any nice barmaids who had the misfortune of working in there.

'You always play the same songs.' Steve said, handing over one pint. 'Every time we go anywhere with a jukebox you rock up to it and I know full well what's going to come on.'

''That's not true.' Dave sipped the head from his lager then took a deep swallow.

'Aye it is. "I wanna be your dog" then "Lust for life" then "The Passenger.'

'So? They're good tunes.'

Steve considered a moment and substituted a drink for a reply. Smacking his lips loudly he held his glass up across the table.

'That's another one we've gotten in on them bud.'

They touched glasses and drank. The first went down far too easily. It really hit the spot and they both relaxed properly. The next was just as good, if not better and the third was definitely ticking all the right boxes. They chatted back and forth, loosening up a bit as the lager began to work its magic. Once the third was gone, Steve didn't even bother asking before taking the glasses back to the bar and getting the fourth round in. Dave was happily not watching the television and listening to the AC/DC selection he'd gotten up to choose just before the Iggy Pop had finished when the door opened and Mark walked in. Giving Dave a nod, he went to the bar where he greeted Steve in the passing and ordered a pint. Watching the back of his head as he leant on the bar waiting, Dave was struck by the weirdness of the set up they had here: the two of them were Police and everyone knew but didn't care. Mark sold hash with that lanky idiot Deek and everyone knew but cared even less. The glass that landed in front of him brought him back to reality.

'Here, Steve? How come we don't just go round to their gaff and bust them both for possession with intent?' His eyes were still fixed on Mark with his bandanna and earring now moving (as expected) towards the bandit. 'It's not like they even try to pretend they aren't up to anything.'

Steve took a thoughtful sip and replaced the glass on the beermat. There had been a time when he too was just starting out and although he had never managed to muster up the zeal that his compatriot seemed to he could understand his frustration. Police work was not the sheriff kicking in the Saloon door and gunning down all the criminals any more. Far far from it.

'You know full well that we need a warrant or anything we seize can't be used in court. I mean, you are the walking police handbook after all...' Instead of the usual dirty look Dave laughed into his pint just as he went to take a sip and ended up spraying foam all over his face. Emboldened by the unusually buoyant mood of his partner, he continued. 'Besides, all they do is sling a bit of hash. It's against the law and illegal and drug dealers are scum blah blah blah but I'll tell you one thing.' Leaning forward and speaking a little lower he pointed back over his shoulder with his thumb. 'If we busted they two muppets then someone else would be shifting their stuff and the rest within days. And who knows who it'd be. I'm well aware that I'm meant to hate them but I can't. Neither of them has ever used strong violence. Or sold smack or even a bit of ching. All they do is hash and green and they do it with as little outfall in the community as possible. Better the devil you know I guess.'

Dave had listened intently while drying his face repeatedly with his right hand. For some reason the explanation seemed to make sense to him as he watched Mark returning to the bar for more change. Most of the dealers they ended up taking down were pushing big amounts of class A's or enforcing their collections and defending their territory with bats and blades. The booze was making him warm to the man with the long hair feeding pound coins into the bandit.

'That almost makes sense man. I guess I can see that.' He took another sip and wiped his face once more to make sure it was clean of foam. 'Bit of common sense policing.'

'That's out of a handbook isn't it?'

'Maybe.'

They both laughed. Suddenly, Dave realised that it was the final chorus of his last AC/DC selection and jumped up to pick more songs.

'Any requests?'

'I fought the law? Anything by Sting and the Police?'

'You don't even like these songs. You're just on the wind up.'

'Yup.' Steve took a sip. 'I request that you just pick some tunes and stop harassing me.'

Dave fumbled for a coin and went across to the jukebox with it held tightly between his finger and thumb as is it would escape if given half a chance. On the way past he ruffled Mark's hair and all he could smell was grass.

'What you saying Markey Boy?'

'You're seeing it all officer.'

He hadn't even turned away from the machine. From across the pub Steve had seemingly found a recommendation after all.

'Floyd. Bit of Pink Floyd man.'

Giving a high thumbs up so he could see he'd been heard, Dave began the increasingly laborious task of typing on the touchscreen to get his selections. Steve was waiting at the table watching him and wondering how badly he'd be read the riot act for what he was going to suggest. It had been many years since he'd worked alongside Luke but he knew that he was going to at least give him a heads up with what he'd been told. A nudge in the right direction. Dave returned triumphant to his pint just as Mark walked away from the bright lights and sat forlorn two tables away from them.

'Right. Mind that guy who came up to us on Arthur's Seat at the cordon?'

'Aye. Thought he was just gonna be wanting a look at the body or something. There's always a few sickos who want to clap eyes on a corpse if you've got one about.'

'Yeah, well I worked with him before I did this. He's a top guy. Really is.'

100

Even through the booze, Dave could feel suspicion rising inside himself. 'I'm sure he is man. And?'

'I want to call him and give him an update on what we know so far.'

He had his eyes down, watching as he carefully swirled his lager round and round the bottom of the pint glass and waited for the inevitable.

'You know we can't comment on ongoing investigations.'

Dave made a mental note to never attempt to say "on ongoing" while drinking again. It had made him feel his tongue was going to drop out of his head. Steve stopped swirling his pint and took a small sip. He looked up at the younger man's face.

'I know, I know. Thing is he does some sort of investigation stuff nowadays. Kind of off the books and under the radar sort of thing. Tried to look into it once: no one seems to admit to employing him. Anyway.' His hand waved dismissively between them. 'If he was up there that early he knew about it as soon as we did. And if he took the time to come up and see himself chances are he thought the body could be whoever he was looking for.'

'Or his man had created it...'

Steve accepted this point with a tilt of the head and a pursing of the lips.

'Also possible. That forensics Sergeant I spoke to at end of shift. Jeffries? You know him?'

'Only to see.'

'Also a good guy but that's by the by. Told me something that could help Luke rule out a few things or point his questions in the right direction.'

Dave was now looking into his pint glass but instead of swirling it, he was going for a slow tilt that was making the amber fluid climb one side of the glass then the other.

"I'm not sold man. You knew I'd be against this so why did you even tell me?'

Steve exhaled slowly and scanned the pub. Mark had finished his pint behind them and was collecting a few bags of shopping from behind the bar. He gave them a wave on the way out which they both responded to with a raised glass.

'I guess I didn't want to do anything behind your back. No use in us starting to sneak around on each other really. Recipe for disaster that.'

Dave considered this carefully. It was actually fairly flattering to him to have his consent asked for breaching protocol. The difficulty now was to manage some form of compromise which let them both leave without feeling bitter or let down.

'Just how well did you know him before?' Steve looked up quickly but Dave held his hand up apologetically between them. 'I don't need details man. I just want to understand why you're willing to risk the sack to give him pretty pointless information.'

Steve took a very careful look around again and rubbed his chin thoughtfully. There was very little he was allowed to disclose about the unit he had served in under Luke Calvin and even less that he wanted to remember. He chose to give his partner a small morsel to appease him.

'He saved my life in Kosovo. Got shot in the ribcage for his trouble and nearly died himself.' Dave was looking at him in astonishment and Steve could tell he was struggling to keep his promise to not ask follow up questions. 'Like I said; He's a good guy.'

There was silence between them for a minute while they both appreciated the gravity of what had been disclosed and heard respectively. Eventually Dave broke the silence.

'How about you phone him up and tell him he might find something of interest in the forensics report? That way we're sort of covered and it's still on him to find out what he can.'

Steve smiled across the table at his partner.

'Good man.'

Chapter 15

Grant had left for the pub with plenty of time in hand and was ambling down Pilton Drive with his hands in his pocket. Depending on which side of the street you were in or which postcode you happened to have the house prices around here could fluctuate wildly. It used to be that no one ever chose to live down here but that was changing. All the new builds springing up were appealing to the young professionals and slowly changing the face and reputation of the area. It still retained aspects of its character from before while developing a glossy facade – that was the way he saw it anyway.

Somehow he'd got to thinking about Rab and how much disaster seemed to follow along in his wake. No matter how many promises of good behaviour were made or threats issued by Grant, both veiled and blatant, there always seemed to be some form of carnage occurring whenever he was around. It had gotten to such an extent that anytime there was a reasonable length of time passing without incident, Grant could feel himself become more and more anxious as the weight of the inevitable unknown that would shatter the peace built. It was like the sun rising in the morning: – no matter how much you thought it just might not happen this time it always turned out the same way and you felt you had no right whatsoever to even be surprised. There was the time he'd gotten too bevvied and thrown his pint in the face of a local hard case with head tattoos and a bad attitude. Or the time he'd gotten too stoned before a gig and threatened the security when they wouldn't let him in because he was blatantly mangled. The time he'd taken too much acid and just wanted to sit in the hall cupboard with the door open for a couple of hours. And these were just the ones that the two of them could recall with at least a hint of amusement. Grant stood by the one mantra he felt like he had repeated over and over so many times that it should have lost it's meaning by now but he somehow had to keep making himself believe it – He's not a bad guy really.

The Fluke was at the foot of Pilton Drive (technically on Granton Road) and its normal clientele consisted of locals of all ages and professions. Come five o clock there were painters finished for the day, plasterers stopping in for "one" on the way home and all others in-between. During the daytime, the older generation held court, watching the horse racing and nipping back and forward from the bookies in between races to put money on or collect winnings. They played "pitchy" against the bar while the barmaid pretended not to notice. There was a swathe of guys that Grant had gone to school with that drank in there on the regular so he was always guaranteed a bit of chat and a game or two of pool.

As he was approaching The Fluke, he noticed that Luke was already waiting outside in the same jumper and jeans he'd worn to the pub, smoking against the wall. Luke's head was back against the roughcast blowing rings upwards into the sky and trying to make them go through each other. Taking in his appearance, Grant was unable to pin down what is was about his newest associate that had made him seem intimidating. There was nothing imposing about the lightly built physique or the frankly rather scruffy hairdo and facial hair that would worry anyone in their right mind. Nor was there a coldness behind the eyes or a mad dog stare and swagger that could threaten anyone who didn't know better. The only thing he seemed to be able to hang his hat on was some quiet confidence that emanated from him and that was a very shoogly peg indeed on which to base an opinion. As they made eye contact and Luke peeled himself away from the wall to greet the big bouncer, Grant extended a hand to shake and mentally agreed with his assertion the previous night that he very much still fancied his chances if it ever deteriorated into violence.

'Grant. How's it?' Luke overshot the offered hand, linked his thumb over the bigger man's and pulled him towards him to bump shoulders. 'You well?'

For the second time within a single day Grant Ferguson was hugged against his will, although he had to admit he didn't feel any sort of butterflies this time round. Patting Luke's back firmly and extracting himself from the embrace he scanned around to ensure no one had seen. The last thing he needed right now was a ribbing from any locals about his "boyfriend".

'You're seeing it all.'

The non-committal phrase seemed to draw a laugh out of a surprising number of people. It had never made sense to Grant but he believed in giving the people what they wanted and if people thought it was a clever and witty response then who was he to dispel that myth? He pushed the door of the pub open and ducked inside without even checking if Luke was following. Inside the first set of double doors there was an entrance area that the management had the audacity to refer to as a "foyer" although in their defence they actually had both male and female toilets coming off from it as well as the overwhelming stench of both smoke and urine. Especially when it was raining, dark, cold or a day ending in "Y" people had developed a habit of sparking up in this no man's land before stepping outside and the smell never seemed to properly leave. If the weather was particularly unkind and the bar staff especially lenient, many didn't even bother to go fully outside at all.

There were two rooms both served by the same bar of which only one was ever open at any time, one ostensibly for functions and the other for normal night to night drinking. It was the "Saloon" side that the noise was coming at this point in time so Grant continued through a second set of double doors on the right into the pub itself. There were cushioned seats running around the outside of the expansive room with tables at seemingly sporadic intervals. The bar ran along the entire length of the right hand side and had high metallic stools with footrests but no back to them. The pool table and dart board were down the furthest end of the room and for the moment there were very few people drinking and no one playing either. Grant went up to the bar and ordered a couple of pints while Luke, who had followed him, was now sat in a corner at a table looking every bit as if he'd always drank there. He had his notebook and pen out on the table and was scribbling carefully on the top of a new page when Grant arrived with the beers.

'Lager OK for you man? Just assumed. My head's still burst from last night.'

Luke stopped writing, set his pen down and took a deep drink from the glass before toasting Grant across the table. Grant returned the gesture and took a huge gulp which caused him instant acid reflux but settled both his mind and the frayed nerves that seemed to accompany his every hangover nowadays. To be totally truthful he could have probably done with a lager shandy or a "tops" at the very least to take the edge off the bitterness but his pride hadn't allowed him to order it. Especially not in his local. He'd never have heard the end of it. The internal thought process was interrupted by Luke.

'Spot on man. Never turned down a pint in my life yet.'

There was a silence between them where they both took the time to look around and think about just how little they actually knew each other. Up to this point their interaction had consisted of a 5-minute conversation outside a pub and a 30 second phone call. Both were thinking that if they'd called a girl the day after they'd first met her she'd probably have run a mile. As it happened, here they were and the grand total of four other drinkers had barely acknowledged their existence far less how weird it was between them. It was Luke who finally spoke.

'How you wanting to do this then bud?'

Grant took a second slower sip that felt like it was beginning to hold down the acid in his stomach and he reckoned he might have a fighting chance of not spewing his ringer in the next five minutes.

'How'd you mean?'

Luke was continuing to look around before settling back on the bouncer opposite him. He smiled and made a gesture that could have been interpreted any number of ways.

'I mean you wanting to tell me something? You wanting to ask something?'

There was no reply from the big man with the ink and the rapidly disappearing hangover. It looked to Luke as if her were trying to make up his mind about something and he sincerely hoped it wasn't a reconsideration of whether to paste him or not. He quickly continued-

'We can just chat? Or I can get a bright light and shine it in your eyes in a dark room? Talk about "the easy way and the hard way" and all that other nonsense?'

Grant paused at this last part with the glass almost at his mouth and fixed Luke with a mad dog look that had reduced so called hard men to apologetic poets up until this point. The hangover was making him paranoid and the mention of an interrogation landed badly with him. In his mind he was trying desperately to remember if

Luke had said he was a cop or not last night. Luke was clearly beginning to enjoy himself now-

'I can roll out my one man "good cop, bad cop routine"? I've been told it would go down well on stage. I also have a borderline offensive German bit if you'd prefer? Involves a few actions and loud voices but tends to get results'

Both men descended into laughter and the tension vanished. Grant could maintain a threatening persona in the face of a lot of things; fear, intimidation, violence; but he could not try and eyeball a man that was treating all forms of implied threat with terrible comedic disdain. Once he had suppressed his laughter, it was Grant who spoke first.

'Aye man, slap the cuffs on and lock me up.' Taking another thoughtful drink, he carefully placed the pint on the beer mat and continued. 'Not even sure why I called you to be honest. Just seems like you're a decent guy and we might be able to help each other out.'

As soon as he said it he felt that it sounded beyond stupid but Luke was nodding and agreeing. They had both seen off almost half their pint so far in the two minutes they'd been sat down and Grant's worry was beginning to soften off almost entirely. He was fully aware that the hair of the dog method was simply making the eventual suffering worse but like all objectively terrible ideas it seemed like a good decision at the time. Luke had not picked up his pen again since they had sat down and at this particular moment it seemed very important to Grant that he continued not to.

'Here man, I forgot what you said you did last night.' Taking another swallow that almost drained the glass, Grant attempted to keep his voice casual. 'You did say you weren't a cop eh?'

Luke also paused with his glass just before his mouth and made a grimace towards the bouncer.

'I never said I wasn't a cop Grant.' The bouncer's eyes were now fully focussed onto him even though Luke had begun casually staring at the window that you couldn't even see out of. 'But I'm not a cop.' In his peripheral vision, the big man had inflated then deflated within the past five seconds. 'I've never been a cop and I really don't think I'll ever be so desperate as to become one.'

Draining his pint, Luke stood up and took his glass with him as he went to the bar to get another two pints in. Grant had finished his own beer and had pulled the notebook across the table towards him. Lifting it close to his face he studied it intently and took longer than necessary to discern that there were no personal details written down at all so far. All that was scribbled was the date that had been underlined over and over again. He put it back on the table and moved it back across as Luke came back and set the glasses down again.

'See man, I'm no narc.'

Grant accepted this with a shrug and a sip. He sat back in his seat and crossed his arms across his chest, flexing his biceps briefly before relaxing fully.

'So what's your story then Luke? If you aren't with the filth and you aren't doing it off your own back, I don't know who you're working for.'

'I'm working for Geoffrey Reid the now. I told you that.'

Leaning forward again and resting his elbows on the table, he collected his glass in one big mitt and pointed it across the table with a smile.

'You know what I'm asking.'

Luke thought carefully before replying. On the one hand there was literally zero benefit to telling this man the whole truth. There were Official Secret's Acts and other ominous sounding pieces of heavyweight documentation to consider although they'd never given him much pause. But he wanted Grant to trust him. He was looking like the best source of information he was going to be able to get at the moment – a veritable oasis in the otherwise barren desert of the missing boy and his terrible father. He decided to give him some truth but not the whole: no lies but not full disclosure.

'I was in the army from when I was young. Nearly 20 years ago actually, went in when I was 16 and never left until a year or two ago when I was 33. Ended up in special forces doing "covert ops": All these grand sounding words for a pretty ugly job. Got moved into the sort of officially deniable stuff that they need done but can't be seen to do. You know, like where if you get killed or captured they just deny you ever existed?' He paused and resumed his viewing of the window. 'Saw a fair bit of action. A bit too much to be honest, so I wanted out. I'd done my time and then some. Guess I got into my 30s and realised I might want someone to at least admit I existed if I ended up dead. They didn't want me to leave so this is our compromise.' He took a long swallow. 'I do private investigations. Same sort of under the table nonsense but it's my own city and I'm on a pretty loose leash.'

The bouncer across the table didn't seem to react in any way that Luke could notice. The impression he got was that this unexpected bout of honesty had bought him a fair bit in the mind of the bigger man. Unusually, all of it was the truth. In fact, he wasn't sure he'd ever given someone such an honest, in depth personal history before.

'Fair play man. Doesn't sound like a bad gig. What are the hours like? The jobs any good?'

'Hit and miss.' was the honest reply. 'Some are exciting, some are boring. Some are rewarding, some are borderline reprehensible.' He saw a bit of confusion across the table. 'I like doing some and I feel bad about doing others. But I don't get to say no.'

Grant thought carefully. 'If you're doing a job you don't actively hate, you're doing better than most.'

Luke took a swallow in agreement. Again they sat in silence but it was no longer uncomfortable. It was more a break in conversation between two friends. This time it was Grant who broke the silence.

'So what do you need to know about Rab? What do you know so far?'

The glass spun in slow circles between Luke's hands under the careful eyes of the two of them.

'Nothing that gets me anywhere big man. I know his father's a piece of work.'

He took the snort from across the table as a form of agreement. It was an agreement that was readily expanded on.

'Aye, he's something else. Never had time for the guy. Slimy, you know?'

Slimy was as good a word as any for the Magistrate who cut about in his expensive suits and phoned in his concerns about his missing son. There was a deeper level to his deceit that Luke felt he could unlock if he could just tap into the knowledge and experience inside the shaved head across from him. He opened his unofficial enquiries with an innocuous question.

'What's Rab like then? Geoff told me a bit but I get the feeling he's not exactly squared me up. Tried to play me the highlight reel when I'm after the behind the scenes.'

Before making any response, Grant picked up the pen from the table and tucked it firmly behind one cauliflower ear. The request for it to be "off the record" was not exactly subtle but was accepted by Luke through his lack of response other than drinking.

'Look, he's not a bad gadge. Not at all. He just...' It was now Grant's pint that was spinning slowly between his hands. 'He just overdoes it. So does everyone though, you know? Everyone's had a few too many and made a holy show of themselves right? But he just does it every time. It gets a bit old but there's nothing more sinister to it than that. It's not like he's out topping prozzies or pushing smack to kids or kicking in randoms up the town every weekend. He's just a bit of a liability.'

With every example of what Rab wasn't doing, Grant had gestured with his pint and the effect had been somewhat lost on Luke as he was fixated on how close the lager was coming to the edge of the glass instead of the points being made. The big man had begun to ramble now and was building up steam.

'He isn't a radge. You never worry that he's going to bottle some guy for looking at him wrong or get you kicked out because someone's taken his seat. He just goes a bit overboard and instead of apologising when he gets pulled up he'll start yammering on about his money and how important his dad is.'

Luke was considering all of this carefully. It didn't sound any different from hundreds of other people. In fact, his memory was dredging up varying embarrassing examples of when he'd been informed he'd behaved similarly the morning after. Maybe not the money and parent stuff but the unapologetic self-certainty that comes with a belly full of spirits and a head full of nothing. Grant had stopped talking and spinning his glass, clearly at a good place to stop and waiting on Luke's response.

'Sounds about right. I've had a few nights like that myself truth be told.' Grant indicated his agreement. 'He a fan of the chemically altered lifestyle as well?'

The laugh from across the table was sufficient answer by itself but Grant felt it necessary to elaborate anyway.

'Yup. Hates a bit of something. Anything really.... Not too fussy.'

As he was making this explanation he turned in his seat and caught the barmaids eye. Raising his empty glass and pointing at Luke as well he faced back inwards. Luke was impressed -

'Didn't realise they did table service here man. Very slick.'

'Usually it's for the older guys who can't get up to the bar easily but if it's quiet they don't seem to mind.' He winked at Luke. 'Especially not for two handsome young guns like ourselves dragging the average age down a couple of decades.'

They were both still laughing when the pints appeared and Grant placed a note in the barmaid's hand before waving off the idea of change. He extracted the pen from behind his ear and threw it onto the notebook before making a childish writing gesture.

'Better get something useful done here before we just end up scooping.'

Picking up the pen, Luke underlined the date another two or three times before writing a single bullet point in the left hand margin of the sheet. He was focused entirely on drawing and redrawing the circle, waiting on the information and feeling the effects of the quick drinks working inside his head. He didn't even need to re-read what he had jotted previously because he knew it all inside out already. There was nothing concrete there and he was in desperate need of some sort of direction to work towards.

'What's the chances of him having been killed by someone?'

'Not likely in my book.' Grant belched. 'No benefit in it really.'

'OK, but I was up at a body discovery early this morning that Geoffrey directed me towards...'

'I don't think that's him.' Grant's interruption left little room for discussion. 'Don't ask me why but I don't reckon it's him. Makes no sense.'

Luke scribbled a little while taking a sip. He also felt that the body being Rab was an outside possibility but he couldn't work off hunches even if they were in common with another few people.

'Why not? You know something I don't?'

Grant was shaking his head before the question even finished. More an indication of his inability to explain his disbelief rather than a firm negative. He was mentally going over the list of people who would want to hurt either Rab or the Magistrate and managed to

111

dismiss almost all of them out of hand for one reason or another. Luke was still speaking.

'What about the dealers he buys from? He ever get anything on tick or rip anyone off?'

'Nope, he's a dealer's dream. Cash up front, return business... There's nothing bad about a guy with cash in his pockets and an appetite for destruction from a business point of view.'

'From a friend's point of view though?'

The only reply was a tired exhalation of breath. Luke had written precisely nothing down and placed the pen carefully on top of the paper again. Folding his hands together in front of his glass he fixed his eyes on Grant across the table.

'You called me man. I'm coming up short every avenue I look down at the moment and I need to get something. I've got feeling you actually want him found and you know something that'll point me in the right direction.'

During the pause that followed he studied the bigger man across from him and fancied he could see some cogs turning in his head. There was something that he was contemplating giving him that Luke knew would at least be a nudge in the right direction but he decided not to attempt to influence his decision. Grant made it in an instant anyway.

'There was one thing that the Magistrate said to me that sounded pretty suspect at the time. More so now given what's happened. In fact...' He took another mouthful of lager. 'In fact he called me this morning to make sure that I hadn't taken him up on his offer without letting him know.'

'What kind of offer was this?'

The pen was back in the hand and poised beside the only bullet point so far.

'A wedge of cash to encourage Rab to disappear.'

'How much?'

'£10k'

Luke let loose a low whistle as he jotted quickly on the paper. The bouncer saved him the hassle of asking the next awkward question.

'I didn't do it. In fact, I told the slimy git where he could shove his cash.' The intensity with which he was holding Luke's gaze now was

112

enough that he'd have felt obliged to agree with him even if he'd just said that the sky was green. 'Rab's my mate and I'm not the sort of man who'd take any amount of money to send one of my pals elsewhere. Either literally or...'

'Metaphorically?'

Grant pointed the glass at him and touched the point of his nose with his free hand. It felt like they were the worst team ever to play charades. He retreated back into a thoughtful silence as Luke wrote a little more before stopping.

'Any chance he made the same offer to a few folk? Anyone serious enough to misunderstand it and do the deed or stupid enough to follow through?'

The thoughtful silence continued. Someone had slipped money into the jukebox at some point during their reverie and a country song about a scorned woman and a dog was blasting out dolefully from the ancient speakers.

'Anyone serious enough to do it would be sensible enough not to.'

There was a concise sentiment to these brief words that summed it up nicely. The few people that were capable of disappearing someone, those that they would agree were "serious", would know that no good would come of knocking of Magistrate's son. Even with his implied blessing. And anyone stupid enough to actually think it was a good plan lacked the muscle or ability to carry it off.

'Well put Grant. Anyone you can think of from the top of your head that would fall outside these categories? Just to ask a few questions, I'm not in the business of busting heads for information.'

Stroking his chin roughly he eyed the smoke stained ceiling cautiously. It didn't make sense to him that these stains had persisted despite the smoking ban having been in force for so many years. Surely someone would have taken the time at one point during the years that had passed to wipe a cloth over it at least? How long would it have taken? Two minutes?

'Grant?'

'What?'

'Anyone you can point me in the direction of?'

'He insists on buying his hash from a pair of muppets out Craigmillar. Most of the rest of the stuff he uses he gets hooked up with on a time by time basis, these guys are the only regulars. Reckons they're pals, I dunno.'

'I'm assuming you disagree.'

'Nothing against the boys, just seem to be every stoner cliché wrapped up in two bodies. Always beyond blazed. Not a bad bone in their bodies but they can't have more than 5 brain cells left between them.' He drained his pint slowly and then took the notebook from Luke. 'And that's coming from me. Kind of like being called short by a midget eh? This is their names and the address.'

Luke reached for the notebook but Grant held onto it a moment.

'I'm not just being nice here Luke; they aren't bad guys. I hear you battered them or kicked them around then you'll be answering to me. Special Forces training or not.'

They smiled at each other.

'Understood. You have my word. If I hear anything at all I'll hit you up.'

With that, he stood up and left the pub with his notebook secured in his pocket. The information about the dealers was pretty weak stuff but finding out that the Magistrate had been offering five figure sums to be rid of his flesh and blood shortly before becoming very concerned with his whereabouts was definitely worth mulling over. There was always the chance that a friend had simply helped him relocate, but the frantic search that Geoffrey had set in motion was indication enough that he was worried this was not the case. Lighting up and beginning the walk up Pilton Drive, his phone rang and he was surprised to hear a hungover sounding Steve on the other end.

'Aye man. No. Aye, still looking. Nah. Can you no just tell me? No worries, I'll check it out. I'm due you a drink man, be good.'

Replacing his phone, he carried on up Pilton Drive but now looking to continue on past Fettes and Broughton to the Police Headquarters. Even if he was choosing to be all cloak and dagger about it, Steve wouldn't ever send him on a wild goose chase so it was worth looking into. Two leads in two minutes? His progress rate had just skyrocketed from 0%.

Chapter 16

Fluorescent lighting ran across the roof of the lab, reflecting off the chrome and linoleum interior. Everything about it was clinical from the tools lying carefully organised within their trays and slots to the bottles of chemicals sorted neatly in the drawers and on the racks. On a gurney in the centre sat the remains that had been discovered earlier that day having endured the painstaking examinations that had become progressively less methodical as the true nature of what was happening became clearer.

Sgt Jeffries was entering through the swing doors at the far end of the room, dressed in full protective equipment as per protocol regardless of how unnecessary he felt it now was. He was making every attempt to remain professional because the man accompanying him to view the remains significantly outranked him and had insisted on confirming these finding with his own eyes. Jeffries had his arms held upwards from the elbow and held the door with one covered shoe as the Chief Superintendent entered. Even in their identical outfits the Superintendent managed to cut an imposing figure – he walked tall and maintained an air of confidence despite having close to zero experience in this field. Jeffries had assured him prior that there would be nothing discussed that would not be understandable to the layman and the Chief Superintendent was not a man to attempt to dazzle with technical buzzwords. Jeffries followed him to the gurney and picked up a pair of forceps out of the tray, carefully indicating a number of small but key points that the Superintendent had no trouble following or accepting. Once the brief explanation was concluded, the senior man thanked the Sergeant for his time and left the room, stripping off his face mask and protective hood before even reaching the door. Jeffries watched him leave and turned again to skeletal remains in front of him.

The discovery had been surprising but had quickly ruled out almost all sinister situations as unlikely at the very best. The

Superintendent's interest in seeing for himself had been surprising but not unheard of. The promise he had made before they suited up to maintain the suitable level of confidentiality was worrying him only because he had voiced his concerns to Steve at the scene. Sighing as he replaced the forceps he could only hope that Steve was sensible enough to keep that information to himself.

Back in his office the Chief Superintendent was sitting once more behind his desk and thinking carefully with the phone in his hand. Contrary to the popular idiom, no news did not necessarily mean good news when it came to situations like this. Regardless of the fact that this put them back to square one, in some manner it was preferable to this being the route they had to go down. He dialled the Magistrate's number to let him know what he had probably found out already through the numerous people who worked for the Superintendent officially but whose loyalties were to the Magistrate first and foremost. It was picked up almost instantly.

'Hello? Superintendent?'

'Yes. How did you know it was me? This number is private.'

'For most people I imagine it would be.'

The Magistrate's response was characteristically evasive and the Superintendent was wondering what sort of unofficial and probably illegal set up was installed in that office on the Mound. Even if he had been so inclined he knew that there would be not a single trace of it remaining by the time his men knocked on the door with an official search warrant. With a man like Geoffrey Reid the key was to pick your battles by avoiding them all until you could rout him in the final conflict.

'I'm not even going to ask Geoffrey. I have some news.'

The silence on the other end of the phone told him many things at once. Firstly, the Magistrate had been aware of the bodies discovery. That was to be expected – these things can never be kept totally under wraps even from members of the public, far less from a man who has intimate knowledge of the system and contacts within it. It was almost certain that he had had eyes on the scene from the second that the police had showed up – they could even have been the same guys. Given that, the lack of immediate response and questions led him to believe that he was already privy to the additional information that he was going to disclose. In that moment he decided to give him

116

only the basic details. There was no point showing your hand if you were folding anyway.

'We found a body this morning on Arthur's Seat. Our guys have determined that there is no possibility that it can be Robert's.'

There was the briefest exhalation from the other end and the relieved tones that started gushing down the line sounded false to the experienced ear of a veteran police officer who had heard thousands of lies and unlikely truths alike over the years.

'I'm so glad to hear it. I've not been able to sleep since I heard. All the worst scenarios were just running over and over in my head.' He exhaled slow and deep for the benefit of no one. 'Have you got any additional information for me? My own investigations are still ongoing and there doesn't seem to be much in terms of direction.'

'Nothing to report Geoffrey. Check in with your man, I was assured he's the best.'

'Certainly. Certainly. Thank you.'

The line went dead but the Superintendent sat with the receiver to his ear listening to the static then the dial tone then nothing. There was plenty about this situation to make him uneasy and he was trying to get it all straight in his head. The fact that Geoffrey had come storming into the headquarters less than a day after Robert had gone missing was strange. The fact that he knew about the discovery was almost expected but he got the impression that he'd already known the outcome of their investigations before it was officially disclosed to him. The Magistrates own sources were clearly being put to work at a frantic pace.

Despite the fact that they were ostensibly on the same team, he had developed a chronic mistrust of the Magistrate and a deep seated dislike for all aspects of how he conducted himself. There should be no place for a man like that within the system that the Superintendent professed to love and truly did. The unavoidable fact was that the walls were going to come crashing down on Geoffrey Reid at some point, but it just never seemed to have actually happened so far. Carefully, he dialled the Major's number to get his own update.

'Major? Yes, it's the Superintendent here. Just a few bits of information to pass on to your man with regards to the Reid case.'

Luke entered the station through the glass doors at the front and wandered up to the information desk. There was glass running all along the lower levels facing out towards the high school across the street. On the walls were posters encouraging people to report crime and domestic abuse and to the right and left of the desk were doors that required security passes to enter or exit. The lost property section operated out of a small windowed booth and Luke was grateful not to be sat waiting on the seats opposite with a hangover and a sense of being in the last chance saloon as he had been on too many occasions previously. Behind the desk, a middle aged man was either busy on a computer or trying to appear to be. Luke leaned forward onto the counter with both forearms and waited. The desk officer was tapping away and tapped his return key with an air of finality before turning with a smile towards Luke.

'How can I help you?'

Luke was concentrating on interlocking his fingertips slowly one over the other.

'I was wondering if Sgt Jeffries was around?'

The tapping resumed and Luke looked around the room idly, waiting. He knew full well that the man at the desk knew off the top of his head whether he was in the station, off shift or out on a job but the facade had to be preserved.

'He is currently still on shift here so I'm afraid he would only be available for work related business if that's what you need him for?'

'Sort of.'

The smile behind the desk seemed to grow slightly as he took his hands off the keyboard and spread them in a sympathetic gesture.

'I'm afraid you'll have to get him another time then.'

Luke tapped the desk twice gently and returned the smile before turning around to leave. He had no specific information with which to justify pulling the Sergeant to the desk for a chat and there was no point in antagonising the man behind the desk. Pausing outside the door to light up his mobile vibrated in his pocket and he took it out quickly. It was the office.

'How's my favourite wife today then?'

There was a pause on the end of the line as Laura decided whether or not she found this remark amusing or not. The overly official tone that responded gave him the impression that the deliberation had not gone in his favour after all.

'I've been instructed to ask you for an update.'

Sometimes she could be so serious that Luke was becoming suspect that these unofficial, top-secret lines were in fact being monitored for training purposes. It was never any fun to antagonise Laura if she wasn't in the mood for playing the game as well.

'I have very little to update. Chasing up a few bits and pieces but struggling to get a foothold.'

'Did you go up to Arthur's Seat this morning?'

'No Laura, I took a day trip to the Isle of Wight instead. Lovely this time of year.'

Again, nothing. Zero out of two – something had definitely rattled her cage. He took a draw as she came out with her response.

'And there was nothing of note?'

'Nothing so far. I have been meeting a few people to try and get some more insight but it's not proving easy.'

'Can't be, from the Isle of Wight...'

Can't really give it out then choose not to be a good sport when it's being given back to you can you? Luke allowed himself a grin.

'I guess that's my mistake.'

Laura continued on immediately.

'The Major has just phoned with a bit of news from the police side of things.'

'I'm actually at the station the now as it goes. Banging my head against the brick wall.'

'It must be nice for you to be there of your own accord for once...' She was definitely smiling down the phone again. 'Instead of drying out at her Majesties pleasure.'

'Yeah, but they don't give you a free breakfast when you're just visiting.'

He had actually woken up in the cells once or twice but she had no way of knowing that. Even with her apparent supercomputer and bottomless knowledge, she couldn't know that right? The paranoia dropped away as quickly as it had appeared. What difference did it really make anyway? Laura interrupted his thoughts.

119

'The Chief Superintendent has been in touch to let us know he will give you any assistance you feel you need. Albeit unofficially. Make of that what you will.'

Now this was surprising. Although there was an ongoing friendly relationship between himself and the police force it was mainly forged on personal relationships at the ground level. There was no protocol that required sharing of information between the two parties. In all reality the police knew that if they made the effort to ever drag him in and try to extract information, there would not even be enough time to have him sat in the chair with the bright lights on before someone who outranked them significantly swung the door open and threw them out with their careers in tatters. He knew that he could have demanded information through the official channels and it would be given to him but no one liked to have their hand forced and playing hardball with the men on the front line would cost him every tip, hint and nudge that would have come his way after this point. It was a delicate balancing act where each acted only on good faith and in the interests of keeping a working relationship going.

'I wouldn't have expected a cooperation order from anyone that high up.... Has the Major forced this on them?'

'Not to my knowledge but even if he had, you know full well I wouldn't be allowed to tell you.'

'You would anyway though wouldn't you?' he asked coyly.

'I would not Mr. Calvin.'

The short response and return to proper names indicated that she was no longer willing to joke with him. He still remained confident that she would tell him should the occasion arise. The cigarette between his fingers had burnt down a fair portion with very little interaction from his end. Remedying that with a couple of short pulls he looked through the window at the officer behind the desk who was busy on his computer again.

'I don't want to have to pull rank on everyone to get what I want.' The cigarette was spinning between his index and middle finger, flipping over and under and back to where it started. 'That's how guys in my line of work get shut out. You start throwing weight around and you'll get a brick wall every time you need anything after that. Good for bashing your head off but not for anything else.'

She seemed to be thinking it over herself before responding. In the brief silence he realised he had not given any thought to how he imagined she was dressed today. Clearly he was losing focus with all this confusion all around.

'Maybe try and confirm it with the man himself before you start using this trump card to earn the hatred of every policeman in Edinburgh.'

A fair point well made. 'Yeah, I think the fact that half of them already hate me is more than enough for now.'

Her sudden laugh seemed genuine. Maybe she was in a summer dress – it was getting to that time of year and even his dear Laura must lighten up every now and then.

'I'm more amazed that half of them tolerate you!'

'Well I never. How rude.' His indignation was of course false. 'I've never been so insulted.' Pausing a moment to finish his smoke and crush it out in the ashtray but there was no reaction. 'It isn't that they *tolerate* me Laura.'

'What is it then?'

'It's that they haven't even met me yet.'

'Lucky them. If you need anything else let me know. And keep us posted please?'

'Anything to hear your voice again dear.'

The disappointed sigh that had preceded the line dying was only mildly exasperated and Luke congratulated himself on annoying her somewhat less than usual. Squinting in the sunlight that was streaming over the playing fields he tapped his phone thoughtfully against his hand while thinking about what his next move should be. It was nice to have an Ace up your sleeve but you never wanted to use it unless you had to. It wasn't playing the game straight and that was an unforgivable sin to any man with integrity. Or even to a cop.

The only hint that Steve had given him was to look into the findings of the forensics team and here he was outside the building itself having been given permission to do just that, all above board. There was something more to all this that was beginning to come together but he couldn't for the life of him see what it was yet. Running his hand through his hair briefly he knew he was going to go back inside and try and get the information without treading on too many toes. Maybe then he could understand all this sudden assistance. It was one thing to come up against a whole load of nothing in the early days of an investigation – it was actually expected – but to suddenly be allowed this level of access was highly suspicious.

'Only one way to find out.'

Having accidentally said it out loud and rather startled an old dear making her way inside he could only smile apologetically, hold the door open for her and wait while she conducted her business before he readdressed the desk sergeant who viewed his return with no enthusiasm but maintained the large smile plastered across his face. Luke attempted to make light of the situation:

'Me again. Any chance of the Superintendent this time?'

There was no attempt made to mask the incredulity this time. The officer eyed him over the desk as if he were a 17-year-old who'd walked into the Ferrari showroom and asked for a test drive. He made no move towards either the phone or the computer.

'The Superintendent? Could you tell me what it's regarding?'

'It's a private matter. Nothing too important.'

Luke was well aware that he was being viewed as a man on the wind up now. After all, from his new friend's point of view he had come in, been knocked back, left to smoke and then returned asking for the highest ranked policeman in the building. It wasn't the sort of behaviour usually exhibited by the men who came to call on him.

'Do you have an appointment?'

Shaking his head deliberately and slowly, Luke could see the irritation beginning to bubble across the desk between them. The sergeant put one hand slowly across his face while emitting a low whistle.

'So. The Superintendent will be happy to see you? Just out of the blue?'

Nodding and grinning, Luke found he was deriving a perverse sort of pleasure from this exchange. He had to compliment his opponent on his ability to maintain his cool. His poker face had barely slipped for a second. He had no idea he was holding a losing hand.

'Would you mind just trying his secretary? See what she says?'

After a long searching look, the phone was taken off the hook and brought up to his ear. Never taking his eyes off Luke who was now leaning forward onto the desk with both arms, he pressed the button and had the call picked up in the big office upstairs.

'Afternoon. Yes, I have someone here who wishes to see the Superintendent. No, no appointment.' He shot a glance back across the desk. 'His name?'

'Luke Calvin.'

The desk sergeant quickly scanned his memory for any relevance to the name and found nothing.

'Luke Calvin.'

His eyes were still on Luke with a withering smile which faltered after a moment before slipping entirely. The ashen faced look became drawn and concerned and there was a confused air as he removed the receiver from his ear and glanced at it as if expecting some response. It was extended across the desk between them.

'He.... he wants to talk to you.'

With a smile and a wink, he took the offered receiver and gave the worried officer a thumbs up that he thought was reassuring but could just as well have been interpreted as confirmation that he'd messed up. He'd sort the poor guy out after he was done talking with the Superintendent.

Chapter 17

Abandoning the relative comfort of the Fluke for the dusk outside, Grant found himself a little unsteady on his feet. He'd stayed for another jar or two after Luke had left, ostensibly to take the edge off his hangover but in reality just because they were going down so well and he was starting to enjoy himself a little. Sitting at the corner table by himself he had ignored the people that came and went as he thought carefully about the ongoing situation from every viewpoint possible. He was making his way back up towards the flat when his phone rang and he fumbled in his pocket to find it.

'Hello?'

'Orite big man. It's Luke. Got a bit of news for you.'

Grant stopped where he was and braced himself.

'The body isn't Rab. Had it confirmed by the cops. I'll let you know if I hear anything else.'

Hanging the phone up, he considered calling the Magistrate but assumed he'd already know. He wanted to call Claire but she'd probably already know as well. Regardless, he still felt like calling her but it wasn't a good idea when he was half canned. He resigned himself to just heading back to the flat and maybe taking a nap. Continuing on his way he felt like a load had been lifted and he was far more buoyant. There had never been any doubt in his mind about the outcome but now it was confirmed. All that was left now was to find Rab and decide whether to be happy to see him or to knock him out.

Sgt Jeffries found himself in his slicker suit and face mask for about the fourth time in one day and accompanying yet another layman through his area of expertise. The sad fact of it seemed to be that this non-event had triggered a good sight more interest from outwith his own department than any of the technically rich cases prior. The only thing that was keeping the smile on his face behind the mask was the fact that the Superintendent had pulled him aside before making introductions and asked him to render all assistance to this Mr. Calvin or whatever rank he held.

Despite being initially wary, Jeffries had slowly realised that Luke's initial connection was through Steve and since he was now helping him officially, his slight oversight in spreading confidential information was caught up in a perfect loop of happy coincidences where he might even get to keep his job. As such, he once again held his forearms straight up while holding the door with his foot, as a surgeon might to avoid contamination, and allowed his new student to enter the room ahead of him before crossing to the gurney and picking up his forceps once again ready to deliver his succinct presentation. Just as he was leaning forward to make his first point he saw that Luke was holding up a gloved hand, gesturing for him to stop.

'One thing Doc. No technical stuff. I'm no surgeon.'

'Neither am I. Trust me, none of this will be hard to get.'

As he cleared his throat to begin he could have sworn he heard the faintest "I'll decide" from the other man's mask but had no way to prove it other than the mirth behind the goggles. He had no idea how this man had ever managed to become friends with moody old Steve. The skeleton that was laid out between them both was stripped of all clothes and flesh and all but intact. This was actually the first point that Sgt Jeffries made, hovering the forceps over the length of the remains with a long sweeping motion.

'Notice a couple of things here before we get into particulars. Remains are entirely skeletal...'

'Aye, it's all bones doc. With you so far.'

The Sergeant pretended not to have heard and resisted the urge to inform him that he was no doctor. Instead, he focused in on the shoulder joint nearest to him, probing the bone delicately and gesturing over the rest of the body with his free hand.

'No soft tissue of any sort remaining on any part of the body.'

'Aye doc. No eyes or skin or that. Got it.'

Jeffries paused again but continued, this time directing attention towards the elbow. He knew that "Humerus" was the term for exactly where he was pointing but given the reception that "skeletal"

125

and "tissue" had elicited he was not willing to further make a rod for his own back.

'More than that Mr. Calvin. No tendons or ligaments. No muscles or fat. Not a bit of flesh or a vein or artery to be seen. The amount and variety of tissue you would expect even around a simple hinge joint like the elbow here...'

'Humerus doc. Even I know that. Where'd you get your medical licence? Plumbing school?'

Sergeant Jeffries laughed and shook his head slowly. 'Are you always this difficult? Or should I feel special?'

In a minor breach of procedure, Luke itched the back of his slicker suit hood with a double gloved hand and thought a moment.

'I'm usually worse actually. Kind of on good behaviour since you're helping me out.'

Jeffries found himself warming to him. There was something about a man who acts with such flippancy in the face of the usual expectation to conform to manners that was refreshing. Grossly unprofessional, yes, but a breath of fresh air none the less.

'You wanting the quick version then?'

Receiving a wink, a click of the mouth and an honest-to-god finger gun by way of response he beckoned Luke towards him from the other side of the gurney and gave him the details.

'Here's the main bits. Bones are totally clean. Bleached actually. Normally we'd have to wait for tests to confirm it but I'd bet my house on it. And look here. ' He indicated to a small powdery hole in the base of the left wrist. 'There's one like that in almost every single bone of the body. Some more obvious than others but all there. So, any thoughts?'

'Maybe they left the body in strong acid for a while? You know, like industrial grade stuff. Or a barrel of Lime, then cleaned it?'

'Watching too many TV shows Mr. Calvin. When's the last time you heard of that sort of nonsense going on in Edinburgh?'

In response Luke made ghost motions with his raised hands and whistled the theme tune from Unsolved Mysteries.

'It's much simpler than that Mr. Calvin. All these holes...' he jabbed at around ten in quick succession 'used to hold screws or bolts. There's been a pretty shoddy effort made to fill them in with cheap plaster but on nothing more than a purely cosmetic level.'

126

Luke leaned forward and examined one closest to him. It was exactly as he had said, the spiralling helix working its way deep down into the bone lengthways was faint but there. He straightened up and waited patiently for the final part of the explanation which was duly provided.

'It's a display skeleton. Genuine bones, don't get me wrong, but they've been cleaned and treated before being placed back together with screws and wires to be used for display purposes only. What we're looking at here is probably a stupid joke or a prank of some sort.'

Luke accepted this with a small nod of his head. Back to the drawing board, but at least this wasn't his man laid out in front of him. He dreaded to think what the Magistrate would have made of that.

Geoffrey Reid was still in his office as the evening drew in across Edinburgh's Old Town. Standing at the window, looking out over Princes Street and beyond where the street lights were coming on and the vehicle taillights stretched out in every direction carrying with them the noise of the city. They were all people heading back from work to their homes, heading out to start nightshifts or travelling in anticipation of a night out. Claire knocked tentatively on the heavy office door and ended up entering anyway when there wasn't any response. Peeking her head round the frame, she was surprised to see that he was just standing with his back to her not doing anything in particular and hadn't seemed to hear her knock or come in. She stepped into the office and let the door close behind her. The soft click of the latch slipping home was unexpectedly quiet for such a large door but it seemed to be enough to startle Geoffrey as he spun round quickly.

'Sorry Sir. Is there anything else you need from me tonight?'

He seemed to be looking right through her. She noticed that he appeared to have aged in front of her eyes over the past few days, looking more drawn and tired than he had up until this point. His eyes suddenly refocused and he saw her as if for the first time and attempted a weak smile.

'Nothing else Claire. Thank you. I'll see you tomorrow.'

With that he turned back around with his hands behind his back and continued staring aimlessly out the window. Claire paused at the door, officially dismissed but under the impression that he wanted her to stay. She had one hand on the handle before she turned back over her shoulder and asked one last time.

'If you're sure?'

The lack of reaction was taken in the affirmative and she re-opened the door as quietly as she could manage and crept out in the adjoining reception area. Her bag and jacket were ready to go on the chair and she collected them as she left, taking the lift down to the ground floor deep in thought. As she exited into the crowds on the Royal Mile she looked up and down the street. To get back down to her flat she would turn to her left and follow the gentle downhill slope across the cobbles but she didn't feel like going home just yet. The day had been long and confusing. Too much running around with very little idea of why. What she needed now was a drink – after all she was still dressed in her skirt and blouse and the bow she put in her hair was going to be wasted if she just went home.

There were easily upwards of forty pubs either on the Mile or within a five-minute walk of it but she had already turned to her right to walk uphill before turning right again and walking down the Mound, reaching the steps that would take her all the way down and out on Princes Street itself. From there it was only another fifteen or twenty-minute walk to the Bull on Leith Walk. She was passing close to a hundred alternative establishments on her route but she had the feeling only a drink in the Bull would satisfy her. As she descended the stairs she found her phone in her bag and texted Grant to see if he was working. Before she had reached the street level he had replied that he wasn't but that he'd planned on going there in about half an hour for a drink. How convenient for both of them.

Grant had just fallen asleep on the sofa entirely by accident when the text message had come through. Waking with a start he had tried to decipher how long he had been out and read the message at the same time, succeeding in successfully accomplishing neither. Rising into a seating position he realised he'd been asleep for no more than fifteen minutes but his head was almost entirely clear. Squinting and refocusing he saw Claire's message and felt a jump in his chest.

Having had no intention whatsoever of leaving his flat for the rest of the evening he was on his feet and phoning a taxi before he even bothered replying. The cab would be there in 12 minutes which gave him enough time for a shower (5 minutes), brush his teeth (2 minutes) and find clean clothes to wear (time unknown). Tapping a quick response that he hoped came across as casual he hurried into the shower and left his phone on the side. Most planned nights out tended to be disappointing purely because the build-up and hype could never match the actual events but a spontaneous outing like this filled him with a bit of quiet hope. Glimpsing himself in the mirror he hoped that his eyes weren't too bloodshot and the toothpaste would drag the smell of booze out of his mouth sufficiently to make a passable impression.

Mark was alone in the flat he shared with Deek in Craigmillar. Sprawled out on the sofa his long hair was untied and spread out behind him. Teasing a bit of it between his fingers it felt greasy and he was trying to remember the last time he washed it. On the TV there was a DVD playing – one he had seen close to a hundred times before now. Without even watching it, he would know which line was coming up and every now and then he'd find that he'd actually let his eyes slip shut but could stick picture the exact image of what was on the screen. It was early evening, not that you could tell with the flat's curtains being almost permanently closed, and Deek had cut out a couple of hours prior after receiving a phone call which had seemed to upset him. It was unlike Deek to get upset about anything – in fact, Mark thought back to try and remember if he'd ever seen him worked up and so far, was failing.

The day that Derek had been up in court to receive his prison sentence, Mark was sat in the gallery feeling like the biggest scumbag that had ever walked the earth. There hadn't been a huge number of people in the courtroom for the final sentencing – it wasn't headline news and frankly Deek probably had more chance of seeing family members in jail than out – so Mark was feeling rather conspicuous. He wore dark trousers with "proper" shoes and a shirt and had even taken the time to tie his hair back in a ponytail and removed his earring for the proceedings despite the fact that he wasn't even on trial. Derek was wearing jogging bottoms and a polo shirt and Mark had cringed as soon as he walked in and saw him. "At least TRY and look presentable dude!" had flashed through his mind as he returned the enthusiastic wave thrown his way by the man in handcuffs. In direct violation of all the instruction that he had doubtless been given by his court appointed lawyer, Derek shouted to his friend.

'Orite man. Cheers for coming! Good to see you.'

Mercifully the judge had not yet entered but the few other attendees all fixed their eyes on Mark who hastily parked himself in whatever seat was nearest. A man in a suit beside Derek reached up the considerable distance to his waving hand in order to attempt to drag it back down and whispered upwards towards his face. Derek's rapturous grin froze a minute and he blinked slowly, clearly remembering the sincere promise he had probably given his lawyer not 5 minutes earlier to sit quietly and politely. He gave Mark a final thumbs up with the sort of face a schoolchild would make if they'd forgotten their homework and turned back around to face the front. He was taller than the lawyer sat beside him and when the judge entered, he was nudged gently to stand up. Ungainly as ever, his body seemed to unfold upwards until he stood straight, nearly a foot above his lawyer looking every bit like a manacled insect of some sort and its bespectacled handler. As the judge began to speak, Mark was finding himself rather impressed with this lawyer as he managed to keep Derek's natural enthusiasm down just low enough to avoid any contempt of court issues. It put him in mind of a toddler at a church service who wanted to react to every sentence and express his interest with no ill will whatsoever. The details of how the arrest occurred and the charges being levelled were given to the court and Mark's shame grew, spotting his cheeks crimson. He hardly needed reminded of the events of that fateful evening.

The basic information given to the court was that officers had entered the premises with a valid search warrant by way of a battering ram as the defendant had not answered the door. In one of the bedrooms they had discovered a substantial amount of Moroccan Brown hashish with a street value of whatever made up number they chose to use that particular day. The quantity was high enough that there was zero chance of getting away with pleading "personal use" but nowhere near high enough to warrant the picture that was being

130

painted of Derek in court as being the hash kingpin of the Lothian and Borders area. This hadn't stopped Deek saying it was all his and even when confronted with sets of scales and hundreds of small plastic baggies he had insisted that he had them so he could carefully track how much he was using. What caused Mark's guilt was not the fact that his mate had got busted or even as most people assumed, that he had just so happened to be out of the flat when the raid happened. Neither had it been that his own staunch denial coupled with Derek's assertion that he lived there alone meant that only the latter was being prosecuted.

Snapping back to the present the judge had begun his sentencing. There had been little doubt from the beginning that he would have to take some time inside due to the fact that the charge was "possession with intent to supply" and even with a class C drug it carried a custodial sentence. The judge himself was practically ancient to Mark's eyes, easily in his 60's, but was far less harsh during his summing up than the prosecution had been. The tone of it was not as ominous as he had expected and when the proclamation came that the sentence was 12 months there was a sense of relief from Mark, Deek and his lawyer, matched only by the frustration of the prosecution service who never seemed to be pleased with anything short of the gallows for anyone involved in drugs. Derek had raised his fist discretely towards his lawyer for a fist pump which the confused man in the suit had grasped and shaken up and down. Mark made a note to catch up with the wee specky guy and buy him a pint – after all the guy had been appointed to take the case rather than taking it for any financial benefit and had done his mate proud. As Deek was led away he caught Mark's eye, gave a shrug and shouted.

'Catch you up bud. Be good.'

Then he was taken below to begin a sentence which wouldn't even last 6 months before he was back out with good behaviour.

Back in the flat in Craigmillar, Mark was still staring at lengths of his hair between his fingertips, bending it slowly, looking for split ends. The courtroom had been surreal but even then his lanky pal hadn't allowed the harsh realities of life to get him down. If life was something you couldn't take seriously and get out alive then all that would be left at the end would be Deek and a bunch of very chill animals. As strand after strand failed the inspection on cleanliness and being intact, Mark was thinking about calling him to find out if he was OK. It wasn't like him to keep things from him and he had seemed a bit upset when he rushed out. On the other hand, Mark was pretty baked and the paranoia that was gnawing at his subconscious could have contributed to his misreading of the situation entirely. He sat up and took the joint from the ashtray and lit it again. What never really helped in these situations was that despite Deek's behaviour since returning from prison a few months prior giving nothing to justify this worry, Mark always thought back to when he had left on the night they got raided. Thought about the subtle advice he was given in the pub to maybe stall there for a couple of hours. Thought about how he hadn't even phoned Derek. How he had sat and drank and listened to the sirens screaming past and sat drinking long after they had departed in the other direction. Every time he was left alone in the flat too long he thought about the drugs in the other room and waited on the door being broken through by the police in retribution for his betrayal. Instead of checking in with Deek on the phone he just carried on smoking and watching the film as the evening slid by outside the closed curtains.

Chapter 18

Victoria Street in the Old Town was beginning to liven up again with the evening's revellers as Luke sat in his window seat with his coffee and cigarettes. The notebook that contained all his notes so far was sat close to hand and he had opened a new, clean one and begun the laborious process of translating the scribbles and lines into something more coherent and legible. The idea had always been that once the notes were correlated and collected into one clean copy the solution would present itself to him. The "Eureka" moment would jump out of the paper and ink and he'd leave with his deer stalker atop his head, opium pipe close to hand and pull away the curtain of deceit from in front of whoever had erected it leaving the clear truth exposed to the light. This was always the theory and never the practice but there was no harm in cleaning up his notes on the off chance it would happen eventually.

The only loose end at the moment was the Magistrate's highly suspicious behaviour from the very outset and beyond which was hardly something tangible that he could pursue. The lines on the paper were beginning to fall out of focus after his long day and bizarre anatomy lesson at the police station. Putting the notebooks aside he turned his attention back to the window, watching the people walking up and down on the pavements far below in groups spanning the entire width of the walkway or in single file, awkwardly squeezing past one another. Along his eye level were the terraced walkways above the shops, the back of St. Columba's free church and the upper level of the High Street where taxi drivers carefully negotiated the small roundabout through the thinning crowds of tourists and carried on under the castle towards Lothian Road.

The Castle was still visible above it all and Luke found it hard to believe that it hadn't been more than 48 hours since he had sat in this exact spot, unable to sleep and watched the castle peering out of the late night gloom. The sheer number of new people that had entered his life since then and all the questions and difficulties that they had brought with them were threatening to cloud his head even more than the dreaded boredom of not working had up until that point. Despite the brief period where there had been a sense of concern from some parties that the elusive junior Reid might be laid out on a pathology slab, Luke had not been able to shake the belief that his quarry was still around somewhere: both he and Rab were able to see the same castle night after night. Based on that fact alone he was sure that he'd be able to track him down and bring him back to whatever sort of life he was leading up until now, just as soon as he got a decent foothold from which to launch his search.

The strangest feeling he had was that the skeleton was in some way connected to the whole scenario. All he had to do was work out how and every other piece of the puzzle would just slot into place. With that in mind, his best option at this point in time was to sift through the list of former employers of Rab and pay them a visit when he had a chance and pray that then the answer would present itself. That was the theory anyway. He sighed. As simple as that.

On the chessboard by his side there was a puzzle laid out that he had set up some point previously. He couldn't recall exactly at what point in the past three days he had done it or where he'd copied it from but he had done little more than glance at it. Now it looked positively inviting compared to trying to untangle the confusing mess that his thoughts and notes were becoming. Every candidate move he considered resulted in him losing significant material on the next move and he carefully manoeuvred one piece after the other before replacing them back in the starting position. The pointless shuffling was strangely reminiscent of what he felt he'd been doing himself the past few days. Moving uncertainly from place to place before returning to the original location with nothing visibly different. There was probably some deep seated psychological reason why he continued to persevere with his pursuit of chess despite the fact that he remained poor at it but his internal train of thought was abruptly derailed by the buzzer going at the door. Getting up to answer, he was surprised to see Old Tam's figure at the door. The great beard and long silver hair were impossible to confuse with anyone else even through a small display from this far off.

What he was doing out of his local area was the main concern. He picked up the phone.

'Hello?'

'Orite son. It's Tam.'

Luke's confusion at having Tam show up out of the blue was quickly replaced by a very real concern regarding whether the old man would manage the three floors up to his flat. Realising that it was improbable if not impossible, he made the decision to go down himself and see what he wanted.

'You wanting to come in Tam. It's a long way up....'

'No son. Nah, just come down for a chat if you have a second.'

'Be down in a minute.'

He grabbed a hoody from his room as well as his phone, wallet and keys and headed out the door as quickly as possible. Pausing briefly, he returned for his notebook and then applied the locks on the way out. What did it seem to be recently with people too unhealthy to survive three floors worth of stairs and appearing at his door uninvited? Hurrying down the three flights, he opened the front door to see the smiling whiskered face of Tam beaming back at him. Dressed as always in a shirt and tie with his massive overcoat, his head was uncovered and alarmingly his walker was nowhere to be seen.

'What are you doing all the way up here without your walker Tam? You learnt to fly or something?'

'I got a lift up son, don't worry yourself. Take an old man to that Irish pub I see there' he pointed downhill towards the Grassmarket 'and buy him a stout or two.'

The evening had grown chillier gradually but neither man seemed to feel it since they both had enough layers to keep out the worst of it. It hadn't quite yet gone 8pm yet and the foot traffic would get heavier again before the clubs opened. They walked side by side, Tam's dodgy knees and ankles setting the pace. Luke lit two of the cigarettes from his packet and handed one to Tam who took it and popped it in his mouth without as much as looking. He rambled on about everything and nothing as they walked towards the pub which was less than 50 yards from Luke's front door but took a lot longer to reach due to his companion's numerous physical ailments. Luke knew better than to ask him what the purpose of this unexpected house call was – Tam never parted with his information until he had his alcohol based fee within his hands.

As they slowly meandered into a small fenced off courtyard that contained the main way into the pub the two men on the door barely gave them a glance on the way past. Tam spoke to them anyway, gabbing about this and that. His sincerity and warmth never drew anything except favourable responses, even when he managed to get off on a tangent trying to remember what the name of the place was a few decades prior (probably before the other three men were even thought of). Eventually coaxing him into the place itself, Luke steered him by the elbow and towards a quiet table mercifully near the door. Once Tam had settled himself down, removed his coat and looked around appreciatively he let Luke slip away to the bar while he remonstrated with himself about the previous name of the pub.

The place itself was adorned on the walls with paintings of various sports of Irish origin or that they at least excelled in. Unlike most other establishments of the same ilk, there was very little about the "Irish" part of this pub that was entirely manufactured. They had traditional music sessions throughout the week put on by whoever happened to turn up that evening with their instrument in tow. Admittedly a few of the regulars played songs from the Scottish traditions they were more familiar in but in terms of legitimate Celtic feel and habit, this was the place to be. The stout and the whiskey flowed freely and the boys on the door very seldom had need to sort out any issues as most were handled in house. Luke enjoyed it in here for the music and the proximity and waited patiently at the bar for his stout and a half with two nips to be prepared – this place above all understood the correct pouring procedure for a perfect pint of porter that was overlooked in favour of speed in many other places. Once he had all in possession he crossed back over to Tam bearing his payment and settled down across from him in their booth. The light in Tam's blue eyes never seemed to go out but it always increased when he had a drink almost within his grasp. Taking a small hit of the spirits and chasing it with a quick swallow of stout which left an additional moustache above his own he looked approvingly at Luke and settled himself more comfortably in his seat.

'I've done yer job for ye again son.'

'I'll decide.'

Tam smirked at him over the glass and made a camp drawing motion with his free hand.

'Better get your wee diary out.'

Luke obliged and extracted it from his back pocket. Taking the pen and laying it on the table he waited for whatever big revelation had taken Tam all the way up town to see him in person.

'I've been telt that yer boy's alive.'

The statement failed to land with the impact he had expected. Luke raised an eyebrow at him and remained motionless.

'Top drawer Tam. Really pulled it out the bag there. The guys not dead. Excellent. Well, I'll just phone up my man the now and tell him shall I? "Call off the search. Bring the troops home. Tam's told me that he isn't dead."'

The older man laughed and shook his head. He was still giggling as he took another sip from one glass then the next and expanded on his point.

'Come on son. Ye really think I'd just have that for you? Nah, I ken he's no dead because I ken where he's been.'

This time the statement did land. Despite his best attempt not to react there must have been a tell somewhere in Luke's face or demeanour because Tam's reaction was to laugh again and raise his glass.

'Ah ha. My info is worthwhile again. Your gonnae hae to start puttin me on yer payroll at this rate son. I'm surprised you didn't snatch up yer wee pretty pen as soon as I opened my mouth.'

For the briefest moment Luke entertained the idea and it was a bizarre image and thought indeed. Classic noir style - the two of them sitting in a smoky office; a weathered sign above the door and cheap bourbon on the desk. A pair of hard boiled detectives running the streets, or shuffling as fast as Tam's legs would allow. Pulling Magnums on hoodlums in dark alleys while steam rose from the sewers and they made cutting remarks to each other about how they were cleaning up this dirty town. Luke could threaten the coldest of gangsters without violence, choosing instead to leave them in the interrogation room alone with Tam the Mouth, who would talk their ear off until they confessed to everything they'd ever done.

137

Settling for taking a long draught of his pint, Luke eventually succumbed to the temptation and picked up his pen from the table to much delight from the man opposite. Writing a heading and underlining it carefully he attempted to pay no mind to the sniggering that was purely for his benefit. Satisfied, he raised his head and met the eyes that were moist with glee.

'Tell me what you know then.'

'Mate of mine, Eric. You know Eric? Aye you do, old Eric? Fae the bowlie. Aye ye do son, we all played dominoes that one time. Anyway. Eric's moved out Niddrie way see, on account of his hip operation. Had it done a month ago and he's no been managing the stairs in his old bit. Ye ken the big flats in Muirhouse? The lift's always broken or full ae junkies and wee bams so the cooncil moved him to a ground floor bit. Makes sense ye see? Mind when I goat the walker first time and they punted me to a new bit? No too bad every now and then they council gadjes, treat the old boys alright.'

The only responses that Luke had offered during this verbal barrage were nods and shakes of the head. Through many years of experience, he had come to the realisation that with even the slightest prodding, Tam would divert down a long and meandering side road of conversation that was a joy to listen to when they were sitting killing some time and beer but a real drag when there was information that he needed to hear. The difficulty was always in deciding exactly how much to allow as cutting him off felt rude but letting him talk unchecked could mean losing the rest of your days. So far all he had written down was "Eric?". Tam had quenched his thirst and resumed his onslaught.

'So Eric's out in his new bit and ye ken yersel that Niddrie isnae as bad as they say. Few folk spoiling it fer aw the rest, ken? I goes oot to see him the day, just to check in. He's no as young as mysel so ye've goat tae keep an eye.'

Luke snorted into his pint and tried to turn it into a nod of agreement. Tam remained unperturbed.

'He's orite oan his feet an that again, trying to get back to walking a fair bit every day. Likes his independence ken? So we're chatting a bit and takin a wander down tae Craigmillar. There's a boozer doon there he used to take a pint in years back when he lived oot that way with his Jeannie. Ye willnae have met Jeannie will ye son? Ah, she wis a gem. A real diamond. Must be gone aboot 15 year easy by now. Poor soul. Well, we get's to talking aboot this an that and aw the rest an I mentioned yer boy that you were after. See, always oan shift me. Tam's always keepin his one gid eye oot for his pal.'

Reaching across and punching Luke's shoulder, he drank again. Now Luke was leaning towards him across the table. Far from being frustrated at the useless information that was being mixed in he found himself enjoying it. It seemed to make the build up to the final reveal all the more gratifying as he tried to mentally sift through the words being spat at him like a machine gun and catch only the pertinent. Tam seemed to have stalled at this stage in the story. Whether he was waiting on being questioned or caught up in some memory was impossible to tell.

'So, I'm assuming Eric knew something then?'

'Aye, aye.' Tam was back on track. 'Thing wi Eric is that he's good wi faces. It's uncanny, he'll clap eyes oan some radge from across the shop or the boozer and tell ye exactly who it is and aboot a hundred other bits and pieces that ye don't need tae know but that's how it is. He likes tae yap a bit an it's better just to let him.'

It was taking a superhuman effort for Luke to keep his eyes down and pretend to write. At least he hadn't laughed out loud this time.

'I showed him that wee picture ye left wi me from ma wallet and he tipples right off. Ken's the boy eh? Well, just to see like, but that's kind of the point. If a gadje is missing and no ones seen him, if ye ken the boy to see ye've cracked it eh?'

'When had he seem him Tam? He's only been officially off the radar for about three days so unless it's been within that time then...'

'I'm no daft son. I'm auld and half blind but am no daft. Says he seen him just the day afore.'

Writing steadily now, Luke completed the line he was on and kept the pen poised by the side of the page. He took another swallow of his pint and replaced it carefully on the beer mat.

'I know you aren't daft Tam. If you're able to tell me everything you can remember about what he told you then there might be a chance of me making you my partner yet. This is the only bit of good info I've had since I've started all this nonsense'

Tam was seeing off the last of his whiskey and then laboriously drained the stout before arranging both empties square on their respective mats.

'I don't want tae show you up son. Keep me as an ootside contractor and pay me in booze. That'll suit us both lovely.'

Luke took both the hint and the empty glasses and went back to the bar for a second round. If Tam had wanted a full bottle he'd have probably bought it for him at this stage. Looks like the old man was about to really come through for him after all.

After he had all the details in his trusty notebook and had safely deposited Tam in a taxi with a twenty that would more than doubly cover the fare, Luke waved them off and began the short walk back to his flat. All he had to do was nip in to grab a few things and then he'd be straight back out. As he climbed the stairs he composed a text on his phone with both hands to give Grant a heads up on the developments. More and more he was feeling like he had done very little so far to justify his role as investigator in this case but he was sure that situation was about to remedy itself. Once the text message had gone, he replaced his phone, opened his front door and prepared himself to go to work for real and earn his money.

Inside The Bull on Leith Walk, Claire was sitting at the bar and stirring a cocktail with a straw. The whole walk down she had been confident and retained purpose in her stride but now that she was sitting waiting on Grant to appear she wasn't entirely sure what had caused her to be so certain that this was the right idea. Every time the door opened, she turned to look over her shoulder and turned away again after seeing that it wasn't him. Her head was dropping lower towards the glass with each disappointment. She had finished the French Martini in front of her and was waiting on the second being mixed up when the door opened again but she didn't even turn around this time. To her right, she was aware of a weight on the bar but kept her eyes fixed on the bartender who was extravagantly straining her cocktail from a great height into the glass. Once he had finished he took the shaker away to clean and as she was reaching into her purse for money a voice beside her spoke.

'I'll get that.'

Grant had arrived. In that moment all the trepidation and worry evaporated and she felt a flush enter her face that she was sure was just alcohol. Turning in her seat to look up into his face she smiled and found her hand wandering once more to the bow in her hair to touch it slowly. He had worn a black button up shirt with jeans and some newish looking dark trainers. She could smell the slightest whiff of aftershave from him that certainly hadn't gone on trimming his stubble but could only conclude that he had, despite himself, made an effort.

'No need for that Grant, let me get yours for you.'

He dropped his right shoulder to lean on the bar with his elbow and looked at her. She had a grin across her face again and almost all the hardness inside him disappeared. The bartender was in the middle of pouring Grant's lager and watched both the combatants engaged in this war of manners with interest. After a prolonged moment of eye contact, the big man with the ink and scars gave way to the secretary with a polite shrug.

'If you insist. I'm nothing if not a gentleman.'

The giggle that escaped from her as she rummaged in her purse with a victorious air made his smile even wider. His cheery grin only faltered briefly when the barman also had a chuckle to himself at the idea. Grant's head snapped round and silenced the barman with a look that would have melted steel as he became furiously interested in polishing an already spotless glass. Reaching underneath himself, Grant extracted a stool that was leaning against the bar and lowered his massive frame down onto it. Once the transaction was complete his pint glass gently touched her Martini as they both nodded to each other in a display of mock manners that would have embarrassed the most pious of teachers at a finishing school. They sat beside each other listening to the music and looking around at the general clamour of the pub – it was fairly busy as always. Grant caught the eye of a few regulars and returned their head nods with the same. It was Claire who eventually spoke.

'So. How's things?'

It felt so formal and she instantly regretted it. She wasn't sure exactly what mood she was wanting to create for the evening but that had felt wrong.

'Good aye. Yourself?'

In place of a vocal response she just nodded and resumed stirring the colourful concoction in her glass with the straw. Once again they both looked round the pub and took it in, avoiding the others gaze. A couple of the older guys that had drank there since before it got renovated sat in the corner and gave Grant the subtlest wink they could muster in unison. Grant laughed to himself – there would be no end of ripping from them next time he was in. It was bad enough having them clock him in here on a date but there was no chance he'd give them the satisfaction of seeing him on one that looked like it had gone badly. Ignoring the fact that he himself wasn't even sure that this was even a date, he turned back towards her and poked her shoulder so that she stopped stirring and looked at him.

'Here, got a bit of news off that Luke guy on the way here.'

'Yeah?' Her excitement was real. 'Has he found him then?'

'No, nothing quite like that just yet but he's making some headway.' He drank briefly before launching into the explanation. 'There's an old dude that stays round my bit. Used to be a bit of a handful in his day apparently but now he just goes around the boozers chatting with folk and knocking down more sauce than you'd think was possible. Tam knows everything about anyone or at least where to ask and Luke reckons the old boy's come through for him.'

Her straw was poised motionless above the glass and her full attention was on him. Grant couldn't stop looking from her eyes to her lips and back again – it was throwing him off his game somewhat. Making a deliberate effort to focus on the pint in front of him instead, he continued.

'Well, he reckons someone's seen him kicking about Niddrie and Craigmillar. Nothing more than that the now but I'd be surprised if he wasn't following it up himself in the near future. Said he had one or two other things to look into first. Not exactly concrete but it's something. Reckon the Magistrate would be interested in knowing?'

The straw began to slowly circle the glass rim again and Claire's brow furrowed in thought. Grant was left wondering if there was anything she could do that wouldn't cause him to stare like a slack jawed idiot. The straw paused just above the surface of the liquid and she brought it up slowly to her mouth and licked the residue from it. Reinserting it into the glass she kept her eyes on it as she replied.

'It would probably make him worry a bit less. He's been totally losing his head over this.'

Grant snorted before he responded. 'Let him lose his head for all I care. In whatever sense you choose to take that.'

Claire shrugged with a smile. He was fairly sure that she too had imagined the portly man in the expensive shoes decapitated and it hadn't exactly been an unpleasant thought. There was no love lost between Geoffrey Reid and pretty much anyone he seemed to encounter. The poison of his character eventually got to everyone. Even Claire found herself being dragged down by his brashness and arrogance. She offered a timid compromise to her glass.

'I guess I could let him know. What do you reckon?'

She had turned to face him again with the last statement and he quickly turned back to the bar as if she had caught him looking. He pondered for a bit before replying.

'I say let him stew. Whatever this is, it's all of his own making. Rab's no angel but no one deserves the disdain that that waste of skin piles on him. He'll find out soon enough, you know how he is. Pudgy fingers in every pie.'

'OK by me.'

They brought their glasses together and revelled in their concrete alliance against the scourge in both their lives. The agreement brought a new camaraderie between them and the awkwardness slowly slipped away. They sat facing each other. They sat closer. The drinks kept coming and as dusk spread into evening Grant Ferguson couldn't stop smiling. He found himself even hoping that she would try and hug him again. She laughed and touched the bow in her hair and hoped that her makeup was still in place. When she put her hand on his in the midst of a particularly wild bout of laughter he didn't pull it away and she left it there, hoping that he would want to kiss her before they left.

Chapter 19

By the time Luke Calvin left his flat again, it was approaching 10pm. The street lights were on and the evening crowd were now out in full force, lairy and loud, walking the pavements. Mercifully his first stop was relatively close by, just up the street in fact. As he crested Victoria Street and turned right he was on George IV bridge which happened to have the unusual attribute of not looking like a bridge at all when you were walking across it. Unless you stopped and looked right and left at exactly the correct moment you would be forgiven in thinking that it was simply a quaintly named street. The bars and pubs on both sides of the street were sounding lively and the different music that spilled out into the street created a bizarre cacophony of all styles and genres that sounded like a radio being retuned from station to station as he made his way past them.

His first port of call was going to be the natural history museum where he knew Rab had worked for close to a year previously. A visibly drunk student type accosted him en route and asked for a light which Luke provided happily, lighting up himself at the same time. Continuing on his way, he went over his plan in his head – as rudimentary as it seemed. Since there was now definite confirmation that his man was in fact alive and kicking there was only the small issue of getting a hold of him to provide his "doting" father with some measure of proof that employing Luke's services had not been a waste of time. Or money. It was already too late to head out to speak to old Eric tonight but much like the young, happy and drunk crowd that thronged around him, Luke had the unshakable feeling that the best was still to come.

The museum was long closed by the time he arrived but that was exactly what he had anticipated. Through the glass he could see the darkness broken by a light behind the security desk and the guard sitting behind it. From the desk light and the glow of whatever he was using to watch either TV or a film Luke could barely make out any features aside from the fact that he was completely bald which invariably made placing him in an age bracket all more difficult. More than anything else he looked thoroughly bored. Luke waited in a dark corner outside the granite building and waited for him to come out – night security guys in his experience almost always smoked and even if he didn't it was more than likely he'd come out for a change of scene at some point. No sooner had the thought run through his head than the security guard seemingly received it telepathically. Stretching upwards and yawning wide he rose wearily to his feet and came round the desk towards the revolving doors. Instead of going through them however, he used his keys to unlock a fire door to the side after tapping at the console on the inside briefly and stepped out into the night. As he extracted a cigarette from a packet in his pocket, Luke did the same and walked out from the shadows in front of the building. Luke patted all of his pockets several times, feeling his lighter exactly where it should be but paused and let out a sigh of exasperation before resuming his frantic pocket searches. A voice from the doorway interrupted him.

'You needing a light pal?'

Luke acted startled before smiling and climbing the massive stone steps up to his saviour. The security guard was just shy of the 6-foot mark and looked to be the wrong side of 40. There was a tiredness in his face that was not entirely related to the unhealthiness of being stuck on constant nights. The hand that offered the lighter had A.C.A.B tattooed across the knuckles and Luke imagined there would probably be a spider web lurking under the shirtsleeves around the elbow. He smiled, took the lighter and lit up. Returning it to his new friend he stood beside him and they smoked in companionable silence. It was like the taxi driver and bus driver situation all over again as Luke could feel the only obvious question to ask bubbling forward in his subconscious and he eventually asked it.

'On the nightshift mate?'

A stroke of genius. Sherlock Holmes had nothing on him. Who else would be able to discern that the man who deposited himself behind a desk in the museum overnight was doing it as a job rather than a hobby. The guard merely seemed happy for the company as he graciously overlooked the idiocy of the question and answered it anyway.

'Aye man. 7 til 7 in the morning.'

Letting out his breath through pursed lips, Luke shook his head in sympathy before extending his hand.

'I'm Luke by the way. Cheers for the light.'

'Gavin.'

The handshake was not the usual bone crushing effort that seemed to be part of the job requirements for any security job. It had even been administered with a smile.

'How do you like the work Gav?'

'It's OK I guess. Apart from the unsociable hours all I need to do is be here and take a walk around every hour. Rocket Science it ain't.' He paused briefly to smoke. 'What do you do yourself?'

Luke considered lying but reasoned that it never seemed to work out for him in the end. There was no doubt in his mind that it would not land well in Gavin's camp given his interesting body art.

'I'm an investigator of sorts. Kind of freelance. It's hard to explain.'

As expected, Gavin visibly stiffened and his tone hardened.

'Why are you here?'

'Just chasing up a lead.'

'About what?'

Luke was keeping his eyes forward looking at the buildings across the street and the people milling around outside the pubs. He was fairly sure he wasn't going to get hit before he got his point across but he was more alert than he let on.

'Missing person.'

From the corner of his eye he could see Gavin relax slightly and turn away from him to look across the street as well. The sudden hostility had not been surprising but it's intensity had been. Luke was weighing up how to ask about it without getting head butted when the situation was resolved for him.

'Got a little bit arsey there didn't I? Sorry man, just been a bit on edge this week. Thought you might have been from the company checking up on me. Had a bit of an incident a few days ago and they aren't very happy with me.'

146

The impression he was giving was that he wanted to talk about it so Luke remained silent. Sure enough, Gavin continued in due course.

'It's the most ridiculous thing. It's actually unbelievably stupid but I'm getting my collar felt for it at the moment and I don't find it as funny as all the other guys seem to.'

'What happened?'

Gavin looked up and down the street slowly before continuing, avoiding Luke's eyes.

'I'm the security guard here on a night, right? Just me. So anyone that goes in and out is my responsibility. I sign the cleaners in and out and the staff if they're working late or coming in early. We keep the records in the sheet back there.' He gestured towards his desk inside. 'Just pen and paper, no need for an electronic copy or that. It's just boring basic stuff.'

Luke was unsure of the significance of any of this but maintained a polite interest. He was still studying the opposite side of the street and smoking. Gavin's story had ground to a halt and he seemed to be faltering so Luke gave him a gentle nudge.

'OK. I get that. So what happened that they're on your back?'

The security guard was carefully eyeing the toes of his boots and scuffed first one then the other off the top of the step. The action made him resemble an overgrown toddler.

'Something went missing.'

'What went missing? If it was something worth a lot of money surely they'd have canned you first and investigated later?'

'Nothing expensive man. Just stupid. The boys have been riding me for two days over it and I'm sure the company isn't believing me that no one came in or out except for the people on my list.' His tone was becoming pleading. 'I was at my desk all night. I never leave apart from coming out for a tab and I need to punch the code in at the door before I go out and come back in. I need to use my keys as well.'

Slowly, the cogs in Luke's head were turning and he was beginning to get an inclination of where this was going. Any self-congratulation on his idea to come by here in the first place would have been premature – he needed to be certain first. Finishing his smoke, he looked around for an ashtray and seeing none turned back to Gavin who was in the process of flicking his down the steps and onto the street. Luke followed suit and asked a question as casually as he could.

'It wasn't a skeleton that went missing by any chance was it?'

Gavin's head whipped round so fast that Luke was shocked he hadn't snapped his neck clean. His mouth was hanging agape and he seemed genuinely shocked.

'Aye. That was it. A stupid display skeleton from the first floor. Worth nothing as far as I can tell but it's genuine human bone, you know? These crackpots donate their bodies when they die so that folk can gawp at them. Just assumed it was some weirdo during the day and no one noticed for some reason. How did you know that?'

Luke's hand found the other man's shoulder and he smiled.

'Just a lucky guess for now I reckon. You fancy showing me all the ways in and out of the building? If I'm right, then I think we both just might be home clear.'

Princes Street Gardens were closed to the public of an evening to dissuade people from sleeping rough or drinking in public. There was no real reason beyond the fact that it was so central and so well known that it would be nigh on impossible to police effectively, especially under the cover of darkness and the other areas of greenery in Edinburgh had not traditionally fared well when it came to acts of physical violence and other forms of depravity in the dark. For this reason, the gates in the high, spiked fence that ran around it were closed and locked every evening and reopened every morning.

Much in the same way that a lock is only a deterrent to an honest man, 5 feet of railing with spikes never have been enough to keep anyone out who desperately wanted in. Such was the case again tonight as a figure stalked down the mound and along Princes Street heading West, keeping close to the fence. The difficulty, they had found, was never in the act of scaling the fence. It was always in finding a location that was quiet enough to do so unnoticed. On they walked, hood raised up to shroud their face and head with hands thrust deep into the pouch style pocket in the front. The warmth of the day was quickly becoming a distant memory as the dark stole away any residual heat that was left. The pavements were busy but somehow the figure managed to walk straight down without turning to the left or to the right – ordinary members of the public tend to acquiesce to the actions of the most insane looking or acting – and the West End itself began to stretch upwards into the sky. Busses and taxis flew past bathing the pedestrians in light and noise before passing on by into the distance, the red lights out the back blinking and flashing as they pulled up to stop after stop after stop. The hooded figure was quickly getting out of breath with the exertion and the pace but the shoes that scuffed along the pavement kept pounding out the rhythm that was looping around and around in their head – "Hurry up. Hurry up. Hurry up."

Turning left onto Lothian Road, they found themselves in front of a church. The denomination was unknown to them and frankly of no interest. All that mattered was that the front gates were usually left open to allow tourists to take pictures or inspect the ancient gravestones out front. The church itself of course remained securely locked. Slipping inside the courtyard, the figure bent close to one tombstone after the other, tracing the carved letters carefully with their finger. They read the names that they never knew the dates and years that had all long since passed. Moving from one to the next methodically, they gravitated towards the darkest area at the very back of the church wall where they quickly scanned for anyone taking notice from the street before jumping up, grabbing the rough stone with their hands and pulling themselves up and over in one smooth motion. Landing in an almost controlled sprawl in the dirt on the other side they remained motionless and waited for shouts of challenge from the street but none came.

Between the wall of the churchyard and the gardens there was the characteristic fence but out of sight from everywhere there was time to make moves carefully and avoid a spike through the foot. One more hurdle and they found themselves in the gardens. The noise from the streets and pavements was dampened by the foliage and when there was a gap in the trains that departed and arrived seemingly constantly, there was a peacefulness to be found here especially in the night-time. Breathing slower and deeper, the figure adjusted their hood to ensure it was still giving them as much coverage as they wanted and started walking back the way they had come only this time at a leisurely pace and without anyone to avoid them. Staying close to the treeline, they continued East with the railway lines to their right and beyond that the steep crags that rose into the sky with the castle sitting atop them.

At the same time, Geoffrey Reid was leaving his offices and locking up himself. Having let Claire go three hours previous he had fully intended to catch up on some case notes but had found himself sitting with the papers in front of him, reading and re-reading without taking a single word in. Sighing deeply, he leaned back in his chair and extended his arms behind his head, stretching towards the window. Tilting his head backwards he stared once more at the vaulted ceiling that seemed improbably far above him and remained motionless for a while.

Outside his window the city was darkening and the skyline stretched as far as the eye could see – these historic buildings reduced to jagged dark outlines in the gathering gloom. The jutting spire of the monument; the colosseum style pyramids of the art gallery; the Free Church College and associated buildings rising majestically against the moon and all deep in the shadow of the castle. As he gradually levered himself back into a sitting position he picked the papers up one more time and managed to look at two lines before flinging them to the far side of the desk. He reached into the inside pocket of his jacket and extracted a brass ring that had numerous keys hanging from it, sorting through them carefully until a small grey one was selected between his pudgy fingers. Leaning down awkwardly, he flipped down a veneer cover at the top right corner of his desk drawer to reveal a tiny keyhole into which the key disappeared. There was a click and with a slight tug the entire top section of the drawer pulled out independent of the rest.

A false bottom in a cupboard or drawer was so common it was borderline on the cliché but his secret top did all he required of it. The drawer's twin on the opposite side had no such feature but maintained the 3 inches of solid wood at the top before the split in order to preserve the illusion. Geoffrey Reid had very seldom been in this drawer but liked having it just in case. It contained only two things – a bottle of expensive whiskey from which he had drank precisely twice and a handgun acquired extremely illegally. The only shot he was after at the moment came in liquid form and after he had taken a pull straight from the neck, he resealed it and locked it away.

Feeling emboldened by the alcohol in his system, he had stood, hit the lights and stalked out into the night.

The car that was parked around the corner in his private spot was the very height of luxury, just like everything else that the Magistrate bought and owned. He had paid for it outright of course and ignoring the fact that the ridiculous top speed far exceeded not only the speed limit but the scope of city driving by a degree of measures, he was very proud of it. The amber liquid had warmed him from deep inside and he thought briefly about whether he'd be over the limit – after all it wasn't like he had poured himself an exact measure – but dismissed it out of hand. Waiting for a taxi home and needing to get one back in the morning were both out of the question as far as he was concerned. Lowering himself into the leather seats, he sat for a moment before pressing the "Engine Start" button and allowing the car to idle powerfully on the street. What he needed to combat his anxiousness was a plan of action.

The same two names kept coming up in all his private enquires so far and now was the time to make a move. Deek and Mark, they told him. Mark and Deek. Over and over, they cropped up time and again. It seemed strange that Grant hadn't mentioned them... Still. The plan entered his mind, fully-formed:

1. Get home and sleep
2. Get a hold of Derek Sutherland and Mark
3. Have them brought to his offices in the morning
4. Find out what they know
5. Punish them regardless

The minor details would work themselves out on the journey home or through the night. It wouldn't be prudent to send Grant to pick them up so he'd have to use a couple of cops on his payroll. Even if he was in the mood for administrating the punishment himself, despite his size and strength, he might want Grant around for their meeting as a bit of back up. Slipping the car into gear, he pulled away into the road feeling much better and headed for home through the dusk.

Chapter 20

Out in Craigmillar, Deek and Mark were sprawled across the sofa and floor respectively. It had been a long time since either of them had spoken or checked the time – their only interactions consisted of passing a joint back and forth between them at varying intervals without as much as a word. The stash in the spare bedroom was slowly decreasing and the money in the floor safe was building up. They were both quietly confident that they could shift the rest of the gear and have enough to stay out of the game for a while. Or resupply and carry on. Both talked about the idea of quitting the gig but the money had been easy today with very little effort and when it came to weighing up the pros and cons at the key moment, all the raids, the hassle and the burns faded away in comparison to the days they made four figures of cold cash from the comfort of their living room without even have to turn off the games console. Mark could feel his eyes becoming heavier and heavier. A strand of hair had fallen down into his left eye but from his reclined position, propped up on one elbow, he couldn't seem to muster the effort to free a hand to remedy the situation. From behind him on the couch, there was a coughing fit that slowly abated before the joint materialised over his shoulder.

'What time is it Mark?'

'No idea man. Gotta be gone midnight.'

He took the joint and held it without smoking. Unusually, Mark had overindulged to an extreme that was only usually seen with the likes of Deek. It had been the endless flow of customers in and out all day. One straight after the other, all bearing cash and snacks. All spending a little while in their company, being sociable. All sampling the wares they had just purchased with the happy retailers.

'Here, Deek?'

'Hmmmm?'

'You know what our problem is?'

There was no reply from the couch but Mark knew he was listening. In fact, without even turning round, he knew that Deek would have moved from his sideways position and adopted the "Let it alone Mark, I'm just resting my eyes" pose of flat on his back with his head propped on the end, the lengthy legs well over the other side and his hands clasped delicately over his stomach. This was the final stage his mate went through before succumbing to sleep and passing out properly but it usually took a good quarter of an hour before he'd stop responding.

'Our problem, my lanky amigo, is that we're too nice.'

The slow exhalation from behind Mark made him roll over from one elbow to the other so he was facing away from the TV and towards Deek. Sure enough, he was in the exact position he had expected with his eyes shut. When he replied there wasn't as much as a hint of movement in any other part of his body other than the mouth.

'No such thing as too nice Mark. You can't be too nice to people.'

The simplicity of the statement matched the straightforward nature of the man. It was a nothing statement but to the two minds addled by too much smoking it felt profound. The mouth on the couch moved again.

'How do you mean we're too nice anyway? What would you rather?'

'I dunno. Be a bit more business like I guess?'

'Check you out Mr. Economics. Giving it big licks with the business plan.'

'You know what I mean. We end up baked, smoking with every guy who comes through the door.'

'Yes. Yes, we do.'

A smile cracked on the couch and Mark just gave up on the whole idea. It wasn't like leaving a goat to tend the cabbage after all. It was like they were both goats and Mark was trying to tell Deek that they shouldn't eat the cabbage despite the fact that they both wanted to. He finally reached up and swept the hair clear of his eyes. Or something like that.

For the hundredth time since it had happened, Mark considered telling Deek at least a little bit about the mitigating circumstances surrounding their different luck when the cops had battered the door down. Deek had said time and time again that it wasn't an issue and there was no way that Mark could have known. The element of untruth in that statement ate away inside his mind, sharpened to a needling feeling by the paranoia that seemed to be growing in his subconscious either with age or with an ever increasing intake level of hash. He watched his friends long frame draped over the couch and saw how peaceful his face seemed. For the hundredth time he decided that he would tell him at some point: just not now. The film they had both been watching had finished and was now looping the title menu over and over. Finding the remote with not a little difficulty, Mark pushed the hair out of his eyes again with one hand to get a clear look at it. After much deliberation, he realised that while it was beyond him at the moment to get up and change the disk, he was more than capable of pressing the OK button and starting the movie from the beginning. Holding the remote close to his face, he pressed firmly on the middle button and was rewarded with the opening credits. Behind him, Deek was starting to breathe deeper and he knew sleep would take them both soon. Finding a bag of crisps and the rolling set-up he positioned himself so that he was still on the floor but now with his back against the sofa where the ever deepening breathing led him to believe that Deek had finally given in to sleep. Whatever had been bugging him when he'd rushed out after the phone call was obviously not enough for him to lose any sleep over. Concentrating hard on rolling, Mark felt a hand touch his hair and ruffle it gently before being taken away. A sleepy voice accompanied the gentle gesture.

''Night Mark.'

Mark paused his efforts at a point where he could safely hold the entire arrangement in one hand and reached behind him with the free one. Keeping his eyes focused on the task in hand he patted whichever bit of Deek his hand happened to land on.

'Night dude.'

The clock in the corner that neither had thought to check stated that the time was 00:45. The movie played out the opening scenes for a second time and Mark had one eye on the screen but took none of it in. After this film, he'd call it a day too. All of a sudden he realised that the paranoia had melted away and he felt entirely fine within his mind once more. After all, business never stops and they could well have another busy day tomorrow.

The night was wearing on but there was no rest in sight for Luke. After he had gone over all the possible ways in and out of the building with Gav, he had taken a note of his personal number and left. As he began to walk back the way he had come, up George IV bridge and towards his flat he was too deep in thought to pay much attention to the people who were brushing against his shoulders as they staggered past and on with their night. All that awaited him back in his flat was cold, quiet and dark and in order to think clearly he wanted noise and company. The watch on his left wrist was another cheap plastic one that cost him next to nothing but had served him years and it informed him that the Bull would be long since closed since it didn't have a late licence. His best bet was somewhere open late that wasn't a club – as much as he required background action to focus his mind, there was no sane person in this world who went to a nightclub to try and piece together the pieces of a mystery that were being handed to them excruciatingly slowly.

The chill was setting in for the evening and Luke found himself wishing that he had worn a cap: his hair was being blown all over the place and from long experience he knew that it would be scruffy looking even for him. Running a hand over his head in a futile attempt to bring it back under control he quickly decided to get inside a drinking establishment where he could sit with his notebook and try and put it all together. Whistlebinkies was a live music bar that stayed open until 3am and had the benefit of musicians (of varying abilities) playing all sorts until the wee hours. More to the point, it was a two-minute walk to North Bridge from where he was and only a five-minute walk (or ten-minute stumble) back to his flat from there once he was done.

Walking past the top of his street he made the crest of the Royal Mile and turned to his right, heading down towards the warmth and noise. For the police, proof was everything – evidence and probable cause – but for him, an idea was enough to be getting on with. A skeleton went missing from a museum that Rab used to work at and a skeleton was found buried in a shallow grave just after Rab himself

155

went missing. Coincidences were far more common than most people would admit, but for Luke Calvin they were his bread and butter out of necessity rather than choice. Once he was settled in the pub, he would read his notes again but he knew already where he had to start looking next – every other place that Rab had worked, no matter how briefly. It wasn't likely to be a small undertaking and he was thankful that he'd taken the time to copy by hand the emailed list Laura had sent him right back at the start. For the immediacy though., his hands and nose were freezing and he was sure that his hair alone would have earned him an audition to join the Jackson 5. Pub first, solutions later. Another unofficial mantra that had served him better than most would expect.

As expected, one pint had turned into two and then there. Sitting in a corner seat underneath the stairs that led down from the street he had his notebook in his hand and was re-reading it for the hundredth time. On the stage, an old bearded man in a suit with guitar in hand was belting out country songs and absolutely nailing it. The brief smattering of applause that rippled around the room after each number was nowhere near doing the performance justice. Luke found himself putting the notebook down to clap along with them after each song. The guitar player looked well into his sixties with a pint of heavy sat within easy reach on the stage and a voice that spoke a lifetime of experiences. Luke believed every word that he sang and was becoming irate at the lacklustre reception from the relatively quiet room. Leaving his notebook on the table he brought his glass back to the bar and ordered one more and whatever the guitarist was drinking. He brought the heavy up to the stage just as the latest song was finished and placed it on the table and was rewarded with a broad wink.

'Thanks son.'

Returning to his own table he started a new page in his notebook and put his confusions down to paper. Assuming for a minute that Rab did actually nick the skeleton, why would he go to the hassle of burying it? Especially somewhere so obvious. Even if someone else had done it for him there was still the question of why – there was nothing to be gained from it that he could see. If he thought it wouldn't be found then it was a pointless gesture. If he thought it would then how long did he think it would take them to realise it wasn't the real deal? The main question was where was he now? According to Tam, Old Eric had seen him in Craigmillar or Niddire and even spoken to him. As far as Luke was able to see, there was no logical reason for him to have be hiding out there. He had no connections there at all.... Luke paused with his glass halfway to his mouth and leafed back in his book to where he spoke to Grant in the Fluke. He had mentioned some hash peddlers out that way that he bought from. There it was, Grant had named them as Deek and Mark. Right below it though he had stated strongly that they were good guys and if Luke roughed them up he'd have to answer to him. Luke had dismissed the connection out of hand based on the triviality of it but now these minor points made a suggestion stronger than the sum of the two of them. He highly doubted they were harbouring him but he was almost certain that they would know more than he did.

Writing again in his book, under where he was going to chase up the old jobs that Rab had invariably been fired from, he made an additional note to go and visit Deek and Mark. Closing his notebook, he heard the opening of The Wild Rover echoing out from the stage and settled back comfortably in his seat. Maybe it would be best to speak to Grant first and get the low-down but he had gone from having absolutely nothing to moving in a very definite direction. Tomorrow would be a busy day but his policy of pub first and solutions later had come through again. It was just gone two am and the place usually shut at three.... on the one hand he should probably be up early-ish tomorrow but on the other, a reward might be in order. Collecting his glass and returning to the bar he signalled the barman for one more and leant with his back against it to wait for his drink, watching the old man and feeling fairly content.

'I don't feel happy about this at all, that's all I'm saying. Not that I won't do it, but that I don't feel happy about it.'

Inside their patrol car, Dave and Steve were once again back on the nightshift and for all the action they'd seen they may as well have both been in their beds. Steve was behind the steering wheel staring straight at the road while Dave was turned sideways in his seat trying to speak to him.

'It doesn't seem like the right way to go about it from any angle. If there was no issue with it then why would we be doing it at this time in the morning?'

'Dawn raids are practically Police tradition Dave. Much like racism and acts of wanton violence. Or was that the only part of the exam you failed?'

The bait that had been dangled was promptly snatched up by the younger man against his better judgement and to his instant regret.

'I never failed a thing during the whole process Steve. You know full well I didn't.'

Keeping his hands on the wheel and his eyes ahead, Steve couldn't quite hold down the laugh that the explosive reaction had caused. Dave turned back to face the front and sat in haughty silence as the car prowled the streets past Niddrie and into Craigmillar. The streets were practically empty and there was almost no traffic. In short course they were pulling into the car park behind The Boat and parking up. Dave made a move to get out of the car but Steve stopped him. The door closed again and Steve spoke.

'Believe it or not, I'm no happier about this than you are. I know the whole thing seems a bit crooked but the call was put out and it's better that me and you take the job than some other random hero who has no sense and less loyalty. We can keep an eye on the boys and make sure nothing underhanded goes on. Make sure they get a fair shake of the stick. Know what I mean?'

'I guess so.' He sounded utterly dejected. 'We'd better get going then. You know they're going to freak out at someone showing up at half four right? Far less in uniform.'

Steve laughed as he exited the car and spoke to his partner over the roof.

'I know. I'd have offered to do it just to see that alone.'

They put their caps back on their heads in unison and walked slowly across the car park towards the four storey block of flats on the opposite side from the pub. The façade was less than appealing but unlike a lot of the places around here, the fact that most of the windows seemed to still be intact was enough for it to be considered practically palatial. As they made the entrance, the decision about whether to ring the buzzer or not was taken out of their hands by the fact that the main door had been recently kicked in and hung loose on its hinges. The lobby, if you could bring yourself to apply that term to the place in which they now stood, was a mess of chipped tiles, smashed lights and unknown stains. The lift door was buckled badly and the light was out so they were pretty much forced to take the stairs – on the rare occasions that the lifts in these sorts of buildings actually worked they were invariably trashed and/or reeking of some sort of fluid that you were better off not identifying. They climbed the stairs slowly and single file in the half-light from one landing to the next as the intact bulbs flickered on and off sporadically. When Steve spoke from behind him, Dave nearly jumped a foot in the air.

'It's like the start of a bad horror movie this, isn't it? Just need a couple of junkie zombies to come flying out of the next door and we're all set for Hollywood.'

'Aye very good Spielberg. If you're needing a rest just say so old man.'

Dave was not going to show his fear or trepidation in front of his older colleague. Even with his relatively poor attitude and lack of interest in the job, Steve was known to be hard as nails and his military background was not your usual run of the mill stuff. Despite respecting him immensely, he could be infuriating. Together they reached the fourth floor landing and paused outside the door, neither wanting to be the first one to make a move and knock. Steve leaned his over colleague in the end and thumped on the door with his fist and then they waited for it to be answered.

Chapter 21

As the night passed and began to slide into morning, the flow of traffic all around Edinburgh ebbed and flowed. The taxis and night busses shunted tirelessly through the dark, ferrying people back and forward from one place to the next or to their homes. Behind locked doors and drawn curtains, families, friends, lovers and partners slept soundly in doubles, kings, singles and on couches and floors. Every domestic situation imaginable was represented behind one door or another: all mixes of races, genders and family groups, all united in their slumber. The few that were not part of this unknowing collective were either excluded out of choice or necessity with the latter envying every quiet home they passed. All of them exercising the innate human need to belong, which drives people together and occasionally makes them stay long past the time the situation has ceased to bring them happiness.

At the foot of the Scott Monument, crouched low on the grassy slope the hooded figure sat breathing out condensation into the night sky. These long, cold hours had meant nothing to them as they had first wandered the gardens in relative peace from the West End up as far as the Mound before navigating a tricky train tunnel passage that connected it to the Easterly side where the Monument stood. The tunnel smelt of damp and decay but they took their time, walking slowly and reading the "tags" that had been left previously. The council put less effort into cleaning these off as they weren't even clearly visible from the train windows in the dark of the tunnel – the only people who would read them were workers and others, like him, who were merely passing through. Aside from the usual "mentions" and needlessly coarse statements were the occasional glimpses of some degree of self-awareness. The words "Question Everything" were daubed broadly in the middle of the tunnel and underneath, in black paint, was the one word – "Why?".

The sentiments were mainly of the disenchanted: those who felt disconnected from society or the normal way of life and had no other way to express it. One had written "Choose Life" the iconic statement that Renton had made in Trainspotting: – inspirational out of context, but in reality, a beautifully damning indictment of what people's life become. Underneath the hood the hours outside were starting to show as their nose ran freely and the regular sniffing wasn't enough to keep it in check. The foot traffic they could see on the other side of the monument was still too heavy for them to head across and begin their nightly climb but it was getting close. Crouching and waiting, they wiped their nose on their sleeve and muttered "Hurry up" to the nameless and faceless people that were unknowingly hindering their plans.

The lights inside the holding cells never went out. Sure, it was for the safety of both the person locked inside and the officers who had to check on them through the peep-hole now and then, but it didn't half make it hard to get some kip. Mark had tried lying on his right side with no success. He had tried his left side with the same result. Now, he was stretched out on his back on the small cold cot trying to position his hair over his eyes to block out some light. His feet were cold since they'd taken his shoes but no matter what his discomfort, he knew that Deek would be doubly uncomfortable with his awkward frame. Staring at the light in the ceiling through his makeshift mask he sighed and tried to get his mind to switch off to no avail. This was them for the high jump now – no doubt about it. Banged to rights. It was going to be the big house for him and no questions asked. Lying in the cell with no phone, no watch and worst of all no way to speak to his mate, all he could do was lie back and wait for the full weight of the law to crush him. He was unaware that Deek was already crashed out in the adjacent room.

When the knock had come at the door he hadn't checked the time. He hadn't checked who it was. He'd just opened the door wide, blinked stupidly in the sudden light and lowered his head in defeat as Steve and Dave had entered the flat, politely removing their hats as they did so. Steve had patted his shoulder twice on the way past and motioned for him to come back through to the living room with him and Mark, still out of his box, had followed as meekly as a lamb.

Deek had taken a while to rouse but when he eventually opened his eyes there was no shock or horror to be seen on his face. He sat up as best he could and swung his legs to the ground to make room on the couch and addressed his latest visitors.

'Orite Steve, what you saying man?'

Through the hall, they could all hear Dave inspecting the rest of the flat and the two civilians waited for the inevitable. The door to the spare bedroom was pushed open and he shouted through, barely able to contain his excitement: -

'Steve. Steve. Get through here.'

Steve sat down on the couch slowly beside Deek and reached for the cigarette packet sitting beside what was left of the hash block. He motioned with the packet and seeing a slow approving nod from the sleepy man beside him, took a smoke and lit it. Mark had collapsed into the armchair and was sitting with his head in his hands, his hair fanned out towards the ground like a veil. Steve looked from one to the other.

'How bad is it boys?'

The reply from underneath the mask of hair came softly.

'It's bad.'

Dave stuck his head round the door. His eyes were wide and there was disbelief plastered all over his face.

'You have to see this Steve.'

'No I don't.'

He loitered in the doorway only a moment more before entering the room to join the others and sat beside his colleague on the couch. Deek was blinking very slowly and Mark hadn't made a move. Steve sat further back, resting his foot on his knee and placing the ashtray on his thigh.

'We need to take you in guys.' The expected protest never came. 'What I'm going to do is sit here and finish my smoke. You guys go put some clothes on and come back in here in five minutes and we can all leave together. No handcuffs. No fuss. How does that sound?'

Deek nodded again and stood up as though he were moving through treacle. When he passed Mark, he put a hand under his elbow and hoisted him to his feet before the two of them left the room together. Dave was incredulous.

'They're going to flush their stash Steve. I guarantee it.' His voice rose. 'Guys, if I hear that toilet flush a single time I'm going to come through and smack you with my baton.'

The slow drawl that echoed back through the doorway was Derek Sutherland at his finest.

'Oooh, you promise big boy?'

Even Dave gave in to the laughter that was going around and helped himself to a smoke. He wasn't sure about what Steve was doing but they appeared to be getting compliance without threats or force and that was a lot more than he had anticipated. Maybe his anxiety had all been for nothing after all.

The station was almost silent – there was an officer at the desk and the rest were out on duty. Dave was loitering in the hallway as Steve spoke to the man behind the desk in hushed tones. When he finally came away, the two of them left together and headed for the patrol car that was sat in the parking spaces in front. Steve had resumed his customary silence but walked to the passenger side of the car instead of the drivers. They opened their doors and entered. Dave sat behind the steering wheel but made no move to start the car. He was about to question Steve but the older man had his phone to his ear and the other hand extended towards him in the traditional "in a minute" pose. He waited impatiently for the call to be completed.

'Orite. Aye, I know what time it is. Yeah. Listen, got a bit of info you might be interested in. Nope, couldn't have waited. You'll get why in a minute. You gonna let me tell or you just going to keep giving it big yawns down the phone? Right, call came out earlier tonight to go pick up two boys in Craigmillar, Mark and Derek. Kind of unofficial, definitely off the record. Brought them down to the station and asked the boy on duty what the plan was. He says they're not getting booked or anything, just taken round to see someone in the morning. Any idea who that would be? Yup, got it in one. Your man, Magistrate Reid. Way ahead of you man, we'll come pick you up in the car. Sound, be there in 10 or 15.'

The phone was returned into his pocket and he faced the front again, staring out the windscreen. Dave was eyeing him carefully as he started the car and pulled out onto the main road, driving in silence for a minute or so before beginning his questions. Of all the many queries running through his head he asked only the most general.

'What's happening here Steve? Where are we going'

'Something weird is going on. I'm not sure exactly what but that's why we're heading back into town quickly to pick up Luke. He lives in Victoria Street; said he'll meet us outside when we get there.'

'What's any of this to do with him?'

'He's working for the Magistrate. Looking for his boy.'

'So what?'

The patrol car was behind the number 30 night bus and pulled around it quickly, headed towards the Commonwealth Pool so they could arrive onto South Bridge and follow it down. Steve was picking away a bit of plastic on the dashboard making a scuff into a tear then a rip.

'So it seems he'd want to know if his employer is getting cops to pull in small time dealers in the middle of the night, not book them, then bring them round his offices first thing in the morning.'

'What do you mean not book them? You mean not charge them?'

'Nope. That man on the desk made no note that they came in and doesn't intend to. What Geoffrey Reid wants, he gets. As far as the great police force of Lothian and Borders are concerned, these guys aren't even in custody.'

Dave briefly weighed the gravity of this. As far as he was concerned the days of these dark arrests went out with the "enhanced interrogations" that would elicit a confession to being the second gunman on the grassy knoll if they went on long enough. They no longer battered people in the back of the riot van or had suspects who tripped and smashed their faces off the station steps. They were an upstanding pillar of the community. Weren't they?

'That's pretty shady. So what are we getting Luke for?'

'When the word went out about picking them up, I jumped right on it so that we could look after them. That makes a little more sense to you now eh?' He received a nod in reply. 'So now I'm gonna bring Luke back to the station and we're going to let him talk to them. You and I are going to get him there and give him a while to find out why they think they're being pulled and we're going to make sure that the man on the desk keeps up his nasty little habit of not recording events that occur during his shift.'

Dave nodded again as the car made the turn onto South Bridge and began down the slowly curving avenue towards North Bridge.

'Like an unauthorised person entering a holding cell?'

'Exactly Davey boy.'

'See all that "Special Forces" Kosovo stuff that you mentioned at the boozer? Is he going to take them out?'

The laughter from the passenger seat made Dave jump again for the second time in as many hours and the punch to the shoulder did little to calm his nerves.

'Come on man, he's not a hitman. He's just a P.I or whatever they yanks call them. I'll bet you ten pints that he doesn't even try to intimidate them and still finds out what he wants to know. Just because he could hurt them badly or kill them doesn't mean he's going to.' He eyed the young driver with a grin. "What about my Special Forces training Davey boy eh? You never worry I could take you out with a nerve pinch or my signature karate manoeuvres?'

Steve began as elaborate a series of ridiculous kung fu poses as the cramped space in the car would allow him. Midway through his attempt to get his left leg up from under the glove box to display his much praised "crane pose", he received his reply.

'Nah man. You're too old and slow.'

The two laughing policemen in the car turned left and came up past the Natural History Museum where Gav sat behind his desk yawning and turned right onto George IV Bridge. The next left was Victoria Street and as the car pulled up, Luke was leaning against the wall outside his door smoking: trying to get the effects of the late night pints out of his head with only two hours sleep was proving difficult. Climbing into the back seat of the car where he'd been a few too many times, Luke shut the door and the trio began the return leg of the journey back out to the police station through the breaking dawn.

The Magistrate had not managed to nod off at all through the night. Once his car was safely deposited in the garage he had entered his home and stood in the hall, for once unsure of himself. His housekeeper had left him a meal of chicken and vegetables which he had inhaled and washed down with a glass or three of red wine.

Plonked down in his armchair he had found himself unable to focus on the news or the business reports and his mind wandered.

It had been nearly two decades since his wife had gone and left him alone with Robert. Despite the fact that the long suffering housekeeper had done most, if not all of the parenting, the only person that Geoffrey Reid felt sorry for was himself. His wife needed constant care in a private psychiatric ward after her issues began to manifest and spiralled out of her control but to Geoffrey it was both weakness and betrayal on her part – as if she had chosen to be a prisoner to the voices and thoughts in her head. His son had grown up without the love of his mother and the security of a family but it was Geoffrey alone who had suffered by his estimation. Robert had always been ungrateful for everything and it had got beyond the point of redemption. To Geoffrey Reid, no one was ever in the right but himself. Despairing for the many blights that had been inflicted on his life by everyone around him, he retired up the grand staircase to bed and let his righteous indignation rob the sleep from his pillow.

It was now five in the morning and he resigned himself to the fact that he might as well get up. A night without sleep was not going to be the thing that made him late to work for the first time ever. Absolutely not. Standing in the shower, he washed his great body meticulously before dressing in an especially fine suit. Today there were things to do and much to be accomplished. Descending to the kitchen, he poured himself cereal and brewed a strong pot of coffee which sat on the side, bubbling merrily. Today was the day that he would find out what happened to Robert. If there was the slightest sign of his hand in it, he would have to squash it entirely. The idea that it was in any way, shape or form his fault did not even enter his mind. Today would be the day he got vengeance of some description. Searching deep in the vaults of his memory for to an appropriate quote to guide his day, he found himself coming back to a verse from the Bible that he hadn't even realised he remembered. - "The sins of the father will be visited upon the son...". Shutting his eyes tight he forced it back down to where it came from. Whatever the outcome, he was not to blame. He had never been to blame.

Chapter 22

Just before 5am, Dave and Steve re-entered the police station in Niddrie with Luke in tow. The man behind the desk glanced up then straight back to his computer, clearly uninterested in what he assumed was another arrest. As they had discussed on the journey, they brought him in in handcuffs between them and Steve moved away from him to lean across the desk and beckon the other officer closer.

'He's been kicking off in the car the whole way here. What's the chances of us taking him into one of the holding cells for a wee chat?'

The other man looked across at Luke who was not only making it look like he was attempting to escape from Dave's grasp but coming very close to succeeding. The officer smirked.

'Feel free. I've got the cameras off in the whole holding bit. Surprising how often the tapes get accidentally wiped here.'

He winked broadly at Steve who extended his hand to take the keys instead of throttling the life out of him like he wanted to. Crossing back to Luke and Dave, he jerked the "prisoner" towards the cells.

'Let's go.'

Luke was babbling and raving, thrashing about viciously until Steve brought him to his knees with a very real liver punch that took the wind out of him and made his stomach turn.

'You after an Oscar or something man? Dial it back ya radge.'

'Just you wait until I have these handcuffs off.'

The two men went back a long way and it was unclear to Dave exactly how much of what was going on was show. He was becoming extremely concerned that he would have two men with special forces training attempting to kill each other inside of an 8-foot cell in a minute. They reached the door which Steve unlocked and all three of them entered into the cell where Deek was sprawled snoring across the cot. Relocking the door, Steve took his own handcuff key out and released Luke from his bonds. Taking only a minute to rub his wrists, Luke threw a brutal overhand right directly at his face. Steve didn't even blink as the fist stopped a centimetre from his nose. Luke shook his head with a smile.

'I'll get you one day Steve. One day.' He rubbed his lower back with his right hand and winced. 'I can see going out of shape hasn't robbed any of your power though. How's a man meant to act when the critics are that harsh eh?'

All the commotion had roused Derek who for the second time in as many hours sat up bewildered at the strangers by his sleeping spot. Rubbing his eyes hard he looked from one face to the next, nodding at the two policemen then stopping on the unknown. Standing up to his full height, he towered over all three and extended a lengthy arm.

'Orite pal, I'm Deek.'

'Luke. Sorry for the circumstances.' Deek sat back down and shrugged. 'I'm going to have to ask you a few questions. Nothing too intense, but it would really help me out a lot if you'd answer them.'

'Where's Mark?'

Dave was leaning against the back wall with his arms crossed and his head back.

'Next door Derek. He's fine. Don't worry.'

'Good. Are we getting the jail Dave?'

'It was an awful lot of hash Deek. You know it's gonna be intent to supply. And the drugs and the money together.... You know it brings me no pleasure but it looks like you're for it I'm afraid.'

Derek's head sank between his legs and the calmness that had prevailed from when he was picked up was slowly giving way to despondency and despair. In his head he saw his rap sheet and he knew what was going to happen. It'd be a long stretch this time. To his surprise, his new friend stepped in to save the day.

'I don't know about that Dave.'

Luke was taking his time extracting a cigarette from his packet before sitting down on the cot beside Derek and offering the bemused prisoner one, which he took.

'How do you mean?'

'I mean you busted in there and seen a good amount of drugs and the cash from it. By all accounts my man here should be banged to rights. Except for one thing.'

The statement hung in the air as Luke took his lighter and sparked up Derek's smoke first and then his own. Dave had come off the wall, argumentative and indignant.

'What thing? I like the boys but there's no other way it can go. And you can't smoke in here.'

'I know we can't.'

Luke continued to smoke. Steve sighed and sat himself on the other side of an increasingly confused Derek who had no clue what was going on but was as keen as anyone to hear why he might not spend years in prison. Steve took the packet off Derek's lap, took one out and lit it. He blew a column of smoke towards the ceiling and looked at his angry young compatriot.

'I think you can work out why Dave. Being the smart cookie that you are.'

There was silence again for a few seconds before Deek himself came up with the answer, much to the evident shock of everyone in the room.

'They didn't have a search warrant did they?'

He looked excitedly at Luke and Steve either side of him who both kept their eyes forward and attempted to keep their faces placid. He looked at Dave and felt like he could actually see the air come out of his body in disappointment. Nudging Luke's ribs frantically, he laughed aloud and stood up.

'Ha. No search warrant. So none of it is admissible in court. Brilliant. You told Mark yet? Can I tell him? Man, he'll be doing his nut.'

Both Luke and Steve reached up at the same time with one hand to grab an arm and pull him back to a sitting position. His hands went up in an apologetic gesture but the grin on his face wouldn't shift. Luke leaned forward to look past him at his old war buddy.

'Give me a couple of minutes to chat alone Steve? Then I reckon you can take them back home. Once you've got me the name and badge number of that specimen on the desk.'

Nodding and standing, Steve took the speechless Dave by the arm and they left the cell, leaving the other two smoking on the cot.

'Right. I feel like I've helped you out a little here Deek, so I want something in return.'

'What do you want?'

'I need to find Rab Reid. I don't care what the backstory is or the ins and outs. I'm not interested in the "he said, she said" nonsense. Just tell me where I can look for him because I'm close and I'm getting more concerned for him. His dad's obviously powerful and connected – look at this here. You and Mark both in the cells with no charge, no record and no cameras on. Going to be whisked right round to the offices of the man himself first thing with no one ever officially knowing anything. There's no guessing what could happen there.'

He paused briefly to smoke and let them both digest what was going on. The underhanded nature of the entire affair was worrying enough but the thought of what else had gone on under the radar on the instruction of Geoffrey Reid was even more disconcerting. Luke continued.

'I'm starting to think he only hired me because he didn't think I'd ever be able to track him down. You're his friend Deek, if helping me out gets you in trouble you then I'll take care of it. I promise you that. Help me find him before Geoffrey does.'

Derek Sutherland blinked twice as he considered and took a long pull on the cigarette.

'What time is it?'

'Quarter past 5.'

'Then I can tell you exactly where you'll find him. But I'm gonna hold you to that promise because there might be fall-out from this.'

Luke clapped his skinny shoulder hard and laughed.

'I've got you covered boss. I'll leave you my card and you can hit me up day or night.'

Derek was grinning now too. Not only was he not going to jail, it looked like he might have a chance at helping his friend and getting one over on the slimy Magistrate all in one fell swoop.

'Right man. Here's what you need to know.'

After Luke had slipped out of the station and into a waiting taxi that had been called, Steve and Dave let Deek out of his cell and allowed him to go and wake Mark up at his own insistence. The

170

excited explanation that they were going home – no arrest and no hassle - was too confusing for Mark to wrap his head around and so loud that it brought the officer on the desk running to the holding cells.

'What's going on here?'

All four inside the cell turned to look at the man standing in the doorway. It was Steve who addressed him.

'There's been a mistake pal. Gonna have to take the boys here back to their flat with a little apology. Reckon you might be due them one too.'

'You know full well what has to happen here. If you don't do as you've been asked I'll get on the phone and find someone who will. There's plenty who'd jump at the chance.'

'Just because there's a handful of scumbags doesn't mean we're all in the Fat Man's pocket. Our pal's going to be dropping in on the Magistrate anyway, once he picks up a passenger. He'll know soon enough what's going down. I've also given him your name and number to report to the Superintendent once he gets a second. Turns out they're pretty close.'

There was no reaction from the man in the doorway. He swallowed as he tried to decide if he was being lied to or not. Looking from one man to the next, he settled back on Steve again.

'Go for it. I'll be phoning the Magistrate the now and you two...' he pointed at Dave and Steve 'are finished.'

Dave stepped forward from the cot towards the door and landed a right cross on the other man's chin that folded his legs underneath him and sent him crumbling to the concrete floor. The anger in his voice was evident.

'If doing the right thing means we're finished then I'll hand the Superintendent my resignation in person. I'm sick of everyone on the street thinking all cops are wastes of skin because of idiots like you. All you care about is who's going to line your pockets the most and you police accordingly. That's everything that's wrong with the force now and I am tired of it. Even if it means bending or breaking the rules to make it happen, I'll throw my hat in the ring with Steve and Luke every day of the week when the alternative is you. Go ahead, phone the Magistrate and tell him. Tell all the boys on his payroll that the curtains coming down and we're going to be on the other side of it when it does.'

Looking back over his shoulder at the two stunned "prisoners" and his partner, he nodded in the direction of the door and they all stepped

171

over the prone figure to leave. Whether accidentally or not, Mark and Derek both found their recent waking had made them clumsy and they "may" have accidentally trod on his ribs on the way past. The foursome hurried out of the station to their waiting car and as they all piled in, Dave sat in the passenger seat and it was clear he was shaking.

'I shouldn't have done that. Why did I do that? So stupid.'

Steve started the car and pulled away from the station as the two in the back tried in vain to console the younger officer. Once they were heading back towards the flat, Steve spoke.

'Bit overdramatic, sure. "Bringing down the curtain" aye? Wee bit of the Untouchables there. Still. It might not be "protocol" but what we did tonight was the right thing and that's what's important. The only difference between us and that guy who's probably already calling up the Magistrate the now is the motivation and the result.'

'Is a sense of justice going to pay my bills? Assaulting a fellow officer is no joke. What am I going to do?'

'What we're going to do is drop these two gentlemen off and arrange a pint with them later to make up for the hassle. Then we're going into town to meet Luke at Geoffrey's office. And the whole way there we're going to feel sorry for the poor man that had the misfortune of turning the cameras off in the holding cells before he got his fillings rattled by the single girliest punch I've ever seen.'

Laughter erupted from the back of the car and Dave's head rose and his mouth opened but no sound came out. He thought back, double checking that what he was being told was correct and realised that with no video he had nothing to worry about. The word of a policeman who had turned the cameras off and kept arrests quiet for money against a 10-year veteran, an officer with a spotless record and two independent witnesses.... The laughter in the back was no longer infuriating but contagious. He joined in, relief flooding his body.

'Brilliant. Pints on me the night boys. Pints on me.'

He punched at Steve's shoulder as the older man smiled and kept his eyes on the road. Sinking back into his seat he felt like the luckiest man in Edinburgh. The relief was palpable. Only one point of contention remained.

'Hang on Steve, what do you mean "girly punch?"'

Chapter 23

On the taxi ride into town, Luke Calvin had made a pair of phone calls to Claire and Grant where he arranged to meet them both at Geoffrey Reid's offices at 7 a.m. Both accepted this early morning call with very little complaint and agreed to see him there. Once he had reached the town centre, he asked to be dropped off outside one of his favourite coffee shops on Rose Street that would be open this early and paid the driver. Now everything was in motion and he had gone from getting nowhere to going full speed ahead with little warning. His head was throbbing dully from the little sleep and the lager last night as he made his order at the counter "to go" and waited outside for it to be prepared as he smoked.

The city centre in the daybreak hours was when it was at its best. There wasn't the claustrophobic feeling of too many people, just the buildings and the streets stripped of almost all traffic, glorious in the rising sun. This morning, all Luke wanted was a pair of sunglasses to keep the light out of his eyes – the splendour of the city that he loved would be there to see some other morning when he wasn't frantically closing a case with a hangover. The door to the coffee shop opened and the girl from the counter handed him two large cups of coffee with a smile, addressing him by name. He smiled as he took them and turned right where he could get onto Princes Street, awkwardly ashing his cigarette with movements of his lips alone.

It was quiet enough that he could jog across the road, easily avoiding the busses and cursing the tram lines as he hopped over them. Reaching the black fencing at the Gardens, he passed both cups through the gap in the poles onto the grass on the other side and vaulted clean over the spikes, landing softly. Picking up the cups again, he moved towards the monument with the casual stride of a man who is entirely entitled to be where he is. Despite the fact he could prove his credentials to any overzealous citizen or security guard, the main reason for his lack of worry was that he was too tired to care. He sat down on a bench facing the entrance to the monument stairs and put one of the cups beside him as he drank from the other, burning his mouth in the process. Putting the cup down and both arms over the back of the bench, he sat and waited. He didn't have long to wait.

Geoffrey Reid was screaming across town towards his offices in his car, accelerating aggressively and braking hard. The radio was blaring even though it was just a talk show that was on. The phone call he had received from Niddrie police station had not been to his liking one bit and he had every intention of rectifying the situation personally. Even the simplest of things: - seemingly the simplest of people can mess them up.

The first thing he had done was to phone Luke and find his ranting, raving and colourful language answered only by the cool assertion that he would come to see him at his offices at seven and explain everything there. Slamming the phone down, he had phoned Grant Ferguson next who sounded like he was already awake and took the demand to come to Geoffrey's office entirely in his stride. He considered calling Claire but thought better of it. Let the girl get some rest – besides, the mood he was in today he was likely to do something he didn't want a female to have to witness. He was a good guy like that. His man at the station had told him the names of the two policemen who had set him up and let the hash dealers go but that could be dealt with later. Geoffrey had insisted down the phone that there would be no consequences for his employee's failure (which was of course a lie) and had insisted that under no circumstances would any information regarding the night's events be put out on a channel, either official or informal. His efforts had to be focussed on one thing at a time and for the moment, that one thing was why the man he had employed to find his son had not only failed to do so but had actively attempted to hamper his own efforts. The nerve of the man was enough to give the Magistrate a red hot rage that made his knuckles whiten on the steering wheel and his teeth grind in his head. One way or another, this was being finished today.

The door at the foot of the monument creaked open and a head peeked out, looking up and down the concourse to see if the coast was clear. Seeing the bench across occupied by a tall man with messy hair, it quickly retreated only to reappear a second later. The stranger seemed to be holding up a cup of coffee in offering. When they spoke, their voice was casual to the point of boredom.

'Come here Rab. Have a coffee. You must be freezing.'

Robert Reid was indeed fairly chilly and decided to accept his fate. Sniffing and wiping with his sleeve, he shut the wooden door and locked it with a key from his pocket. He crossed the pavement and took the offered cup, sitting down on the bench. After taking a sip, he removed his hood with his free hand and took a smoke from the packet that was sitting between them.

'How did you know where I was?'

'Spoke to Deek and Mark. They were in a cell at the time, didn't exactly volunteer.'

'Did my dad send you?'

'In a way. He employed me to find you. Guess he thought that was kind of my gig.'

Rab sniffed again and Luke looked at him properly for the first time. His face was drawn and white under his spiked blonde hair which had been crushed by the hood. His ear was pierced on one side and the thin lips and small nose held no resemblance to his father. Only in the eyes, which were watery and grey blue, could any of the Magistrate be seen. "Lucky boy" he thought.

'What happens now then?'

It was Luke's turn to sniff. The morning was still brisk despite the fact that the sun was up. He took another deep drink of coffee and relaxed further onto the bench

'We've arranged to meet your old man at his offices of the Mound at 7. So we have about half an hour by my reckoning to chat a bit before we walk up.' He read the fear in Rab's eyes. 'I'm not going to let anyone hurt you. But if you try to run from me I will have to stop you. Understand?'

Rab nodded sadly. It felt like the end of the line. All that had gone on the past few days, all that he had done over the years and all the problems he knew he had caused all came flooding into his head at once. He had been thinking of running but somehow he believed the man beside him that the only way he'd get hurt is if he tried to escape. Luke was reaching into his back pocket and taking out his wallet. He extracted a creased picture from it and offered it to Rab who took it suspiciously.

'Have a look at that. This is what your dad gave me to find you with.'

There was laughter from both on the bench as Rab looked at his graduation picture from all possible angles before holding it up beside his face and turning towards Luke.

'You must be good if you found me off that.'

'The best.' was the reply in a tone that showed he thought quite the opposite.

Robert looked at the picture for a little longer before folding it up and putting it in his own pocket. He rubbed his hands on the legs of his jeans and held one out towards Luke.

'I guess we might as well be properly introduced before you take me in. Robert Reid – professional disappointment.'

'Luke Calvin – Not a cop.'

They shook hands briefly and returned to their smokes and coffees.

'You know where your dad's offices are by the way? I've never been.'

'Aye. You can see them from up there.'

He was pointing to the observation platform that stood at the top of the monument. Luke nodded.

'Is that why you went up there every morning.'

'Not sure. Maybe?'

Draining the dregs of his coffee into his mouth, Luke stuffed it into a bin and stood. Rab followed suit.

'Come on, let's walk and talk Rab. You're gonna have to fill me in on a few things so we know where we stand when we get up there.'

Geoffrey parked up his car outside and locked it as he left, extracting a large key from somewhere deep inside his suit jacket as he went. Placing it in the lock on the front door he was just in the process of trying to remember the code for the alarm that would still be armed when he realised it had already been switched off. Bounding up the stairs two at a time he succeeded only in nearly giving himself a heart attack. When he reached the first floor and opened the door to the reception room of his office he was panting and had broken sweat. To his surprise, he found Grant was there already there, in jogging bottoms and a black t-shirt, parked in a seat behind the receptionist desk. Even more surprising was Claire sitting beside him behind her computer, typing away. Her hair was tied up in a black bow and she smiled at him as he entered.

'Good morning Mr. Reid. I was up early so coming in to catch up on a bit of paperwork. Found this one waiting outside.'

She dug an elbow into Grants ribs who looked up and spoke himself.

'Aye, got here quicker than I thought I would. Lucky she showed up or I'd still be waiting.'

Geoffrey was too preoccupied to ask any questions and walked past into his office through the heavy door at the back of the room. The other two returned to the computer, wasting time watching videos online. Once they were alone his arm returned to its previous position over her shoulder and she snuggled in against his chest. He placed a single kiss on the top of her head.

'Maybe we'll get to sleep through until morning next time eh Claire?'

Her voice was muffled against his t-shirt and he could feel her speech resonating inside his ribcage.

'Think a lot of yourself Mr. Ferguson. Who said there'd be a next time?'

His laughter made her head bounce against him and they sat together in a sleepy embrace waiting on Luke to come and doubtless wreak his personal brand of havoc on their morning.

In his office, Geoffrey Reid couldn't stop pacing. He trod the rug endlessly, stalking back and forward in front of his window with his hands clasped behind his back. Sitting down briefly, his hand went to his mouth and he found himself chewing on a nail – a habit from his youth that he hadn't indulged in for decades. Standing again to resume the pacing which was the lesser of the two evils, his mind was going as fast as his feet as he wondered what revelation Luke was bringing him that was so important. Despite all previous evidence to the contrary, he may have turned up something worthwhile despite himself. There was no longer than ten minutes until the appointed time and the only thing that kept the Magistrate from opening his drawer and taking a quick shot was not the time of day but the worry of what dark road drinking spirits in the morning led you down. Outside his window in front of the skyline and the sun, his bird had returned and was standing on the granite sill, eyeing him with curiosity. Geoffrey wanted to let it come in. To feed it and look after it. Make sure it never left. But the window didn't open so they stood separated by the heavy glass, able to see each other but destined to exist in different worlds.

Luke phoned Grant instead of buzzing the offices once he was outside. Rab had followed meekly the whole way up and talked incessantly. Tapping the seemingly endless supply of cigarettes that appeared in his captors hands from every pocket, Rab had smoked and talked and Luke had smoked and listened. There only stop had been another coffee shop where Luke stumped up the cash for a grand selection of coffees, teas, hot chocolates and enough pastries to feed a small army. He and Rab continued on their way, now encumbered with food and drink, talking between mouthfuls of pastry. Rab was now balancing two trays of cups on top of each other and it was taking all his concentration to keep it steady. Luke completed his call outside the offices.

'Someone's coming down to let us down. Here.' He took the double stacked coffee. 'I think I'd better take that.'

Bemused, Rab surrendered his burden just as the door cracked open and Grant's head peeked out, looking at Luke and motioning for him to come inside. Luke directed the big man's gaze to his left where Rab stood sheepishly on the pavement, rubbing his right forearm and looking at the ground. Grant exploded out of the door, ran straight to him and scooped him off the ground in a bear hug that probably smashed four of his ribs and collapsed a lung. They spun round like that in the street as Luke watched and waited. Once Rab was back on solid ground but still under the meaty arm of Grant that was now ruffling his hair viciously, he began to stammer his way through what could have been an apology or an explanation but he didn't get far enough to say for sure because he was cut off by Grant.

'Less of that man. We can sort all that later. I'm just glad to see you ya scrawny wee radge. Your old man's been losing his nut even more than usual.'

They both noticed Luke waiting as if for the first time and apologetically took a tray of drinks off him each. He stretched his shoulders and fingers out in mock agony at being left holding the weight for too long and spoke to the reunited friends.

'Is Claire here as well Grant? And yous got here before he did? Good. Right, we'll head up and then we can.... What are you two muppets laughing at?'

Rab was struggling fit to burst and Grant had already gone. The large shaved head inclined down to his pal and came up again in roaring laughter. Wiping his eyes, Rab held up an apologetic hand towards Luke.

'Sorry man, sorry. You've had a big flake of pastry on your face for the past ten minutes. We know this is serious but you need to sort that out before we can look at you.'

Luke had a sudden flash to how the two of them must have been at school and all the time since. He smiled along with them and wiped a hand down his face a couple of times as the two men attempted to regain their composure and finalise the plan of action before they headed upstairs to face the music.

Chapter 24

The door to the office swung open noiselessly and Luke stepped in alone, closing it behind him. The Magistrate was still staring out his window at the bird on the sill, his hands clasped behind his wide back, seemingly uncaring about the intrusion. The thick glass muffled the noise from the street below as Luke helped himself to the seat on the other side of the Magistrate's great desk. There was still no reaction from the man at the window and from his seated position, Luke reached across and could barely grasp the lid of a crystal ashtray that was doubtless for decoration only. Scraping it across the wood so it sat near in front of him, he got his cigarette packet out from the pocket of his jeans and placed it within easy reach. Despite the fact that there was a disposable lighter in his pocket, he searched the desk for one of Geoffrey's own ones to use. Spotting an immaculate zippo on the mantelpiece, he stood again and picked it up, using it to light his cigarette, studying it thoroughly in his hands before snapping the flame out and putting it back. Touching each item on the mantelpiece delicately, Luke examined everything that was so proudly displayed until a voice behind him caused him to pause.

'Mr. Calvin. Will you kindly stop touching these.'

Geoffrey Reid had turned from his vigil at the window and was watching him with growing horror as he had explored all the trinkets with his fingertips. Magistrate Reid now gestured back to the seat that had been recently vacated and Luke sat back down, tucking his leg underneath him and smiling through the thin smoke.

'Good morning Magistrate. How are you?'

The big man in the suit was hovering behind his desk, unsure of whether to remain standing or to sit. In the end his tiredness overruled his will to maintain any psychological edge that would be gained from towering over the seated man. He very much doubted that Mr Calvin would have been affected by it anyway, so it would

180

possibly be an exercise in futility. Ignoring the fact that he was smoking in his office, Geoffrey leaned forward in his chair and rested his elbows on the table, clasping his hands together in between the two parties. Luke continued to smile and ashed into the crystal bowl, waiting on the questioning to begin.

'So. I hear you found yourself in a prison cell last night.'

'Not the first time. Nor will it be the last. Occupational hazard I guess.'

'I'm decidedly curious as to how you happened to be that far out of town that early in the morning, in the custody of the police only to walk out shortly after without as much as a charge sheet being brought up.'

'So now you want to ask questions about people being arrested without documentation Mr. Reid? Do you really feel that's a good line to be pursuing? Given that you are fully aware why I was there.'

The Magistrate smiled back at Luke but there was no warmth in his eyes. It was more like a rabid dog salivating at the sight of fresh meat or a clown from a nightmare.

'So I see that we're both intent on making this as difficult as possible Mr. Calvin. How prudent it is for either party remains to be seen, but I fear it will get us nowhere.'

'I agree. If you have questions, now's the time to ask me. I doubt we'll be seeing too much of each other after this morning.'

'I concur. Very well, as it happens there are one or two things I would like to clear up. Your unprofessional behaviour and lack of results notwithstanding, I find it very hard to justify the money I paid you to find my son when you not only show me zero concrete results of any description but instead actively sabotage my own personal lines of investigation.'

The cigarette pirouetted gracefully between Luke's fingers, jumping from one to the next, spinning round the thumb and continuing its journey round and round. Both sets of eyes remained fixed on it.

'That was not a question Mr. Reid, it was a statement. But I'll answer it anyway out of common courtesy because I've been struggling with that as well these past few days. Everyone I've spoken to seems to think that Rab falling off the face of the earth would be nothing if not a benefit to you. In fact, some would argue that your handprints might be found somewhere along the trail that led to his disappearance if I were to look hard enough. That was a puzzle I only managed to solve very recently and it isn't anywhere as clear cut as I'd like it, but if the shoe sort of fits, you can cram your foot into it.'

Geoffrey Reid's tone was ice cold and he leaned forward. The size of the table meant there was still a considerable distance between the two of them so the action did not have the impact he had hoped.

'If you believe that you can sit in my office, in my employ and accuse me of having a role in the disappearance of my own son then you had better have some airtight evidence to back it up. Otherwise I will body bag you professionally. Then for real.'

'Death threats don't suit you Magistrate. You're too involved to get blood on your hands. Think too much of yourself to do the dirty work personally. In fact, on my way in here I saw a particularly large gentleman with a shaved head and tribal tattoos down to his hands.' He pointed behind him with the cigarette. 'Is that your insurance policy in case you swing for me and I happen to beat you half to death with one of your knick-knacks?'

The Magistrate checked himself and sat back in his seat. The fake grin made a reappearance and he clasped his hands once more in what Luke could only assume was a well-practiced pose designed to defuse situations.

'He is also in my employ. You have no need to fear physical violence as long as you are honest with me Mr. Calvin.' Luke was not in the slightest bit worried. 'I feel you should at least explain to me how you came to be in that police station last night and why you feel there will be no consequences for assaulting an officer of the law for no reason.'

Unfolding the leg from underneath him and swapping it for the other one, Luke adjusted himself more comfortably before he responded.

'How I came to be there is not as important as who I spoke to there. I had a very brief chat with a certain Mr. Sutherland. I happen to think he's a pretty nice guy all things considered and he told me some very interesting bits of information…'

The reaction was instant. The blood rushed to the Magistrate's face and his voiced raised several decibels.

'He's a liar. If you had any sense in you at all you would know that he's a junkie dealer and a liar. Spinning whatever rubbish he feels will buy him a little more grace. If you believed a single word he said, then you are an even poorer investigator than I thought you were.'

The cigarette had resumed its spinning but it was only Luke who was staring at it. Geoffrey's eyes were burning holes through the head of the uninterested man performing the elaborate manoeuvres in between puffs.

'There was only one piece of information I asked him for actually. And it turned out to be entirely solid. So by my scoreboard that puts Deek at a 100% record for tips and information.' He finally met the Magistrate's eye. 'Like I said, he's a good guy.'

'I am telling you now that anything he told you will be lies. There isn't an honest bone in that man's body.' The meaty fist was slamming down on the table with every word. 'He's scum and a waster.' Luke had stood up. 'No good, low life druggie.'

Luke crossed to the door and opened it. Geoffrey Reid's tirade of rage and fury dried up in an instant.

'Orite Dad. How's it going?'

Robert Reid entered sheepish as before closely followed by Grant who stood behind his friend. Luke had known neither as children but could picture exactly how their friendship must have been and how it had stayed through the years, never really changing with regards to the fundamental roles that each played. Rab was rubbing his pierced ear self-consciously as the Magistrate who had risen in indignation returned himself to his seat in shock. The redness that had come into his face with his anger had given way to a paleness and he kept looking from his son to his desk and back, stammering awkwardly.

'Robert... I thought... I was so worried...'

Luke retook his seat and placed his elbows on the table, clasping his hands together between the two parties in a perfect imitation of the Magistrate. He indicated behind him with his head.

'That was the tip that Deek gave me. Where to find Rab. That and only that. According to Rab, he came to Deek pretty upset a few days ago. Needing to get off the radar for reasons that I'll come to in a bit. And Derek, being the good guy and friend that he is, facilitated this in his own way. Robert was squatting in Mark and Derek's old flat that had been abandoned since it got raided and kept a low profile. In fact, as far as anyone knew, he could have left the country, just left the city or been plain old dead, except for the fact that he kept on sneaking up town of a night to wander the Gardens. The only reason I was even put in his general direction was that an old boy happened to spot him coming back in the morning and extracted a conversation out of him. What are the chances?' Luke's cigarette had gone out and he took a moment to re-light it. 'Now, Magistrate. What reason would your son have for feeling like he had to disappear for a while? Any ideas? Thoughts? Opinions?'

Geoffrey Reid wouldn't meet his eye. He wouldn't look at Rab who stood embarrassed in the corner. And he wouldn't look at Grant who was losing his temper beside Rab. It was Grant who addressed the Magistrate next.

'Tell him Geoffrey. Tell your boy what you asked me to do. What you offered to pay me.'

'I said help him disappear. I meant relocate, you know that Grant.'

His voice had become pleading and weedy. His great hands were being wrung together in earnest; a penitent sinner indeed. Rab surprised everyone by lifting his head and stopping his father's attempts at an explanation dead in their tracks.

'I know what he offered you Grant. Because he offered Deek the same. It was the first thing out of Derek's mouth when I came to him for help, he wanted to be up front. Pretty bizarre to realise the value of your existence in cold hard cash. Even worse when it's so abysmally low. £10,000 dad? Really? I know you're a pretty cold man but that is beyond the pale.'

The cigarette between Luke's fingers stopped twirling and hung in mid-air, the smoke trailing up to the ceiling high above. There it was. The final piece of the puzzle. The part that tied it all together and so neatly as well. Ignoring the stammering mess across the desk from him, he turned in his seat to look at Rab who had his head up for once and Grant who was staring at his friend, not entirely sure how to feel about this latest piece of information. Luke pointed the smoke in Rab's direction with a question.

'You didn't tell me Derek had been offered the same deal as Grant.'

Grant was still incredulous but responded with humour.

'Yeah, I'd have offered a discount if I knew it was a competitive market.'

Rab had a laugh to himself as he walked across the room to the far side and picked up two chairs from against the wall and brought them over to the desk on the opposite side from his father. He parked himself down and motioned for Grant to do the same.

'I guess you need the full story to put it all together properly. For starters, when I went to find Deek and he told me, my first reaction was to be worried. That's a big amount of money to anyone, but he said he wouldn't have taken it if it had been a million. And I believe him. I offered him £15,000 cash to help me get off the grid instead but he wouldn't take that either. Most I could get him to take was a couple of notes to get me food, booze and a little something to help with the boredom. Well, first night I was already going out of my mind in that flat. Just the four walls to stare at and the only person who knew where I was having to deny it. I couldn't call anyone. I couldn't go out in the day, so I waited until it was dark, grabbed a hoody, hopped on the night bus and wandered the town. It doesn't sound like much but it kept my head on straight. Even if everyone thought I was gone, I felt like if I walked around among them I'd still exist. Know what I mean?'

'I guess so.' It was Luke who responded. 'By the way I'm assuming that you kept a hold of your old keys from when you worked at the museum?'

'Yeah. That was pretty stupid but it seemed like a good idea at the time.'

'Always does.' Grant said, rubbing his friends shoulder.

'Deek came round the next night to keep me company for a bit. We smoked and chatted round and round in circles until we were talking about how good it would be to get one over on him.' He was facing Grant and Luke but nodded to the right at the Magistrate who was staring at the desk and remaining quiet. 'We got more and more wasted until I came up with the plan. We drove up to the museum, sneaked in the side door with my key and took that skeleton from the display case. We dressed it in some of Mark's old clothes and planted the poor thing on Arthurs seat in the pouring rain. The car was a banger – not even road legal so we just burnt it out and drove back in Deek's car thinking we were the smartest guys in the world.'

Grant and Luke exchanged glances quickly and even Geoffrey raised his head to look at his son with disbelief. It was Grant who spoke.

'Run that by me again man. You're trying to disappear so you nick a skeleton, bury it in a shallow grave and burn a car out? Is that really how you lay low?'

Rab was shaking his head the whole time the question was being asked. He seemed as nonplussed as the rest of them.

'I dunno man, we both thought it was an airtight plan. We were going to leave it a while then Deek would call my dad and ask to get paid. If he wanted proof, he'd dig up the skeleton in front of him and we just sort of hoped he'd accept it.'

There was laughter from both of his companions on his side of the table and even a derisory snort from Geoffrey Reid. Rab looked hurt and ashamed as his head drooped towards the floor once more. Luke offered his cigarettes around as he rocked with mirth and made two abortive attempts at sparking it before managing to not laugh the flame out on the third.

'Do you know how long a body takes to turn into a skeleton Rab?' Luke's efforts to maintain his composure and keep his tone kind were failing. 'Because it's a long time. And they usually aren't bleached, screwed together and dressed in plaid shirts.'

Rab's hand went up to his earring again and his face reddened in the face of the laughs that were being had at his expense from all parties involved. He had realised as soon as they were done how stupid and reckless the plan was but much like every other silly decision he had made, it had seemed like a good idea at the time. There was no viable defence or grounds on which he could claim it was a well thought out plan so he made no effort to.

'Like I said, we realised it was stupid. Even more so when it got turned up less than two days later and the cops got a hold of it. As soon as I heard that, I phoned Deek and he rushed over to try and calm me down. I was all for handing myself in but he sort of reasoned that it would do more harm than good. Besides, how would they ever tie it to us? You know? Who would ever put these things together?'

Luke raised his hand smugly. It was a big dose of luck that had brought him to make the connection but there was no point in letting them know that. If Steve hadn't told him to check the police report, if the Superintendent hadn't given him full access just when he had, if the security guard had kept his worries to himself – any one of these situations had only to be slightly different or occurred out of order for the whole thing to have passed him by, but a little bit of luck was more than you were used to in his game. Rab sounded as if he was finishing up his explanation.

'I should have probably turned myself in. Or phoned Grant at least to let him know I was still alive. I'm not proud of what I've done but I felt backed into a corner. I've worried a lot of people and caused a lot of hassle for my own reasons and I am sorry for that. Although I have no sympathy for him.'

The "him" in question was sitting quietly behind his desk with his hands folded in his lap and his head hanging. There was a defeated air to the Magistrate that seemed very out of character. He looked like he was deep in thought and searching frantically for a way out. Luke was still smoking and turned from Reid Jr to Reid Snr.

'So. Looks like I've done what you asked me and we can all be happy. There are a few minor points that might need looking into however.' The Magistrate's head came up slightly. 'For example, the whole "conspiracy to murder" problem you seem to have.'

'It'll never hold up in court and you know it.' Geoffrey's voice was tight but seemed tinged with fear. 'What do you have other than the word of a convicted dealer and a common thug?'

The arm that Luke stretched out to restrain Grant was not needed as the big man took the insult in his stride and remained seated between Rab and Luke with his muscled arms crossed and a sneer on his face. Luke was still holding court.

'But it doesn't have to hold up in court does it Geoffrey? The merest whiff of this latest scandal and you'll be ruined.' He leaned forward to make sure his former employer was listening. 'Especially on top of all the previous suspicions. The miscarriages of justice. The bribes. You name it, you've been accused of it. From what I've been led to believe, you've been sitting very politely in the last chance saloon for a long time now with a list of people as long as your arm just waiting for a slip up and an excuse to toss you out on your ear.'

Geoffrey seemed to have regained some of his composure and raised his head all the way, looking all three men in the eye carefully. He had made his mind up about one thing or another and his opponents waited for him to show his hand.

'You might be right Mr. Calvin. There have been many accusations and not a single one of them has held up under scrutiny. That notwithstanding, there is likely to be nowhere else for me to turn if this does get out. What you're doing to me could be interpreted by some as blackmail, no matter how noble you feel your motives are. All I wanted was a son that I could be proud of. Not one who bounced about from job to job embarrassing me with his drug fuelled antics and vulgar displays of power that he hadn't earned. I gave that boy there every chance to earn my respect and he never took it. Everything that's happened to him is on his own head.'

Grant's tone when he replied was measured but the fury bubbling below the surface was tangible. Luke eyed him warily, suddenly very aware that if he were to launch himself at the Magistrate there would be little that he and Rab could do in the immediacy, if either of them felt the urge.

'That's you all over Geoffrey. Never made a mistake in your life. Always the victim somehow. No matter what happened or who it happened to, you were never to blame. If you'd taken more time with Rab maybe he'd respect you more. Have the slightest inclination to make you proud. Man, the fact that he's even still here speaking to you after all this shows that he's a better man than I am – if I had the severe misfortune of having you as a father I would be sitting in jail for your murder ten years ago and I'd be in there with a grin on my face.'

There was no one in the room that disbelieved him for a second. The intensity in him had bubbled over and gone off with both barrels. Rab's eyes never left his father but he placed his right hand gently on the front of Grant's shoulder. To Luke, it was bizarre to see this slightly built man defuse the giant with not as much as a word but Grant acquiesced to the unspoken request and leaned back in his chair, his rage now simmering.

'I've no doubt you would Grant.' Geoffrey was rubbing his chin thoughtfully. 'I fully believe that you would. My attack dog. Doing whatever I asked as long as the price was right. Funny how you develop morals just when it suits you.'

'If it wasn't for him I'd have been in serious bother well before now Dad' said Rab 'and you know that full well.'

'Be that as it may.' The Magistrate clapped his hands and rubbed them together. 'So boys. What's the plan from now? Since you seem to have it well in hand up to this point. First.' He raised one finger. 'My own son turns against me. Second' He raised another finger to join the first. 'my loyal enforcer throws his hat in the ring with' the third finger came up 'the man I paid a lot of money to find my son in the first place. Well isn't this just a mess.'

'What happens next is up to you.' Luke ashed into the crystal once more. 'There are going to be consequences of some sort for your behaviour and your disregard for the law. I'm sure we could try and have you arrested but I doubt a man with as many coppers in his pocket as you would take long to get out. And there is no doubt in my mind that as soon as you can, you will make it your mission to exact your own brand of revenge on every single one of us sitting here.' Geoffrey nodded and smiled. 'In short, I don't see any way in which we can all leave here this morning satisfied and happy. So we have once again reached an impasse.'

The Magistrate reached into his pocket and extracted his small key. Moving the veneer cover to expose the keyhole, he opened the disguised drawer and placed the bottle of whiskey on the table. Reaching into it again, he brought out the handgun he had acquired and levelled it across the table at Luke's chest who continued smoking, unconcerned. Grant also remained motionless but Rab recoiled, leaning his torso as far away from the muzzle as possible.

'There is a solution to our problem as it happens gentlemen. Mr Calvin here is the only one outside of this room who is aware of any of this confused story. If he were out of the picture, then that would be the end of it and we could all go on pretending like none of this happened.' His broad grin had returned. 'How fortunate it seems to have but the one loose end at the end of this convoluted escapade. And how unfortunate for you.'

Rab was doing his best to keep his body well away from the business end of the gun that was being pointed while making a futile attempt to placate his father.

189

'There's no need for that Dad. Geez, have you lost it? How are you going to explain that? You can't just shoot the guy in your office and expect nothing to happen. Just calm down. Put the gun back down and we'll talk about it.'

'I'm afraid not son. I should have expected you to disappoint me again but it still always surprises me somehow. This is the only way that the rest of us can go about our lives. This has to happen.'

Luke glanced over his shoulder to the door where Claire had just appeared and he saw Steve and Dave loitering in the passageway. Impeccable timing for once. He took another indulgent draw from his cigarette and turned back to face the Magistrate who hadn't noticed his secretary entering and most definitely not the two uniformed men looking in with quiet interest. He kept his eyes on the Magistrate as he shouted to her.

'Claire. Did you take the bullets out of the gun like I asked you?' He addressed Geoffrey. 'See, I phoned her up ahead of time. Made sure she got here before you. Took a few precautions.'

Geoffrey looked horrified and glanced open mouthed at the gun in his hand as if he would be able to see if it were loaded or not from the outside. Claire shouted back from the door with a reply that neither expected.

'Sorry Luke, I didn't know how to.'

The blood in his veins turned to ice and the bottom of his stomach dropped out. He had planned it all so well and never even considered this possibility. He should have checked. He should have double checked. The grinning face of Geoffrey Reid had his imminent victory plastered all over it. After all these years in war zones, all the times he had stared death in the face, he was now going to meet his end in a frankly garish office at the hands of an overweight Magistrate because he had assumed a secretary would have a working knowledge of firearms. It was a rookie mistake. A schoolboy error. There was no time to move or react as the podgy finger applied pressure to the trigger. Rab stuffed his fingers in his ears and dove off his chair. Luke sat where he was and closed his eyes tight. Grant didn't move a muscle. The "click" from the gun ushered in a deep stunned silence. Luke warily opened one eye as Grant leant his head towards him to speak.

'I did it for her, dude. She didn't have a clue.'

Chapter 25

In the reception area, just outside of the office, Luke, Rab, Claire and Grant were still sitting around. The mood was light and the unpleasantness that had occurred only next door seemed to be already mostly forgotten. Rab and Grant were somehow involved in a play fight that the former had no chance of winning and after a brief tussle, Grant sat proudly on top of Rab's wheezing body, flexing his arms and striking poses. Luke was still chain smoking, trying to recover from the scare that they had given him. Once the gun had failed to go off, Steve had charged into the room and tackled the Magistrate clean off the back of his chair. Dave wasn't far behind and by the time the other three had stood to assist there was no need for help as he was handcuffed and restrained face flat on his own carpet. The two policemen had radioed for an additional car and once it had arrived, whisked Geoffrey Reid away to a cell. There was going to be no talking his way out of this one and after a brief chat with the back-up that had arrived the four of them found themselves alone. No one had spoken for a while until Grant snatched the bottle of whiskey off the table and brought it to Claire's desk where he poured himself a generous shot in her flower patterned teacup, re-poured and offered it around. Luke rubbed his right eye hard – tiredness had come over him all of a sudden. He addressed the back of Grant's shaved head as he was pulling a laughing Rab back to his feet with a force that would probably wrench the arm out of his socket.

'Lucky you were here Grant. That gave me a bit more of a scare than I'd like to admit.'

'No need to admit it.' said Rab 'you were so pale that Casper would be embarrassed for you.'

Claire had taken at least three teacup shots and her face was flushed. She chirped up from behind her desk where she was reclining with her feet on the desk.

'I'm sorry Luke, I didn't think about how it sounded until after I'd said it.'

Grant sat down beside him and ruffled his curly hair. When he spoke there was whiskey on his breath and excitement in his voice.

'I'm not that sorry man. Sure, you might have had a heart attack, but him pulling that trigger is attempted murder. He had no idea I'd unloaded the gun. Now he had to go down.'

Luke had stopped rubbing his eye under this renewed assault and smiled weakly at Grant. That point was entirely fair. The years that the brief moment of terror had put on him were worth it for the end result. Picking up the bottle and refusing the offered cup he took two big mouthfuls and enjoyed the burning as they slid down.

'I guess so. I'm just imagining if you'd showed up after me. Or Claire.'

'Nah man, we shared a taxi up.'

Luke nodded and took another hit from the bottle. It was making his worry slip away and he was beginning to appreciate the happy mood in the room. Grant was nudging his ribs again.

'Dude. I said we shared a taxi up.'

He looked from Grant's smirk to Claire's red face and downturned eyes and he understood. He toasted Claire with the bottle, causing her to look down again with a happy blush, which Grant and Luke used as cover to deliver a furtive fist bump. Taking one final long drag he offered the bottle to Grant who passed it to Rab. Rab had calmed down from the excitement and was looking in danger of becoming depressed again.

'Listen guys, today's been...' he searched for the correct word... 'an adventure but I need to know how much trouble I'm in. I mean with the car and the skeleton and all the stupidity.'

Thinking carefully about his response, Luke's hand went out and Rab supplied the bottle to it once more. Taking a shot for deductive reasons and that alone, he ran his hand through his hair, catching on tugs that had come into being when he hadn't had time to shower properly before being picked up.

'It just so happens that the Superintendent himself gave me his full co-operation for some reason a few days ago so the outlook might not be as bleak as you expect. The car being burnt out is not going to come back on you unless they decided to waste time, effort

192

and money sending the forensic squad over it – which they won't. Breaking into the Gardens every night is not only hard to prove but pointless to prosecute since you caused no damage and didn't hurt anyone. I highly doubt you were the only one in there either so you're clear on that one. Actually stealing the skeleton is possibly a difficulty but only because the Security Guard on nights is getting heat from the company over it. When I speak to the Superintendent later, I'll get him to call the company personally, explain that they have found the culprit and that he used a key to enter, but do not wish to prosecute due to mitigating circumstances. He might chuck in a mention of how helpful the security guard was with their enquiries and recommend a commendation for him. There's not a manager in the world who will object to that when it comes straight from so high up. That'll get Gavin off the hook and all that leaves is you going up there sooner rather than later and apologising to the man himself in person. He's a sound enough guy so I reckon he'll probably not hit you. Probably.'

Rab was looking more hopeful with every word that came out of Luke's mouth and had returned to his previous state of euphoria by the time he was finished. If an apology was all that was needed to set things straight, then this Gav guy was going to get the sincerest apology of his life. Grant and Claire were sitting beside each other, their fingers lightly intertwined. Luke stood up and handed the bottle off to Rab.

'Unless anyone has any objections, I'm going to get back to my flat. It's been a long night and I need to check in with the office, tell them that once again I've cracked the case and am the best in the business, then sleep.'

All three agreed that it seemed like the best idea and as Luke was exiting he heard Rab being told that he was coming round to crash at Grant's for a few days. No objections allowed. Luke trudged down the stairs towards the front door of the offices, feeling as though he could sleep for days. A shout came from the top of the stairwell just as his hand was on the doorknob. It was Claire.

'Come to The Bull the night Luke. Us three are going and Rab's gonna get Mark and Deek along. Grant reckons you owe us all a pint at least.'

Luke was wracking his brains furiously for an excuse to stay in and be alone. He felt drained. Exhausted. Worn out. The last thing he wanted to do was go to the pub. Grant's voice echoed down to him from somewhere in the offices.

'Jen's on the bar the night....'

Well it was only a pint. I guess it couldn't hurt to be sociable. He opened the door and stepped out into the sunshine on the Mile. If he made his phone calls on the ten-minute walk back, then he could just drop into bed as soon as he got in. Finding his phone in his pocket, he dialled the Superintendent first to bring him up to speed and clear any issues on Rab's behalf. He would also mention the key roles that both Dave and Steve played and ensure they were adequately compensated. After that he could phone the office and fill them in. The Major would be pleased as punch no doubt. Congratulations would be in order.

Only at that moment did Luke think that perhaps the Major and the Superintendent had both been looking for the downfall of Geoffrey Reid the whole time, long before they put him on the case. Dogsbody Calvin. The pawn. The Major could sit with his flying goggles strapped to his face and a handlebar moustache ten-foot-long for all Luke cared this morning, he wanted his own bed and to embrace oblivion for eight to ten hours. He was already looking forward to sleep and as the Superintendent answered, he lit a cigarette and began the uphill walk to his flat as he began to explain all that had happened.

The rain beat a tattoo on the window pane, echoing through the dark. The droplets pooled and raced to the bottom, spiralling this way and that on the glass. The luminous face of his watch told him that it was 2:38 but Luke Calvin was propped in his favourite seat by the window watching the taxis drive up and down Victoria Street, cutting through the dark with their headlights. He was smoking another cigarette and watching the smoke rise lazily towards the ceiling.

By the time he had reached his front door that morning he had informed the Superintendent of all the ins and outs from start to finish and received not only praise but his word that Rab would be in the clear and that both Dave and Steve would be rewarded for their role. Laura had been chatty and happy, which had unnerved him, but the Major's brisk tone had set him back on an even keel. The Major was pleased the job was done and had heaped on the meaningless praise. Once the official debriefing was complete Luke had stayed on the line with Laura until he got home, laughing about nothing and imagining her sitting behind her desk with a sundress and a huge hat. Once they'd said their goodbyes he had hung up the phone and been very aware that the waiting on the next job started again now.

When he woke up that afternoon, there was a message from Grant saying that they were all meeting at The Bull at 6pm and he had showered and dressed in a black jumper and jeans before heading up to meet them. Deek and Mark were there when he arrived and the other three showed up not long after. The drinks disappeared as quickly as they could be bought and the entrance of Dave and Steve at the back of seven was met with a huge drunken roar of approval. They had commandeered the far corner and sat all together; the dealers, the coppers, the secretary, the enforcer, the runaway drug fiend and the investigator; and they had laughed and drank until closing and for a good few hours after. Once the door had been locked after the last customer and the shutters taken down, Jen had come over to join and the merriment had continued. One by one they took their leave until the pub was dark and empty and it was all over.

Outside of the window, the rain was running in torrents down the cobbled streets, sweeping away the rubbish of the day into the gutters. Across the road, the silhouettes of the ancient buildings on the Mound dominated the skyline. As far to the left as he could see was Edinburgh Castle; jutting up into the dark night sky, seeing everything that was being done in the dark. Luke stared closely through the heavy rain at the jagged outline and thought. It may be the middle of the night but until that phone rang again for work he had some time to himself. And at least for a few days, he was more than content to sit here in his window seat in the shadow of the castle.

From the doorway, a sleepy voice called to him.

'Come back to bed Luke. It's freezing.'

Jen's red hair was a curly mess and the shirt that she was wearing was his. It made her look even more tiny than she already was. He put his cigarette out and took one last look at the castle in the rain. It had always had a profound effect on him, even more so now that he realised Rab had probably been looking at it at the same time over the course of his search. These things could all wait until morning though. He walked to the hall and allowed her small hands to grasp his and lead him back to his own bed. A good night's sleep was long overdue.

THE END

19523809R00112

Printed in Great Britain
by Amazon